Come Alive

by Elora Ramirez

RHIZOME
PUBLISHING

Pueblo, CO

Come Alive
Copyright © 2011 by Elora Ramirez
Published by Rhizome Publishing

Cover design by lastleafprinting.com
Original cover art Debra Cooper of debracooperart.com

RHIZOME PUBLISHING
Rhizome Publishing, LLC
Pueblo, Colorado 81003

cultivate@rhizomepub.com
rhizomepublishing.com
On Twitter: @rhizomepub

Press inquiries: publicity@rhizomepub.com

Printed in the United States of America
First Printing: April 2012

ISBN 13: 978-1-61943-005-1
ISBN 10: 1-6194300-5-3

To Russ -
  thank you for being my
  light in a dark place.

Prologue

SUNRISES MAKE ME COME ALIVE. I'M USUALLY UP FAR BEFORE THE SUN makes an appearance anyway, so when the first light of the day creeps its way across the sky I can't help but smile. Sunsets are relaxing - the colors slowly collapsing into a starlit night. But sunrises? Sunrises take my breath away. I think it's the colors. The fluorescent oranges and purples and reds screaming the start of a new day - reminds me to take a breath, embrace a fresh beginning.

It was three months ago, in the middle of a gorgeous sunrise filled with glowing iridescent clouds and trees that looked on fire, I met her. We both arrived at school early, before the janitors came and lights in the classrooms made a dance of electricity. We sat next to each other, completely silent. I fingered my Moleskine, watching the sunrise and waiting for a whisper of a beginning so I could start writing. Writing has always been my escape. Building new worlds and peaceful settings is my way of combating my own surroundings - harsh, violent, selfish - ripping every part of who I was to pieces. But I wouldn't be ruined. I made myself a promise - I would make it out alive. I glanced down at my journal and brushed my finger across the cover. So many thoughts, so many hopes and dreams just waiting to be realized. I closed my eyes and took a deep breath and focused again on the colors in the sky forming a symphony of beauty. When the reds found their way across the sky, I smiled. This was my favorite part - the splashing of color across the night sky. And then I heard it. She was crying. I remember distinctly the feeling of dread; the sniffs to keep her tears at bay interrupted her coughs to cover her muffled sobs; I was stuck. I wrinkled my eyebrows in exasperation - I hated coming into contact with people who cried, especially those who made a habit of it. I always felt obligated to do something - and there was nothing more awkward than feeling the need to comfort a stranger. I struggled with comforting myself, how could I find the words to make it better for someone else? Perhaps it was selfish, but I chose to ignore the tears. I tucked my brown hair behind my ear and focused on the light blue taking over the deep violet of the sky.

"I never should have gone home yesterday."

My insides sank. Was this girl seriously trying to make conversation? My eyebrows bent in frustration as if suddenly my nail beds were absolutely fascinating...I hoped her monologue would end there. I didn't need any more drama in my life. I wrinkled my nose at the discovered dirt underneath my fingernails and made a mental note to clean them when I got home.

"I never should have believed him when he said he'd change."

Her words were stilted, interrupted by hiccuped sobs.

Obviously she wasn't going to stop talking. I hesitated and glanced at my forgotten journal - the empty pages aching to be filled with thoughts and questions and descriptions...there wasn't anything I could do but listen, so I did. I turned my face halfway towards hers and raised an eyebrow.

Apparently, that's all she needed.

"I mean, it's not like he's my dad or anything, but he's sleeping in the same bed as my mom. You'd think I'd get some kind of perk besides him trying to crawl in the same bed as me."

She had my attention then. Was she...was she serious? Somewhere in the recesses of my social understanding I found my voice as I tried to ignore the funny feeling creeping inside my stomach.

"Is this some kind of sick joke?"

She didn't pay any mind to my question.

"I had to wait a little longer than normal to get out of the house this time," she shuddered, "He, uh...he fell asleep..." She couldn't finish - the tears continued, streaming down her face. "Listen, you don't have to tell me this."

She turned and looked at me with mascara inked around her eyes like a wet raccoon.

"Do you ever look at the sunrise and feel hope? It's a new day. What's left behind in yesterday has passed and there is nothing you can do to bring it back. It's reliable. The promise of a morning sky supersedes anything I've ever known. It's beautiful. All of the colors, mixing together to create a new shade..." Her voice dropped to just above a whisper. "Without the sunrise I wouldn't feel alive. The sunrise reminds me there's always another day coming..."

I was speechless. Who was this girl? I looked closely but didn't recognize her despite the oversized hoodie, sock sleeves and greasy hair. Somewhere in the distance, birds began to sing, a three note song of hope and promise; glancing at the sky I gasped, the light blue began to mix with the red to create a rainbow of radiating light standing in stark contrast to the few stars remaining stubbornly behind.

I turned to hear more of her story; despite my best intentions, I was held captive by the intricate connection I felt in such a short amount of time. Forgotten were the feelings of disdain at the beginning of our meeting; I wanted to know more. I wanted a chance to ask questions. I needed to know I really wasn't alone. I remember being keenly disappointed when I realized she was gone.

Her words echoed in my brain. How had she known my story? How could someone be going through the exact same thing, but different? I looked around one more time, to make sure I hadn't missed her hiding in a corner or shrinking back undetected, but she was no where to be found. I slumped in defeat. Gathering my bags, I made my way to the front door - glancing the entire time at the faces around me. *Where did she go?* I wondered, *How could she have just...disappeared?* My thoughts were soon interrupted by the first bell, signaling the custodians to unlock the doors so we wouldn't have to wait in the cold anymore. The crowd forming outside quickly disappeared as students rushed in doors to get away from the brisk morning air. I sat there for awhile, dumbfounded. *Should I wait? Should I let someone know?* I glanced around one more time before settling on the mystery. Turning around, I walked through the doors of my school, my thoughts on everything but the homework I still had to complete for my first period class.

That was when I met her, though. That was when I met the girl who changed my life through a single conversation. I never saw her again, even though I constantly look for her in the crowded hallways of the school. Every once in awhile, I remember the conversation with stunning clarity. This stranger, in one simple phrase, threw my world incredibly off-kilter. And regardless of whether I ever see her again or whether she was a figment of my often times active imagination, I don't care. Her words give me a reason to believe. Her words remind me of one simple thing: hope.

One

HIS NAME IS KEVIN MATOUSE. AT SIX FEET, HE'S EASILY A HEAD ABOVE the rest in our class. But he's so cute and every time he gets close to me my knees start to wobble and my hands start dripping with sweat and I start to stutter. A shaky girl with leaky hands and a speech impediment doesn't help the whole, "I'm trying to impress you" vibe I attempt to give off, but it's whatever. We've been together for about a month, and I always promise myself I will stop acting like a complete schoolgirl when I am around him, but it never happens. He looks at me and my heart starts beating against my ribcage and the butterflies shake violently in the pit of my stomach. I just can't help it. Chalk it up to my teenage hormones.

We met at a coffee shop I frequent. I'd seen him before, but never imagined he'd stop to talk to me. That first conversation always brings a rush of blood to my cheeks - it was as if he knew me. We talked for hours, forgetting about homework and families and those around us. We sat there until closing

- when the baristas had to quietly clear their throats to get our attention. I blushed then, and I blush now just thinking about it. Never before have I encountered someone who can completely make the world disappear.

We're not the most likely of pairs. I'm the weird quiet girl who carries around a Moleskine to capture ideas and phrases and quotes to escape from the blindingly boring lectures my teachers feel the need to share on a daily basis. Kevin? He's a football player. And he plays guitar and his family loves each other and well...he's basically my opposite. Except not - and that's the thing. He's not my opposite. Whenever we're together it seems as though our brains are connected. We get each other. Our backgrounds couldn't be any different, but when he looks at me, I know I'm the only one he wants to be around - and that's nice.

I've heard he's not the best guy, and he's not good for me, but these people don't know him like I do - they don't even know me that well. Despite the rumors, despite the whispers when we walk down the hall, there's just something about him. Perhaps it's those baby blues; a girl can get lost in some baby blues, especially when they're paired with shining white teeth and a body with muscles I didn't even know existed. *Crap.* I think to myself. I've gone and drooled on my homework again.

I'm at home now, and all I can hear is my mom and dad arguing. An exasperated breath falls off my lips and I sigh. I think for a second about packing up my books and walking to the coffee shop - from the sound of the words flying across our living room, there won't be any quiet here for some time. I roll my eyes and place my hands over my ears, turning my music up just a little bit - just enough to drown out the biting remarks right outside my door. For as long as I can remember, they've spoken through anger instead of love. My mom isn't brave enough to leave him and my dad can't imagine life without someone to push around. It's their own vicious cycle mixed with infidelity. A nightmare, if you ask me. You would think that after twenty years of marriage, they would have figured out how to get along. I think about Kevin again and smile. We get along. We get along just fine.

Forgetting my homework and the lengthening fight outside my room, I close my eyes and dream about being Mrs. Kevin Matouse with knees that don't shake and hands that don't sweat and words that don't skip.

I'm startled out of my reverie by a loud knock on the door. Obscenities fill the open silence as my dad attempts to twist the handle. I roll my eyes and lean over to switch the lock right as he bursts into the room. The stench of alcohol sweeps over me and I try my hardest not to gag. Last time I gagged it bought me thirty minutes of face slapping and a lecture about respect. I stumble out of my chair and walk toward the corner of my room knowing this probably won't end well. I search his face, looking for signs of what the fight could be about - what could have upset him to the point of explosion.

His eyes are bloodshot. His hands purple from the strain of withholding his anger. This all happens so quickly, in the span of a few minutes. He struggles to keep focus on me - his head having a hard time keeping up with the rest of his body. I know this body language well. Someone will pay for a mistake. The mental checklist roars through my mind: progress report came in today - I made straight A's. When I got home, I spent two hours cleaning the house - just like he always expected. And then the realization.

Oh.

This time, it wasn't me.

Right behind him is my mom. My mom with some other man. I can't even compute what this means I'm so confused...I'm confused and terrified because I see him moving toward me.

"Dad, what are you...."

Apparently it was me because my dad starts throwing punches as soon as he's close enough I can see his drunken eyes.

I feel a fist collapse against my cheek and I gasp.

I can't process my mom standing with some guy because the blows keep coming. The blows keep coming and he keeps yelling and my mom keeps crying. That guy just stands there.

I ask myself: *What kind of person just stands there?*

"You did this, you dirty little whore. You're nothing. Nothing!"

His hands find places to grip and slap and poke that no one would ever see. There will be bruises. There is already blood. My mother weakly argues with my father, begging him to stop simply because the carpet has enough stains.

I barely register that she mentions nothing about him hitting her daughter.

I finally manage to break free and push my way past mom and Mr. I-don't-have-a-voice. I really don't know where I'm headed; I just know I need to get out. My cheek still burns in the shape of a fist. Gingerly, I reach up and touch the bruise forming. It's tender. Swollen. I turn back around to see if anyone is following and trip over my little brother's toy truck. Falling against the wall, I jam my fingers. I don't have time to think about it though, because I can hear the rage building in my room. The man-without-a-voice is suddenly yelling back obscenities at my father. It will only take a few minutes before my dad realizes me gone. As I run out the door, I hear my mom in the background, crying.

I can't help but wonder if she's crying because she was caught or because I'm leaving. My chest heaves with remorse and pain, and I fight the bile forcing itself up my throat. I will not let him win. My head turns reflexively as I shoot a furtive glance back to my house, sitting eerily silent in contrast to the raging argument heard for miles just seconds before. I give up and crumple to the grass in defeat. My body flinches against the icy green blades, but I simply wipe my cheek and pull my hoodie over my head to protect my skin from the burning sensation of frozen water against the most recent scrapes and bruises. My face crinkles in disgust. It happened again. How could anyone ever want me? How could anyone ever find me attractive? I close my eyes as the tears start to fall freely, melting the ice around me.

Maybe my dad was right. Maybe I am nothing. The inner record player rewinds the events of the last hour and I start to wonder. How was my mother's mistake my fault? Why did my father choose to take his anger out on me? I try to push the thoughts out making me think I am nothing more than a human punching bag and reach for positive memories. The last time Kevin kissed me. Laughing with my friends at lunch. Getting my English paper back and noting the "brilliant!" scrawled across the top by Mrs. Peabody. I keep this up until my doubts are replaced with my shaky self-confidence. I am worth something. People do want me. Staring at tiny blades of grass glistening with night frost I force the mantra back and forth through my head.

Just breathe, I tell myself. Just breathe.

I stay there for about thirty minutes. A bit longer than normal, but my father doesn't disappoint - I know the routine: anger, remorse, forced forgiveness and guilt. Compulsiveness at its finest. I hear his footsteps before I smell the residue of his latest bottled conquest. I take a deep breath and pray for strength. I close my eyes and for a brief second pretend I'm someone else entirely.

"Stephanie?" His whisper sounds strained – like he's fighting back tears I know will come.

I motion to him with my hand, not really wanting to get up and feel the tender spots continuing to let me know their existence. His face breaks through the bushes and registers my shivering frame. His shoulders collapse and for a brief second, he buries his face in his hands.

"Oh sweetie. Oh Stephanie. I'm so sorry. I'm sorry. I promised, I know. But I couldn't help it. Please don't leave me. Please."

His earnest words weren't new to my ears; I knew his learned drunken behavior warranted this scene. It always did. I hate this part more than any other - even the fists against skin. How can you not help it? How can you not help hitting your own flesh and blood? I don't get it. His arms reach to lift me off the grass and I shrug away - pain shooting up my ribs and radiating off of my knee.

"Leave me alone." I say it without thinking.

My heart stops and I hold my breath. *Stupid, stupid, stupid* I think to myself - waiting for the inevitable backlash. In my haste and anger, I allowed my voice to be heard. It was the exact opposite of what my dad expects from us. Reconciliation is nothing to him - we reunite on his terms. If I don't feel like it, well...I have to at least act like I want to forgive and forget. His response to my mistake is immediate.

A switch flips and my dad's face blanches in anger. He stands up straight - his hands on his hips and his eyes wide with disbelief. You would have thought I physically slapped him. A sneer crawls across his face slowly and he laughs.

"What? You want me to leave you alone?"

The change in behavior comes suddenly, but not unexpectedly. My father could be the poster child for borderline personality disorder triggered by alcoholic stupor. His eyes darken and I grimace against the melting ice. He turns around and starts walking back to the house, grumbling the whole way there about my lack of appreciation for what I had been given.

"You want me to leave you alone?" he says over his

shoulder, "I'll leave you alone. Find somewhere else to sleep tonight you waste of space."

I stare at his retreating figure for a half second before I realize what just happened. Without thinking, I jump up and run after him, crying the whole way.

"Daddy, daddy – no wait....please! I...I didn't meant it."

My voice starts shaking with hysteria. I trip on a dip in the road, landing hard on my knee. Blood immediately starts forming tiny rivers down my jeans.

"Please...." I whisper, broken.

He turns around and walks towards me, a smirk of satisfaction on his face. Taking the hand he offers, I wince at the force he uses to yank me to a standing position. He brings his face within inches of my own, his breath nearly knocking me over. He reaches out and grabs my arms with such brute force, tears threaten to spill out against my will. I bite my lip, fighting to keep them under control.

He wrinkles his lips in disgust. "I regret the day you were born. You mean nothing to me. Nothing. You're the worst mistake of my life."

His words cut to the deepest places I hide from everyone. Within seconds, my father manages to reach inside and rip open every single wound from every single harsh word ever spoken to me. His retreating figure broke my heart before. Now? I am shattered. Without saying a word, I wriggle from his grasp and turn and walk into the house, ignoring the apparent absence of my mother. I make my way to my room, welcoming the haze starting to form around my brain.

I am nothing. I mean nothing. Closing my eyes, I let the darkness sweep over me as the tears finally gain the freedom to take over. My body, exhausted from the night's events, begs for rest, but my mind wants nothing of it. I spend the rest of the night in a comatose state and it's not until the first light starts peeking through the corner window that I wake. With an urgency that can only be explained as lunacy, I shower and change clothes in record time.

The sunrise. I need to see it. I need to remember.

I leave the house with minutes to spare and am instantly rewarded by one of the most stunning displays of color I have yet to see. I lock the door behind me, stuff my hands in the pockets of my jacket, and begin the long walk to school, eyes glued to oranges and reds and pinks, fighting for a piece of the sky.

I see him before he sees me. He's sitting on the bleachers - my favorite spot - talking to someone on his cell phone. This has been our meeting place for a few weeks now, kind of our way of starting the day together. This morning, he's wearing his typical uniform of letter jacket and jeans. I think of his scent - the way it lingers on my clothes after he holds me - and I smile, the butterflies coming to life inside. His hair falls across his forehead and he reaches up to brush it away. I stop for a few minutes and just watch him. I imagine he's talking to his mom - who else would be up this early? Not wanting to interrupt him, I wait for awhile longer. I didn't know if he would be here this morning because I wasn't able to answer his phone call last night.

Last night.

Memories come flooding back and I try and push them away. I glance again at the sky and remind myself today is a new day with new possibilities and hope. My eyes wander back to Kevin - he looks tired. He's off the phone now, his eyes focusing on the clouds in the distance. His head rests in his hands and every once in awhile his left foot starts to invol-untarily bounce. His nervous twitch. I smile to myself and make my way over to the bleachers. He hears my approach and lifts his head. Smiling, he reaches for my hand to help me up the stairs.

"You started early this morning."

He tilts his head and his grin grows across his face, "What do you mean?"

I point to his phone still sticking out of his pocket and he nods his head in understanding.

"Oh. Yeah. That was uh...my mom." He scratches his head sheepishly, as if he wonders whether or not he should divulge information, and shrugs, "She just likes to know I made it to school okay."

I raise an eyebrow and position myself close to him - away from the chill of the morning air. He wraps his arm around me and pulls me closer still. "Good morning, beautiful."

I smile and blush at his greeting and lean forward to kiss his cheek.

"Mornin'," my voice is a lot deeper than normal - I cough to clear the frog out of my throat and silently curse the evening spent outside on the frozen grass.

I glance out of the corner of my eye as I sit gingerly next to him - my legs still incredibly sore from the night before. I pull my hair down across my face and attempt to make my bangs fall below my blackened eye. I feel his gaze inspecting me - noticing my wincing, my sharp intake of breath, my purposeful positioning of hair across my face...

"Your dad get a hold of you again?" I sigh. He always knows.

"Yeah." I sniff to avoid the fresh wave of tears threatening escape, but he beats me to the punch.

He doesn't even say anything at first. He just grabs my hand and squeezes it.

"Steph..."

"Don't Kevin...please. Not now. I can't handle it."

I look at him through my tears and will him to understand - to not go to those places - the ones where people ask me to leave my home or to say something against the only family I've ever known. They don't understand. They won't ever understand. It's so much more complicated than walking out the door.He glances down at our fingers - now interlocked. He looks at me and gives me the crooked smile that would make me go cockeyed for the rest of the day.

"Why'd you come out here this morning?" He asked.

"To remember."

"Remember what?"

"Hope."

He touches the bruise on my cheek, black against the paleness of my skin, and purses his lips.

"I hate that you have to live like this, Steph. No one should have to experience what you do on a daily basis. How do you do it? How have you not gone crazy? I think about my own parents and...I don't know...it's just so hard for me to fathom someone not experiencing the safety of a family."

He takes a strand of my hair and places it behind my ear and looks at me, waiting for a reply.I have to hand it to him - his approach is different. Instead of asking me to leave, he asks why I stay. He tries to understand. I squeeze his hand as I fight for the words. I look away and focus on the sun's rays bathing the trees in its morning glow.

"I don't know, Kevin. I just...do. I have no choice but to survive. My brother helps - knowing there's someone younger than me in the house pushes me to stay. I couldn't ever leave Pacey knowing what happens when my dad gets angry. It's just the cards I've been dealt, I guess." I shrug my shoulders complacently and look at him out of the corner of my eye, "The only thing I can do is hang on to the constants in my life - writing. Protecting Pacey. The hope of a sunrise." I glance down at our hands and whisper, "You."

He takes my face gently into his hands and kisses me lightly on this lips - briefly touching the scar from the night before - and the birds begin to sing, echoing across the field against the backdrop of clouds that look like fire and mirror my heart - alive and bursting with a new day.

He pulls back and looks me in the eyes, "I'm going to find a way to keep you safe, Steph. I promise."

Seeing the intensity in his gaze, I know without a doubt he's telling the truth. I think about my father - his anger and what he would do if he knew I was talking with Kevin, and my blood runs cold. I look away for a second to collect my thoughts. I'm not used to this feeling - this knowing I need protection but not wanting it for fear of retaliation.

"Kevin...my dad is dangerous. Please don't get involved - I don't want you hurt."

He studies me and shrugs his shoulders, "It's too late, Steph. I'm already involved. I was involved the second I saw a bruise on your skin. Nothing will change that - and I promise I'll be careful. Your dad doesn't scare me."

I take a deep breath and let it out slowly. *That's the problem*, I think to myself.

I feel the fear rising - the fixation and compulsiveness - and silently will them away. Closing my eyes, I rest my head in my hands and wonder how long it will be until Kevin realizes the extent of my dad's power.

Two

EVEN THOUGH OUR CONVERSATION ENDED WITH ME CONCERNED ABOUT his safety, I go through school in a daze and a slight smile on my lips. Every once in awhile I blush when the memory of Kevin's kiss makes its way across my thoughts. I remain relatively unscathed during my classes - I'm a master of pretending to pay attention.

Except for Pre-Cal.

In my daydream I instinctively shut out what Mrs. Houghton asks the class. I never hear her call my name. I spend ten minutes after class, apologizing for my absent-mindedness and promising to pay attention in the future. The whole time I'm there I avoid her constant glances towards the bruise on my cheek. As soon as I'm able, I turn around and brush my hair across my face in a protective sweep.

"Hey Stephanie?" I wince and slowly turn to respond to Mrs. Houghton's question - making sure to plaster a smile across my face so she doesn't see my initial reaction.

"Yes ma'am?"

She glances at me and I watch her toy with the idea of asking me what happened. I see the wheels turning and her decide to forget about it, to not get involved, before she waves her hand at me as if to say, nothing - don't worry about it.

She smiles and simply says, "You did well on your test the other day. I just wanted to thank you for your hard work."

I stare at her for a split second - wondering if she's serious. I'm decent at math and never bomb an exam. My lowest grade on any assignment for this class was an 85 because I forgot to show my work on one problem. Despite my hard work, she's never said anything to me - never praised me for a job well done. I immediately disregard her compliment - knowing it was said simply to cover up what she really wanted to ask. When I realize she really isn't going to give me the third degree about the bruises, I gather my things together and hurry out the door, surprised at the mixed feelings taking over.

Despite my desire to remain invisible, to not bring attention to myself, my heart sinks. I rarely meet anyone willing to get messy for what is obviously a dire situation. All of my teachers gawk at the bruises when they see me. All of my teachers hesitate when they catch my eye after class. But there's only been one who even considered getting her hands dirty at my expense - and I haven't seen her in a long time. With new resolve, I decide to go pay Emma a visit after school. My cheeks blaze crimson at the thought of another person ignoring me, and I force my thoughts on those I know love me. I smile and make my way down the school hallway, stopping by my locker to get my Physics notes. The test I have coming up just might eat my lunch and ruin my average. Regardless of what happens at home, I know doing well in school and getting into college is my ticket out of here. It's the only hope I have, really. I make a mental note to study as much as possible for the test and am out the door as the last bell rings for the day - I need to see Emma. I need to be reminded someone notices what I am going through at home.

She lives about ten minutes from the school so walking isn't a problem. I see her house from a distance and immediately a peace begins to wash over me. It happens every time I'm near her - I know for those few short hours I'm safe. I can be me. She's the calmest person I know - nothing surprises her.

Walking up to her door, I smile at the fall decorations littering her porch. Carved pumpkins, cornucopias filled with fake fruit and twigs of numerous styles, shapes and sizes form a cozy little nook around her two ancient looking rocking chairs. Never one to scrimp on decorations, Emma stocks up on anything to celebrate the current season. Her zest for life echoes throughout everything - even the fake cobwebs hanging from the corner of the railing. I lift my hand and notice a stray cobweb sticking to my palm. I wrinkle my nose. I don't care if it's fake, it looks gross. I shake it off and stuff my hands in the pockets of my coat.

I walk through the door and notice the new air freshener greeting my senses. And cookies - ah - Emma's cookies. I skip into the kitchen, immediately in a better mood, and help myself to the cookies already on the counter. Plopping on the couch, I perk my ears and listen for sounds of Emma. I hear her in the room next to the kitchen - probably doing laundry, I think with a smirk - and then I frown. I can't even remember the last time I washed my jeans. I suddenly glance down at the couch, expecting to see a spot from dirt and grime where I sit. I breathe a quiet sigh of relief when I see no signs of dirt and continue to eat the chocolatey goodness.

"There's milk in the fridge, Steph," I hear Emma call from the laundry room and a slow smile spreads across my lips.

How she manages to make me feel so at home is beyond

me.

"Is it that nasty organic stuff you always buy or soy milk?" I call back - knowing my question would light a fire in Emma's already spunky attitude.

I don't drink soy milk - even the thought of it makes me gag. I head over to the fridge to look for the fresh gallon she promised. I hear something drop in the laundry room and a snort of discontent. Yep. Teasing her is always worth the entertainment. I smile and pour the milk in a tall glass before heading back to the couch.

"Stephanie," she calls from the hallway, "either drink the milk or go buy yourself some milky water substitute for the real thing. You aren't going to find soy milk in this house."

She walks in the room with a room full of clothes and peeks her head above mounds of towels and baby clothes. "Besides. You know I'm allergic to soy."

She throws the clothes on the couch and collapses in the middle of them.

"You wanna help me fold? Benjamin nearly soiled every single pair of onesies he had this week. I don't care what people say. Infants have more mess in them than anyone can ever imagine. I swear if he has another diaper blowout I just may puke."

Looking at me, she brushes the hair out of her eyes and sits up straight.

Well this didn't take long.

"What happened, Steph?"

Her questions are never optional. I think back to when I first met her in my Creative Writing class in high school. She was my teacher. I was her student. Something happened in the middle of the year though - after I turned in a paper explaining my tendencies of self-denial and habitual expectation of failure - we became more like mother/daughter and less like your standard teacher/student. I will never forget the first time she kept me after class and asked me her first question formed as a statement. I had no choice but to respond - and to be honest. Looking back, I know it was her who saved me that semester from some dangerous decisions I was bound to make. Looking back, I know it was her who likely called the authorities due to my continual bruises and quiet tears.

As always, the authorities did nothing. As always, Emma was there - door unlocked, phone ready. I spent a lot of time hiding out from my father that year. I was always nervous he would find out where she lived - he hated anyone getting in the way of his plans and constantly threatened to find out who said something. It took months for him to finally believe it wasn't me. A lone shiver of memory courses through my veins and I wrap the coat tight around my chest. I glance at her and took a deep breath, pulling my hair away from my face so she can see the bruises.

"He got angry again last night."

She breathes in sharply and I put my hand up before she starts stumbling over her words, "It's okay. I survived. He apologized afterwards. And I know it sounds weird, but I know he didn't mean to do it. For some reason he always seems to take his anger out on me. My mom's been cheating on him - I had a feeling, but last night we actually found out the truth. I don't even know how it happened - he was over at our house. The guy just stood there as dad hit me and yelled at me." I shudder involuntarily at the memory and continue - straightening my back as well as my resolve, "We worked it out though."

I look at Emma, begging her to not make a big deal out of what happened, even though I know with every fiber of my being just how big of a deal it is for my dad to do what he did to me - continually. My knee is proof - it still throbs from where he pushed me up against the desk and where I later crashed against the pavement.

A string of curse words fly from her lips and I hide a smile, it takes a lot for Emma to swear. She looks at me and wrinkles her eyebrows - showing her disagreement with my flippant attitude.

"Steph, this is not okay. When are you going to get out of there? When are you going to finally accept it's not your responsibility? You are meant for something great - something big. How can you amount to anything if you are fighting for your life?"

I let her words wash over me. I've heard them before - I heard them from Kevin just that morning. Honestly, much of what she says runs through my head on its own accord. But I know it makes no difference. Nothing is going to change - if I tried to leave, it would only make it worse.

"Emma, I just can't leave. It's not possible. How would I manage? Where would I go? Who would take care of Pacey? There are just too many obstacles right now. Besides, it's only a couple months." I shrug and play with the string on my jacket's hood, "I can do anything for a couple of months."

Our conversation is interrupted by the unadulterated cry of an infant and Emma wrinkles her eyebrows.

"I need to feed him. Are you able to stay tonight? Dinner's going to be ready here in about thirty minutes or so." She turns and looks at me and points at the couch, "Hold that thought. This conversation is far from over."

I stretch against the pillows and fight the urge to run. The last thing I really want to experience is a sense of domesticity - even though I know it's what I crave. One of the hardest things for me to see is a family loving each other, knowing my own family waits at home for me - all too willing to yell my indiscretions to the world as the bruises form on my skin.

Emma walks back in the room and Benjamin giggles at the sight of me. My heart melts and against my better judgment,

I decide to stay. I may get nauseous at the sight of a close-knit family, but I can't ever turn down the affections of this little boy. I smile at Emma and reach for Benjamin.

"You're evil, you know that, Emma? Pure evil. And your timing? Impeccable."

Emma chuckles and passes her son off to me and turns towards the kitchen.

Calling over her shoulder, she says, "Is it really my timing or you being absolutely predictable?"

I throw a pillow at her and miss her retreating figure by mere centimeters. Dang it.

"Watch out for the candles!" She hollers from the other room.

I grit my teeth and glance at Benjamin who stares at me from big, brown eyes. Grabbing the bottle from the nearby table I sigh.

"How does she know, Benjamin? How does she always know?"

He shrieks at the sight of the bottle and reaches for sustenance. For a brief moment, I wonder if my parents ever felt for me what I feel right at this moment - watching Benjamin, a sudden urge to protect him at all cost creeps into my heart without notice or invitation. My eyes began to mist over at the realization.

As if on cue, Emma walks back into the room and kisses the top of my head.

"You're beautiful, you know that girl? Your heart for others is hopeful and pure and trusting. No matter what anyone else has told you, you are worth much to this family and even though you may not have a home with your mom and dad, you have a home here."

I let the tears flow freely then. Leaning against her shoulder, with Benjamin in my lap, I let myself rest for the first time in days. For a few minutes, I allow myself the ability to forget about the nightmare of the past twenty-four hours and to build dreams of the future I hope to create. For a few minutes, I imagine what it would be like to have a home and a family who loved me and cared for me and wanted the best for me. I imagine what it would feel like to be protected at all costs.

And for a brief moment of time, I actually believe what Emma said.

I actually believe I am worth something.

Emma just sits there. Quiet. Letting me grieve and begin to heal.

Finally, she glances at me and asks, "Do you remember that one time in class last year when we did the line activity?"

"Um yeah. It's actually something I would rather forget." I smile at her and shrug my shoulders as I wipe the remaining tears from my cheeks, "Wasn't the most shining moment in my history of self-confidence."

"Do you remember what you said that day?"

I sigh and glare at her as she rearranges Benjamin who has fallen asleep on her shoulder. I know she has a point, but I'm not ready for self-evaluation. Not yet. I grimace, knowing the thoughts will come anyway.

"What are you trying to get at, Emma? I remember that day. I remember what I said. I remember not believing in myself. How can I forget? I used to have razors stashed in the side pocket of my backpack just in case I decided I couldn't handle it anymore. Why are we bringing this up again?"

I can't help it; the anger is already there, waiting for me to tap into it. I love Emma to death, but sometimes her probing irritates me to no end. And this? This memory? It's something I try to forget - it reminds me of a darker time. One without hope.

I would never tell her this, but it was on that day I actually decided to end it all. I was through - done. Bored. Bruised and rejected and so totally fed up with dealing with being absolutely invisible to those who could rescue me. And then she stopped me.

I realized something during the last question of the activity. She had been inspired by Erin Gruwell, the teacher responsible for the Freedom Writers. She placed a piece of tape along the middle of the hallway outside our classroom and asked us questions. If the statement applied to our lives, we stepped up to the line. The goal? To build a familiar atmosphere within the classroom walls. I remember through this exercise my classmates suddenly realizing they weren't the only ones going through things - they weren't the only ones who liked certain hobbies or activities. A lot of our walls and defenses crashed down around us through her questions ranging from what movie we had just seen to whether or not we had tried ecstasy to the last one: whether we believed in ourselves despite anything others had told us. I'm sure she thought it was a gimme question. I mean, who wouldn't step up to the line? Every teenager I meet seems to radiate self-confidence - a sense of immortality and entitlement oozes from every pore. Of course, every one stepped up to the line. Every one except for me. My heart started beating against the prison of my chest and I felt faint - I held on to the wall as everyone around me smiled and glanced at each other in realization of the importance of the activity. I just stood there - a blank slate - tears flowing unwillingly down my cheeks. It wasn't until Emma sent everyone back into the classroom for discussion that she saw me - face against the wall, eyes secretly eyeing the blade poking out surreptitiously in my pocket. No one would know. No one would care.

And then I felt a hand on my shoulder.

"Stephanie. What's wrong?" Her eyebrows wrinkled in confusion and she glanced automatically to the list of questions - assuming one had sparked my tears - which wasn't far from the truth. She waited there, eyes focused on mine, until I started talking.

"I'm fine, really Mrs. Stevens, I just...the activity was hard." I looked at her, struggling to spit out the words." I couldn't step up to the line because I don't believe in myself." I shrugged my shoulders and wiped my cheeks, "Realizing that, scared me."

Her shoulders sagged and I immediately felt guilty for being such a downer to this teacher who had done nothing but care for me everyday. I was just about to ask to use the restroom when she smiled, drew me into her arms and whispered in my ear.

"You may not believe in you, but I do. No matter what anyone has said; no matter what anyone will say; I have seen what you are capable of and the love you are able to give - and I know without a shadow of doubt you will amount to great things. I believe in you, Stephanie. Don't ever forget that."

Just like tonight, the tears fell freely - staining her white sweater with eyeliner and spent mascara. She didn't mind, though - just like she doesn't mind tonight. I steal a glance her way and see her looking at me cautiously. I suddenly realize why she brought the subject up and I grab her hand.

"Thank you for believing in me, Emma."

She smiles and squeezes my hand.

"You know I always will." She looked at me closely. "Did anyone notice your bruise today?"

I nodded.

"Yeah. Kevin did this morning and Mrs. Houghton started to ask me about it but then changed her mind." I let out a short laugh tinged with cynicism, "It's not necessarily the situation anyone wants to sign up for, you know? And the last thing I want to be is a charity case."

Emma continues to look at me and wrinkles her nose in thought, "Stephanie, you're not a charity case." She goes quiet for a little while - placing a pacifier in Benjamin's mouth. "Do you want me to work my connections again?"

I roll my eyes and scratch my nose.

"Emma. You know more than anyone else what a twisted system we have. Do you think calling this in would amount to anything? Really? CPS has already proved themselves royally inadequate for this situation."

She stays silent, bouncing Benjamin in her arms to keep him calm. He looks at me with wide, trusting eyes - innocent to the conversation we are having and the evil it symbolizes. I say a quick prayer, asking for this innocence to stay as long as possible. Kevin's right. No one should have to face this.

Taking her silence as a sign I was right, I stand up and kiss her forehead and rub Benjamin's fuzzy hair.

"Will I see you tomorrow? I want to stay for dinner but I should probably get going."

She nods, "Yeah. I shouldn't be busy after you get out. I'm second guessing this whole 'take a year off of work' thing. I love being a mom, but...I miss my kids." She smiles at me and says, "You guys were a great bunch last year. Reminded me why I love teaching so much."

I laugh and widen my eyes in mock surprise, "You're the only one. Most teachers questioned their sanity after dealing with the people in my class." I fingered a picture hanging on the wall of her wedding day and turned back around, "How's Jude? I miss him."

"He's good. Busy. Work has him traveling a lot right now, analyzing and building reports about what he sees when observing those assigned to him. It's stressful, but he loves it." She glances at me as she gently lays Benjamin on the couch so he can sleep and her arm can rest. "He misses you too. He sees you as a daughter, you know."

I blush at the term of endearment and nod.

"Yeah, I know. And, if I could choose, I would definitely

have him as a father. He's at least showed me what I deserve."
I walk over to Emma and give her a long hug. "Thanks again for everything, Emma. I will stop by tomorrow after school."

She holds on to me and whispers, "Wait. You aren't going anywhere yet."

I look at her questioningly and she points towards the front door. "Jude is about to walk in and dinner is ready. Sit. Get comfortable. And take off that hoodie - I swear it's permanently attached. Don't you have a jacket to wear?"

I look at the worn down jacket leaning over the couch and Emma frowns. She opens her mouth to speak but is interrupted by the door opening and Jude walking inside. She winks at me and rushes over to give Jude a hug. I turn away only to be enveloped in some of the largest arms I've known.

"Steph! Goodness it's been awhile. It's so good to see you."

Jude's voice booms from his chest and I can't help but smile. There aren't very many men I know I can trust. Jude is definitely one of the few. I'm not sure how much of my sordid and complicated life he would admit to knowing about, but it doesn't matter - I know he cares.

"Hey Jude." I give his waist a squeeze and he steps back to get a better look at me. His face goes dark and his hands tighten for a brief second on my arms. I know he sees the bruises.

"Jude, honey - dinner is ready. Do you want to change first?"

Emma's voice cracks through the air and Jude tilts his head toward me as though he's trying to figure out whether to pursue the issue now or later. He squeezes my shoulders and leans forward to kiss me on the forehead before walking to their room to change. I breathe a sigh of relief and look for Emma in the kitchen.

She catches my eye and smiles, "Don't worry. I'll talk

to him. You won't have to say anything if you don't want to."

I nod and grab some plates to set the table. "I know. He's just concerned."

She stops tossing the salad and looks at me, "We both are, Stephanie."

I hold her gaze for a brief moment, not sure what to say. I glance down at my nails and begin picking at the cuticle - completely overwhelmed at the love I just saw in her eyes.

As always, dinner at the Stevens' house proves to be an event. Emma worked all day on braising beef into some incredible creation. She gives me a generous portion and at first I'm wondering if I will ever be able to finish. Halfway through, I understand this is a far cry from the SPAM I normally eat, and determine to shove every piece in to my mouth.

"How was work today, love?" Emma asks Jude while fighting Benjamin and his attempt to grab every utensil he can reach.

"It was good. Tiring. We've limited our search to a few key players in the field. No names, just leads - but the progress seems promising."

"What exactly are you looking for now, Jude?"

I take a breath from eating in order to join the conversation. I've never known what Jude does for a living - it's always been slightly mysterious and covert. Every time I see him I try to find out more, hoping to see a little peek into his life I didn't know before.

He stops mid bite and catches Emma's eye before answering the question.

"Well, I work for a non-profit trying to partner with local law enforcement. We haven't been fruitful, for some reason the police department is a bit reticent to join with our agency

- which we can understand. We aren't delegated by the government but through our own desire to see justice in our area. We have a rising issue with organized crime - specifically drug trafficking and prostitution. We're trying to get to the bottom of these problems - see if there's any darker force at play."

I struggle to swallow my food - suddenly not very hungry. I'm not sure what I was expecting him to answer, but it wasn't this. I fight for control, to mask the emotions running wild inside.

I fidget with my fork and ask the question I fear I already know the answer, "Could the cops be involved?"

Jude lowers his eyebrows.

"Be involved? Like how?"

"Well, if they are unwilling to help, could it be they're involved with the very forms of organized crime you are trying to prevent?"

Emma clears her throat and gets up from the table to refill her glass. I watch her and catch a single look thrown Jude's direction. I know there's something deeper here - something they aren't saying. I bite my lip at the unspoken irony and turn towards Jude. His fork is on the table now and his hands are clasped in front of him. This is his power stance. He means business.

"That is something we've considered, but we really aren't in the situation to tackle that level of corruption. We do have a few partner organizations who could help us if in fact the police force is corrupt."

His voice is...detached. He turns his head and looks out the window for awhile, making circles with his fork on the plate. He finally turns back and catches my gaze. He smiles - a small, knowing grin that makes me feel safe. Protected.

He continues, a little more present with the conversation, "Whatever the case, we're committed to keep those in harm's way safe. I have guys all over the field - watching and waiting.

We'll be there at the first misstep these guys make. It's been far too long and far too complicated a situation."

I study his face for awhile before nodding and returning to my food. I feel strangely comforted by his words. Emma knows my background. She knows my frustration with the local police's inaction at my expense. But as we finish our meal with the talk shifting to Benjamin's latest antics and words he possibly uttered during Jude's latest trip, I wonder how much she truly knew. How much she would be able to handle?

Three

Even though Emma baked cookies, she also found time to throw together a beautiful concoction of chocolate cake and strawberries. She pulls it out of the kitchen and both Jude and I groan. There's no way I can place another bite in my mouth, but I know I'm certainly going to try.

"So, Stephanie have you looked at colleges lately?" Jude asks as he takes a knife to the cake.

"Um, kind of? I mean, it's not really a priority. I'm most likely staying local, you know - to take care of Pacey."

"Hey hon, didn't you tell me you found something for Stephanie? A college she might enjoy?"

Jude and Emma exchange a glance and she passes me a pamphlet.

"I found this college on the internet. It's low residency - which means you travel to the campus three weeks every semester for work with the professors. The rest of the time you take classes and correspond via the internet."

I take the pamphlet and flip through it nonchalantly.

"I guess I'll need to find internet then, huh?"

Emma's eyes widen and she shakes her head, "Duh. We have internet. You could come over here and work. Or there's always the coffee shop - they have free wi-fi."

I raise an eyebrow and tuck the pamphlet into my pocket.

"I doubt my father would understand me frequenting your house and I'm pretty sure he'd freak if he found out I came over here to take college courses. But - thank you, Emma. I'll take a look at this."

The clock's chime echoes across the living room and my eyes make their way to its place on the wall. I sigh when I notice the time. My dad is not the worrying type, unless it deals with me not being there when he needs me. I stretch and push myself off the couch, making my way over to where Emma and Jude are sitting.

"I should probably go, guys. Emma - I'll see you later this week? I may need some help on a paper I'm writing for English." I lean forward to give her a hug.

She accepts the embrace, rubbing my back a little before she lets go and looks out her window, glancing back at me in concern.

"It's pretty dark outside, Steph. Are you sure you're going to be okay? You didn't have the van when you got here and that's a long way to walk."

I'm almost out the door when I stop and turn around and give her a smirk.

"No offense, Emma, but I'm pretty sure I can handle myself. There's not much out there I haven't seen."

Emma rolls her eyes and calls out at my retreating figure - "It's not you seeing these things that bother me, Stephanie. It's running into them time and time again without changing your scenery. According to Einstein, that's the sign of insanity."

I laugh and shake my head - letting her know I hear every word she said. Buckling myself against the cold, I brace myself for whatever I find when I walk through the front door of my own home.

She doesn't let me get past her driveway. Running outside with Benjamin already bundled in a blanket, she dangles her keys and motions for me to get in her jeep.

"I'm driving, Steph. I don't care what you do at night or how many times you've walked these streets. You're not walking them with me knowing you're out there when I could have taken you home."

She smiles and places her son in his car seat - still careful not to wake him. The air is getting colder, I could feel the chill of the night sky descending on the neighborhood. I twitch from a sudden chill and wrap my jacket closer against my chest. Climbing into the passenger side, I put on my seatbelt and rub my legs for warmth. Emma opens her door and starts the ignition, heat blasting immediately from the vents. I'm an independent person. I have to be. There aren't very many people I can truly count on, even though that number is slowly rising. Every once in awhile, though - it's a great feeling to allow myself to be cared for and know someone is concerned. Looking at Emma, I'm suddenly glad she decided to drive me home.

Four

MY BROTHER IS WAITING FOR ME WHEN I WALK IN THE DOOR.

"Sissy, where have you been?!" he whispers earnestly as I pick him to give him a hug. He pulls my ear towards his mouth and says, "Dad is mad again. This time at mom. She can't be friends with Tyler anymore. Dad went to the store and told mom Tyler better be gone when he gets back. Mom is in the kitchen crying."

Pacey looks around and rubs his eyes and reaches around my neck. Playing with my hair, he sighs and shakes his head - showing maturity beyond his years.

"Tyler's still here...he scary. Made mom cry."

My heart sinks. *Really?* I close my eyes and feel a deep sense of regret for my brother who is being subjected to harsh realities at a young age. At four-years-old, he already knows the name of mom's "special friend" and by the way he's clinging to my arms, has seen dad hit something or someone since he got home from work. I glance wearily around the living room and head towards my room before I hear the scream.

"Tyler! I. Can't. Leave. Don't you get it?! I can't leave him.

He'd find us. He'd find you. I'm stuck here."

"Like hell you are...," a deep voice answers back and I hear footsteps rushing down the hallway toward the living room. They're heavy and I envision work boots stained with mud and grime leaving marks on mom's precious carpet. It's not long before I hear the ragged breath of someone desperate behind us.

Shielding Pacey from whatever is coming, I turn around and gasp. It's him. Mom's friend. Mr I-don't-have-a-voice suddenly found purpose, and it's built in what strangely looks like a gun. And Pacey is right. Looking at Tyler's bloodshot eyes, I'm filled with an incredible sense of fear.

I'm frozen to the floor. Pacey begins shrieking in my ear for momma because despite my attempts to protect him I am no match to his young muscles breaking free from my grip. He sees Tyler. He sees the gun. His eyes go wild and he continues to scream.

"MOMMA! MOMMA! MOMMA! Where are you?! MOMMA! MOMMA! MOMMA! Why'd you make her cry?! MOMMMMAAAAA!!!!!"

Like a broken record, Pacey's shouts grate against my soul. This just isn't right. This just isn't right and there's nothing I can do about it. Tyler is waving the gun around like a madman and I am stuck between him and what he wants and Pacey is shouting and my world is spinning and this just isn't right and my thoughts fly out of my reach but I don't know what to do and where is my mom? Where is my mom?

My world stops for a split second and I realize where I am - Pacey's death grip on my neck has me focus in on what's going on long enough to understand what I need to do. I gather my thoughts with enough force and pull out my cell phone to call 911. I stare at Tyler's eyes - punch drunk with heroine and whiskey, and pray the operator answers before someone is shot. I can't even hear the telephone ringing due to Tyler hollering.

"Where's your father?!" he cries, "I'm going to shoot that bastard. Don't believe me? Just wait. I'm through dealing with him. Try and tell me I can't see my woman anymore. Try and make me."

His hands are shaking and his eyes are wild.

I snort. *Your woman? Pretty sure your woman is already married.*

Shrugging my shoulders, I push down the words I want to say and plead with my eyes for him to shut up. His words have stopped making sense and sound more like a huge infant spitting out sounds to gain attention. The operator finally connects and I breathe easier with human contact on the other end of the line. In short, staccato phrases I request help with a disturbance, watching Tyler's unsteady hand struggle to keep the gun upright.

The operator seems to notice my voice cracking under the weight of the situation and pauses. "Ma'am, has there been any violence?"

"I-I-I don't know."

I see my mom quietly peek around the corner and I glare at her quickly retreating figure. *Why is she such a blasted pansy?!* I think to myself - *You're my freaking mother. Start acting like it.*

"No. No violence. Not yet. But there could be if someone doesn't show up now."

I close my eyes and count to ten - hoping this is all a bad dream and I am about to wake up on Emma's couch with Benjamin slobbering on my shoulder.

My thoughts are shattered by the voice on the other line asking if any weapons are involved.

I stare at the shiny object shaking under Tyler's nervous fear and rage. Pacey is still screaming and fighting against my grip. I can feel my own sanity crashing around me.

"Yes," I say, "please hurry."

I hang up the phone and continue to stare at Tyler who is continuing to wave the gun around in a drunken rage. I stand there, waiting. Arms around Pacey, eyes closed, waiting for the nightmare to be over.

The police arrive at the scene shortly after Pacey's screams wake up the neighbors. Which of course makes everything perfect - one of my favorite things to provide is free entertainment for the neighborhood. I wrinkle my nose at the crowd gathering and turn my attention to my brother who is struggling to stay awake even though he is standing up and leaning against my knee. I glance at my phone to see what time it is and realize it's already almost midnight. I drop my arm and rub my hand through his hair - reminding myself to wash it later.

"Hey bub. Why don't you go inside and try to get some sleep? You look really tired and it's already pretty late."

He looks about ready to burst into tears again, so I pick him up and kiss his cheek. Knowing this is going to take something more than just a hug, I search for something he's familiar with; something we can both hold on to for strength.

"Who's your partner?" I whisper in his ear.

"...you are," he says, squeezing my neck.

I fight back the tears and squeeze back.

"That's right. I am. And I always will be. I always will be here, you know that, right?"

He nods slowly, his spiky hair brushing against my neck.

"If it'll make you feel better, you can go crash in my bed."

He rearranges himself in my arms and begins to smile - even if just a little smirk, it's a welcome sight in contrast with the terror he portrayed earlier.

He plays with the stray hairs hanging out of my ponytail and quietly asks, "Can I sleep with you tonight?" His eyes dart towards Tyler being handcuffed and mom crying on the porch. His eyes make their way back to mine and he says, "I don't want to be alone."

I close my eyes against his pain.

"I know, Pace. I know."

We're interrupted by my dad's truck rumbling down the street, the exhaust popping every few seconds. It takes less than two minutes for him to jump out of his truck and let the police know how he feels about Tyler being on his property. I find him, a head above the crowd, exclaiming heavily and waving his arms around in anger. I raise an eyebrow as the police just listen and quietly gaze at each other to avoid my dad's gaze. For once, he didn't cause the disturbance, but the police are all too familiar with my house and Sam Tiller's lack of control. His empty threats mean nothing to them, they never have - which is why I'm still here - stuck. I watch the show for a little while longer before I can't take it anymore and turn away from those who have done nothing to protect me and everything to cause me pain.

I make my way over to my mom sitting on the porch steps. Despite my lack of respect for what seems like her wimping out on the family, I recognize the basic human need for touch all too well. I sit next to her and lay my head on her shoulder, bony from lack of eating in order to please my father's expectations of a woman's body. Her body still heaves with hiccuped sobs, her head hangs almost below her shoulders in defeat. She looks absolutely pitiful and if it weren't for me knowing what she's done to get here, I would almost feel sorry for her.

"You know, mom - everything's going to be okay." I ignore her sharp intake of breath and keep talking, "I know you don't want to hear that right now and I know you didn't necessarily sign up for life coaching with your teenage daughter, but everything will work itself out. It always does."

I place my hand on her knee and she glances down - tears falling of their own free will. She bats at them in frustration and looks at me, her eyes desperate for some type of hope.

"Right before your dad left he gave me a choice: either move out or quit seeing Tyler. He didn't even let me spend the night last night. I slept in a sleeping bag on the back porch like I was a dog or somethin'."

I look at her out of the corner of my eye - realizing all too quickly this would be a conversation I wish I didn't have to experience with my own mother. She doesn't even notice my unease and continues, "I called Tyler to let him know what your dad did last night and what he said this afternoon. He freaked out - went crazy - promised to take care of it." Her voice falls below a whisper, "I had no idea this is what he had in mind." She whispers a string of cuss words and drops her head into her shaking hands. I imagine they're shaking from withdrawal as much as from fatigue and worry of the past few hours.

Before I can comfort her, she continues: "I just don't know what's scarier - living without Tyler or dealing with your father. My life is a mess," she whispers, "and it all started with you. You were the mistake. We never meant to have kids and then we got pregnant with you."

Her eyes grow cold and she stands up to walk inside.

I close my eyes and silently wish this night would just end. The conversation with my mom doesn't surprise me but it strikes a chord inside - partially because of my disbelief of the whole situation and her selfishness, but also because I have a sudden desire to escape to my haven - the corner of my closet already decorated with pillows and blankets and well-worn books. Many nights I spend in this space - aching to get away from arguments or fists. It works well. My own paradise in the middle of hell.

The gravity of tonight's events slowly start to hit me. Tyler came over to shoot my dad. The scream came from my mom when she saw Tyler pull the gun out of his jeans and understood his plan. Apparently she wanted away from my father and our family but not that bad. To be honest, I kinda wished my dad showed up hours ago while Tyler was still drunk and bent on taking what belonged to Sam for twenty years. As far as I was concerned - nobody deserved it more than my father. I eyed the gun as the police officers cuffed Tyler and fingerprinted the weapon. Oh what a different world I would be living in now had it only been thirty minutes sooner....

Not wanting to entertain those thoughts, I leave the chaos out in my front lawn and walk back to my room. Pacey found himself a cocoon inside my comforter. I pick him up to carry him into his bed. He jerks in protest and grabs my arms - holding them as tightly as his little hands will allow.

"No, sissy...," he barely whispers. "No. Let me sleep with you...please."

His voice fades as he falls back to sleep and I have no other choice but to let him sink back into his protective shell of comforters and sheets and Ninja Turtle pillows he snuck in from his room. Watching him sleep, I sigh and pull out my journal. I keep one ear tuned to the conversation right outside my window and the other plugged into the latest Swell Season album. I need comfort and I can always count on Glenn Hansard to provide a soothing melody late at night while writing. I glance wearily at my door and wait as memories of the night before leave and my muse slowly creeps in to my thoughts. Shoving the headset further into my ear, I pull my long hair back into a pony tail and settle in for the night. It's going to be a long one and I haven't even started my homework yet. I look at the empty page and feel the welcoming words come to life within my heart. Setting the pen to paper, I etch my feelings with ink, spilling out my insides in order to keep the chaos outside. I feel my eyes start to close despite my best efforts and I place my pen inside the binding of my journal while I rest for just a second. Within minutes, writing is forgotten and homework is the least of my worries as I fall asleep, exhaustion finally overtaking me and allowing me a brief moment of reprieve.

Five

I WAKE IN THE MIDDLE OF THE NIGHT TO A SHORT TAP ON MY WINDOW. My breath catches in my throat as pictures of Tyler waiting with a gun roll through my brain before I realize he wouldn't have enough patience or intelligence to get at us through a piece of glass. He'd try and pick the lock with a paper clip before realizing the door has been unlocked the whole time. I grab my robe and buckle it tightly around me to counter the cold floor and lack of heat in my room and peak through the make-shift curtains.

Kevin's face stares back at me - smiling. I jump back when I realize who it is and run to the front of the house and out the door - forgetting about my lack of clothing or make-up.

"Kevin?! Wha...why are you...is everything okay? What's going on? It's the middle of the night..." I stop mid sentence when I notice his smile.

"Everything's fine, Steph. I just wanted to take you somewhere." He shuffles his feet in nervous anticipation when he sees my look of incredulity. "I can't tell you where we are going," he explains, "It's a surprise."

I'm not sure what to think. It's in the middle of the night and cold and the last thing I want or need is some rendezvous going incredibly sour. I scrunch up my eyebrows and cross my arms against my chest.

"Kevin..." I hesitate, "this is crazy. I have my brother with me tonight and if he wakes up and I'm not there he's going to freak and..."

He interrupts me by placing a finger on my mouth and moving a stray hair behind my ear.

"Trust me, Stephanie. You want to see this." He holds out his hand and asks, "You coming?" in a voice so appealing I would have agreed to take a space shuttle to Mars had it been a different situation. I breathe deep and nod.

"Let me just go put on some warmer clothes and I'll be right back."

"Perfect!" Kevin exclaims and fist pumps the air. "It's like we're on an adventure," he whispers as he leans close enough to my face I can feel his breath against my cheek. I go weak in the knees for a split second before I realize where I am and force myself to stay in the moment.

Separating myself from him before I forget to change, I motion for him to be quiet and walk back into my house. Running into my bedroom, I shuffle through my drawers before I settle on jeans and a hoodie under my heavy jacket. Grabbing gloves and a hat, I quietly rush outside and meet him in the middle of the driveway. I briefly notice my dad's truck isn't there and frown.

Where can he be this late? Knowing I really don't want to know the answer to the question, I focus on other thoughts and walk over to where Kevin is standing in the middle of our lawn, watching a stray cat make its bed on the hood of a nearby car.

"This better be good, Matouse." He turns and looks at me in surprise when I use his last name - a handle used often by people at the high school but never by me in our conversations. I notice his lack of belief in my threat and I lightly punch him in the arm, "I mean it! You're encroaching on quality sleeping time for me." I widen my eyes to show him how serious I am, "What time is it anyway?"

"Just past 1:30 - which means we should probably hurry."

"Oh really? We should hurry?" I say as we start walking down the street. "Why? It's not like we have anywhere to be or we are breaking curfew or it's below freezing out here...I mean, this is completely normal. Two teenagers, walking down the street in the middle of the night, with only one truly knowing where they are going." I look at him and nudge him with my shoulder, "Right?"

Kevin snorts and I stop short and jump on his back in protest. Laughing, he takes off in a sprint as I fight back the shrieks of glee and absolute...life. For a brief moment, I feel completely alive and I can't even catch my breath to take in the beauty of it all. I remember one of my favorite books and how the main character mentions feeling infinite - and for the first time, I finally understand what that truly means. I bury my head in Kevin's neck and enjoy the ride.

"So, where is this mystery place you are taking me?" I look at Kevin and smile.

He looks like a kid at Christmas - anxious and eager to give a gift. Our impromptu piggy back lasted for a little over a block until he finally had to put me down because he was so exhausted. So now we are walking, hand in hand, down the street - dodging cop cars on patrol. It wouldn't be in either of our best interests to be caught past curfew.

He looks at me out of the corner of his eye and laughs. "You certainly are persistent, aren't you? Just be patient. We'll get there soon enough."

We walk past neighborhoods and into a more secluded area of town. He stops and looks around, a shadow of sudden realization crossing his face.

"Oh! We're here!"

I stop for a moment and look around, and all I see are weeds. We've ended up in one of the nearby fields. Totally forgotten, the grass has gotten pretty high. I follow Kevin into a clearing where the grass is slightly shorter. Tall grass or short grass, it doesn't matter to me. I'm not what you'd consider "outdoorsy." I can't help but make a face at the possible creepy crawlies inhabiting this area and try not to think about the time Pacey brought home a snake he killed in this very field.

Kevin's staring at me.

"What? I can feel your eyes burning a hole in my cheek."

I meet his gaze and immediately look away because of the intensity in his stare. I'm still getting use to looking people in the eyes and seeing trust instead of hate - or something more sinister. Kevin pulls me closer to him and shields me against the cold.

"Are you going to talk about what happened tonight at your house?"

I look at him, my eyebrows pinched, "How'd you know anything happened?"

"Steph. I live around the corner. I heard the sirens." he glances at me sheepishly, "I also walked over to see if everything was alright. After last night, I was worried." He puts his hand up as I open my mouth to quiet my protests, "I stayed behind the crowd. And when people started leaving, I took a spot around the corner. I didn't want anything to happen after everyone left." He gently touches my chin, "So...what happened?"

I scratch my nose and play with the tips of my hair - something I do when avoiding a question or distracting myself from what was going on around me. It doesn't work this time, though. Like Emma, Kevin's question wasn't meant to be ignored. He wouldn't settle for anything less than an answer. I frown and pull a hair out in rebellion and then turn to look at him - waiting.

"Tyler showed up tonight with a gun. He, uh...he wanted to shoot Dad."

Kevin looks at me in shock and shakes his head with disbelief, "You've got to be kidding."

He watches my reaction - waiting for the punchline. Realizing I am serious, he rubs his face and returns my questioning stare.

"What happened?" His voice is barely audible, almost hesitant - as if he doesn't want to know the answer.

I snort and shrug my shoulders, "Who ever knows with my family? Substance abuse has a funny way of making you behave differently than you were meant to and everyone I know has some type of addiction except for you, my brother and Emma." I shudder, "It was terrifying. Pacey was freaking out and the police took forever to get there and my mom was eerily silent and hiding - as usual." I start wringing my hands in nervousness. Sighing, I twist my lips and look him in the eyes, "It's hard to ignore what suddenly becomes so commonplace in life, you know?"

Kevin closes his eyes for a split second and touches my cheek.

"Steph, you know this isn't okay, right? You know parents aren't supposed to act like this; there has to be a way out. I just...I don't understand why you insist on staying."

I laugh.

"A way out? Kevin, I realized a long time ago my life isn't a

Disney movie or Friday night sitcom. It's just something I'm going to have to accept. It doesn't mean I'm okay with it, it just means I was dealt a crappy hand of cards and it's what I have to work with - nothing more, nothing less."

I smile to reassure him - although the smile doesn't really reach my eyes.

"You keep mentioning being dealt this crappy hand of cards - and I understand - sometimes we aren't able to choose where we are born or who our parents are."

Kevin looks at me and places his hands on my shoulders and lightly touches my chin so I will look up at him.

"But. Even though our cards may not be the best in the deck, we still have the ability to make the most of the situation. To change our surroundings. Stephanie, don't let your family poison you. You're too pure."

His words hang on the air - I know he's waiting for me to respond. But, how do I respond to something so against everything I believe? Pure? I fight the wave of laughter threatening to take over. I realize then just how little Kevin knows about me, and I'm filled with fear. What will happen when he finds out the truth? What will happen when he finally understands just how tainted I am? I wait a little while before speaking, hoping my voice won't give away how much I'm shaking internally.

"I think it's easier for someone to talk about changing his hand when he was dealt with easier cards to begin with - it doesn't make you wrong or insensitive," I grab his hand and wipe a stray eyelash off his cheek, "it just means we come from different worlds. And, different worlds require different rules. Sometimes, those rules are broken. Most of the time, they aren't and you remain stuck." I let go of his hand and stretch my shoulders, "Don't get me wrong, Kevin. I want out of my house. I'm counting the days until I can ride off into the sunset and never look back. I want to make something of myself - I refuse to fail. But. For now? I can't leave. It's just something I've had to learn."

He looks at me and starts to protest, I can see it in his eyes. I lean forward before he can start talking and give him a peck on the lips.

"Thank you for caring, Kevin. You're one of the only people I know who truly care about me. It's refreshing to know I am protected."

I still see the questions in his eyes and I ignore them; I cough to break the tension and change the subject.

"So. Why are we out here again? I see, um...a field and some grass and I'm pretty sure a spider just crawled up my leg but I don't really wanna look."

He hangs on to my gaze for a few seconds, probably to make sure I really want to drop the topic of my family. I know he still has questions, but right now, I want to forget about myself for awhile. He sighs with acceptance and wraps his arms around me.

"You're looking in the wrong place, Steph."

He motions for me to look up by pointing to the pitch black sky.

"Um. It's black. No surprise, though - that's usually what happens at night."

He laughs at my confusion and just says, "Wait."

And then it happens. A sudden shower of shooting stars - brilliantly streaking across the sky. I gasp and cover my mouth with the beauty of the night sky unleashing its power.

"Kevin, how on earth did you know this was going to happen?"

My words are still hushed and awestruck - I've never seen anything like this. I've never given myself the opportunity to look at the stars because normally when I'm out late, it's because I'm running from someone.　　He pokes me in the side.

"It's simple. I pay attention in Science."

I glare at him and sit down in the grass - the icy blades poking through my jeans. I grimace and look around before deciding to lay straight on my back so I'm facing the meteor shower. It looks like tiny pieces of glass tearing themselves against a black velvet tapestry.

"It's beautiful," I whisper.

He sits down beside me and nudges my shoulder.

"I figured you might like it," Kevin says, "It seemed to be something you would understand - complete beauty found in some of the darkest of places."

I turn and look at him, the blades of grass poking my cheek. I grab his hand and hold on for dear life.

"What do you mean? Why would I understand this more than anyone else? You can't deny the beauty here...it's - stunning."

Kevin meets my gaze unwaveringly. "Yes. It is. But you were about to completely dismiss it. What did you see when I first brought you here?"

"A field with snakes and spiders," I answer, suddenly feeling a little itchy around my ankles.

I push the thought out of my head while I try to keep my eyes on Kevin's face. I can tell he is thinking about something. Something he has been mulling over in his head for quite awhile. He seems confident. Sure. I wish I could take some of that confidence and bottle it up to use with my family.

Kevin laughs.

"Yeah. A field with spiders. But if your face would have been stuck in the grass, you would have missed the show."

His face turns serious and he places his hand on my cheek.

"It's just like you, Steph. There's a lot of dark places inside. Places you don't want anyone to see or know about. Places where you hide your insecurities and used razors and bruises you don't deserve. But you're beautiful. You're the most beautiful person I have ever met - inside and out - and I think if you let yourself look around, you'd find some beautiful places you never thought were there."

"Kevin..."

"Steph, don't try and explain this away. Don't try and tell me I don't know where you come from - because I do. Don't try and tell me I don't know what I'm getting myself into - because I'm already in too deep. Just promise me you'll join me."

I bite my lip. No one ever made commitments with Stephanie Tiller. No one ever paid much attention to her. And here I am - face to face with a boy I could very much fall in love with - and he's asking me to promise him I will join him. I close my eyes and say a prayer for strength and take a leap of faith. When I open my eyes, Kevin's grinning ear-to-ear. Our silent promise hangs in the air for a brief second before it floats up and away, joining the millions of stars shooting across the sky in a celebration of love and promise and hope.

"You know what this reminds me of?" I ask.

"What?" Kevin turns his head and flinches when a piece of grass pokes him in the eye. I giggle.

"There's this Tori Amos quote I heard once," I close my eyes and try to remember, "'I love feeling alive; I love walking out in the cold in my bare feet and feeling the ice on my toes.'" I smile as I wave my arms around and touch his shoulder, suddenly thankful it's pitch black so he can't see me blush, "This reminds me of that. It reminds me of feeling alive and living in the moment. The cold grass inching through my skin, the smell of night in the air, the stars falling all around us..." I turn and look at him and squeeze his hand, "Thanks for bringing me."

We sit there for awhile, resting in each others' arms and sharing secrets and dreams and hopes and expectations. When Kevin finally thinks to look at his phone we realize it's almost four in the morning. I laugh at the thought of sitting through classes today after being out all night and then I start freaking out. A test. I have a test today. I turn to Kevin and have a minor melt down.

"My physics test! I forgot all about it. I have to study...I have to pass."

Kevin laughs and rubs my arm, "You're going to be fine. You still have a couple hours to sleep before you have to be at school."

I roll my eyes and wriggle free, standing up to gather my things. I start pacing and wringing my hands and throwing Kevin withering glances.

"You don't understand, Kevin. This test determines whether I pass for the semester. You know, that's important for a senior - passing." *And maybe getting out of this town,* I think.

Kevin looks at me and smiles - "Well...I haven't eaten in awhile and I have some cash on me from mowing my uncle's lawn this past weekend. Do you want to go share a cinnamon roll from Cloud Nine? We can sneak in and grab your bags on the way there. I'll help you study for the exam. You know I got an A in that class?"

I squint my eyes and cross my arms - "Who are you?" I ask.

Looking around, I take in our surroundings again and I force a laugh at the absurdity of our situation. Turning to look at him I poke his chest with my finger, stepping within inches of his face for a split second before retreating into my own space.

"You have me staying out all night and watching meteor showers in the freezing cold and now you want to take me to breakfast so I can study? Kevin Matouse, you absolutely are the most fascinating person I know."

He grabs the nape of my neck and gently pulls me closer

to his side so we can walk as close as possible to stay warm.

He leans over and kisses my temple and just responds, "Not as fascinating as you, Stephanie. I'm pretty sure you're the only girl I know who would stare down an intruder while calling the police and asking them - calmly - to come and handle the situation while the crazy drunk continues to point his gun at you." He squeezes my shoulder and lowers his voice a little. "In all seriousness, Steph. Next time something like tonight happens, please call me...after you call the cops, of course."

I look at him and nod.

"I think I can manage that - as long as you don't join Tyler in taking my place of pulling the trigger on my father. If anyone should have the privilege of ending his life....it should be me."

Kevin looks horrified and I laugh - "I'm kidding, Matouse. Kind of." I wink at him. "Now, let's go get me hyped up on sugar, shall we? I need to stay awake through this Physics test."

And with that, I smile and take off running - leaving Kevin confused for a split second before he laughs and starts chasing after me.

Six

We get to my house, out of breath and exhausted from our midnight run.

"You're pretty fast, Steph. Have you ever considered going out for track?"

I laugh and look at him with complete disdain, "Are you serious?!" I look down at my figure and continue, "I'm not the most athletic person. I trip on my own two feet walking on level ground. The only reason I was able to outrun you is because, well..I've had practice." I shrug my shoulders and wrinkle my eyebrows - "Not necessarily something I like to make known to everyone, you know? Running from your father who is in a drunken stupor and completely out of his mind isn't every girl's dream. So, no. I've never considered track. I think I'll just stick to my pen and paper - I'll leave the nasty sweaty stuff to you." I smile to reassure him, and then wink, "Now, be quiet while I go inside and grab my stuff." I look at him closely. "No noise, got it?"

He holds up two fingers, scout's honor, and whispers, "I'll be a church mouse."

I laugh quietly and turn away with only a fraction of doubt in his ability to stay quiet for an extended amount of time when all of the sudden I feel him grab my arm and yank me back towards him.

"What the...," I cry, ready to throw a punch to counter the force of his hands pushing me down to the grass.

"Steph...down. Now."

His urgent whisper catches my attention and I immediately pay attention to what's around me. Only then, lying flat in the grass, do I notice my dad's truck pull into the driveway. Kevin must have seen the headlights as my dad turned on to the street because now, pulling in, the headlights were off. I glance at Kevin and he's staring intently at my father. The look on his face equals that of someone who seems ready at a moment's notice to step in between me and whatever force may be coming my way. In any other circumstance, I would probably find it heartwarming - cute even. Not here. I can't think straight with my heart beating a violent rhythm against my chest.

What is he doing getting home so late? I wonder to myself. And then I see her. In the passenger's seat. Giggling and playing with her long, jet black hair.

Valerie.

I grab Kevin's hand and squeeze it - a silent code to see if he sees what I see - he squeezes back and moves his head to watch my reaction. I close my eyes and count to ten, leveling my heartbeat.

Valerie? My heart sinks. It doesn't make sense - not to someone who doesn't know my father. Unfortunately, I do. I know his preference of young flesh all too well. I shudder as memories pass through my mind - memories I thought were over.

My dad walks around to her side of the truck, opens the door and then pulls her down to the pavement. Wrapping her in his arms, they move towards each other in a lingering kiss. I wrinkle my nose in disgust and bury my head in my arm to avoid watching the sordid affair, but the picture is already burned into my brain, along with about a million other pictures I wish weren't there.

"You better go, kitten. You have school tomorrow, dontcha?"

My dad's voice rambles and sways with his body's reaction to liquor.

Valerie smiles, giggles, bats her eyelashes, cocks her hip and glances at my dad so seductively I almost puke right there in the grass.

"Sammy. Don't you remember? I haven't been to school all year. I got my G.E.D - I'm working at Gunther's Law Firm as a secretary. I'm saving money. For us." She winked at him, "But I do need to go. Will I see you tomorrow?"

My dad shuffles his feet against the pavement and scratches his arms and replies, "I don't know. I have to go down to the police station and get things settled with Tyler. I have some money saved and I may try and bail him out if possible." My dad sighs with fake compassion and rubs his forehead. "You know, do I agree with what Tyler did today? No. Absolutely not. Do I blame him? No. He wasn't in his right mind. He needs help. I'm going to make some phone calls to see if I can get someone to talk with him. It's the least I can do to ease some of the bad blood between us."

My eyes grew into tiny slits and I silently curse. He's such a freaking liar. Tomorrow is Thursday. He will be at Dilsey's Pub for dollar long neck night. Besides. He hates Tyler with every fiber of his being. Pretty sure he would knock him out and toss him in the lake without a second glance. Valerie just smiles and places her hand on his cheek, remaining completely oblivious to his dishonesty. A lamb to her slaughter. I fight the urgency to run and pull her from his grasp. She has no idea her fate's about to be sealed.

"You're such an amazing person, Sam. I really don't understand what Stephanie has against you. From what she has told people at school, you would think you were a monster." Her voice turns sugary sweet, "And you've definitely proven yourself to be anything but a monster."

Oh you have no idea, do you Valerie?

My heart sinks in despair and I pray she never has to find out just how dangerous my father can be. He grabs her by the hips and pulls her close to him. I could feel my stomach turning, my reflexes kicking in - I bite my tongue to keep from throwing up everything I ate that day.

"I wanna show you something," my dad says conspiratorially. Valerie's eyes take on a shade of curiosity and that's just enough for my dad to take the bate. He pushes some hair behind her eyes, "What's wrong, baby? Don't you trust me?"

Valerie giggles - showing just a hint of uncertainty beneath the confidence she claims. She nods her head and the deal's done.

"Atta girl," my dad whispers loud enough for us to hear the graphic undertones beneath his words, "Let's go out back. I have a special place just for us."

And with that, they walk out of sight behind the corner of my house, my father's hands tight around Valerie's arms in case she decides to change her mind. I can hear her questions as they walk behind the house and I silently beg her to stop talking. Questions only make my dad antsy. I give in to the disagreement with my stomach, moving away from Kevin and throwing up everything I've eaten that day into the grass. As Kevin grabs my hair to prevent it from falling in front of my face, I squeeze my eyes and heart shut from the image of my father walking out back with one of my childhood friends.

✳

Kevin and I decide not to wait around any longer. I open my window facing the front of the house, crawl in my room, grab my backpack off my desk and turn around to leave all without hearing a peep from Pacey.

"Mission accomplished," Kevin says as I maneuver my way back out of the window without cutting myself on stray wires and shards of glass long past remodeling.

I glance at him and give him a half-hearted smile.

"Can we just get out of here? Please? I really don't want to be around when they come back."

I shudder again and fight back the nausea. Kevin grabs my hand and leads me towards the sidewalk. For awhile, we just walk in solitude, each of us lost in our own thoughts about what we just witnessed. I'd been wondering where Valerie disappeared to - I hadn't seen her all year. We use to be inseparable, always over at each other's houses. In some ways, I wasn't surprised she found herself mixed up with my father. She was always so...curious. Defiant. But underneath was a hunger for acceptance - a target large enough for any creep to see. I'm so deep in thought that I almost forget Kevin walking beside me. He's the first to speak and his voice sounds loud against the silence.

"Do you think we should call the police? I mean, what's going on isn't exactly legal and it may be what they need to put your dad behind bars for good..."

I glance at him and for the first time, begin to comprehend just a little what it would be like to be completely innocent of any familial dysfunction. I carefully weigh my words before lashing out on him undeservedly.

"Have you ever dealt with the authorities coming to your house, Kevin?"

"No," he answers with a hint of curiosity. He knows

I'm going somewhere with this train of thought.

"Have you ever had to hide bruises when CPS came to visit so you and your siblings wouldn't be split up in foster care? Have you ever felt the need to lie - to protect yourself and those you love from the backlash of the truth? It's not as easy as people think."

I look towards the horizon, where the sun's rays were just now starting to greet the blackened morning sky.

"Calling the police is always the safe answer - but it's not always the most prudent."

Kevin slows down his pace a little and glances at me.

"What do you mean? Isn't this pretty cut and dry? Valerie is a minor. Your dad already has a file and has a history of being clinically dependent on alcohol and violently abusive. You don't think this would nail him once and for all?"

I sigh. I really wish we could avoid this conversation, but there's no turning back. For a split second I hesitate. Can I trust him? Will he run from the truth once he knows? I figure I have nothing to lose, so I stop and grab Kevin's hand so he will look at me.

"No, Kevin. I don't. I don't think it will stop my father. In fact, I know it won't." I see his eyes begin to question, and I continue, "I know this because it's happened before. Valerie isn't the first. My dad has a history of befriending my girlfriends."

Kevin looks at me incredulously and asks, "And the cops know this? Your father has been reported? What about the parents? Did they find out? Stephanie...your dad is a sick man. You do know this, right?"

I laugh cynically and turn my eyes towards Kevin - "Yeah, Kevin. I know. And yes, the cops know. My dad's file is thicker than anyone's in the county. However, it's kind of hard to book someone on a crime when you're guilty of it yourself."

Kevin studies my face.

"I don't understand. Who's guilty? Your father?"

This is what I am trying to avoid. This right here. I'm on the verge of telling Kevin something I've never told anyone - and the ramifications are huge. At first I say nothing - as long as I don't say anything he will think of me in the same way. I stay quiet for awhile - continuing to walk down the sidewalk, my eyes fixed on the rising morning, until I feel Kevin gently squeeze my hand.

"Hello? Is anyone home? What's going on, Stephanie?"

And there it is. The question I can't ignore. I close my eyes and focus on something good - a memory I would want to remember - and turn toward Kevin. Opening my eyes, I say the words I've avoided since the moment I saw my father with Valerie.

"My father traded me, Kevin. In order to keep the police from saying anything, he convinced one of his buddies in the force to accept a bribe." I can see a shadow begin to form on Kevin's face as the pieces fall into place.

"You were the bribe."

I breathe in deep and exhale slowly.

"Yeah. Five guys. It started one night when I was twelve. Most of them turn their heads when they see me walking down the street. Some smile and tip their hat as if I should be excited to see them. All of them turn a blind eye to my father's indiscretions." I drop my head and focus on a crack in the sidewalk, "My father is a sick man, Kevin - but he's also incredibly brilliant. He figured out how to cheat the system and he's milking it for all it's worth. I just never imagined to be lumped into his conquests."

The memories are coming full force now. The confusion, the pain, the heavy breathing of the men in the dark room as they continually take everything away from me - innocence I didn't even know I possessed. The first time it happened, I stayed home the next day - too sore to do much. My dad covered for himself, telling mom I had the flu and would probably need to be left alone in my room so she wouldn't get sick herself. She never even came to check on me. No one did. It took about a week to fully recover - physically at least. Now? I don't get the privilege of resting. Sometimes I'm even called out in the middle of the day during school. Still - no one has said anything. I don't even think I've been held accountable for my truancy issues. The fact that there's no accountability involved makes me wonder just how far my dad's indiscretions reach.

Kevin squeezes my hand, bringing me out of my twisted reverie. He makes short ticking noises with his tongue as we continue to walk. We stay like that for quite awhile - both lost in our thoughts and memories and questions of the future. Once again, he's the first to break the silence.

"Does Emma know about this?" he questions, the shock still radiating from his eyes.

"Not directly," I answer. ""She knows my dad has the authorities in a tight grasp, but she doesn't know how he's managed to get away with so much."

Kevin places his hands in his pockets and then pulls them out - blowing on the insides to warm them up and protect them from the biting cold, "Have you ever thought about telling her? What if her and Jude knew? Don't you think..."

"I can't." My words are firm. A warning, "And neither can you."

I purposefully walk a little faster so Kevin gets the hint to stop pushing the issue. I'm a little bit ahead of him and my stomach starts to growl in protest of not getting anything since upchucking after seeing Valerie and my dad. Erasing the memories of their tonsil hockey, I think about the gooey goodness of Cloud Nine and the impending doom surrounding my Physics test. You know, things normal teenagers would think about - not being traded for sex or seeing their dad muck up with one of their friends. The mood swing is drastic; I'm well aware. But, there's nothing I can do to stop it when it comes. It's pretty simple, really. I feel one way, and I don't like it, so I feel something else. Right now? It's hunger. Hunger and worry about school.

I need normalcy and not to think about the fact that I just gave my boyfriend every reason to think less of me.

"Hey Steph - wait up."

Kevin's footsteps strike a quick cadence against the sidewalk as he works to catch up with me. He grabs my hand and pulls me back to walk in step with him. Glancing at me out of the corner of his eye he stumbles through his words.

"Don't be mad at me, Stephanie. It's just...this whole thing frustrates me. And maybe you're right. Maybe it's because we live in different worlds and there are different rules so I don't really know how to respond, but you have to understand, it's absolutely maddening to know someone you care about needs protecting and you can do nothing to protect them."

We continue to stare at each other in silence, frozen to our spots on the sidewalk. I can see the Cloud Nine sign blinking neon in the distance and just past that, on the horizon, a blinding shade of orange bursting into red catches my attention.

"The sky is screaming." My voice cracks against the quiet and startles Kevin out of his thoughts.

He looks at the sky and then back at me.

"What?" he asks, and I note the look of incredulity on his face and smile, knowing he is probably getting pretty exasperated at my change in subject.

I point at the sunrise.

"Look at the sky. It's screaming. The colors are begging us to notice. The reds dancing and making a soft shade of pink on the clouds' underbellies and the blue fighting for its own place in the sky." I look at him and shrug my shoulders, "The sky screams for people to take notice - even when we know no one will. I've said it before. The sunrise? It's my constant. Despite nights where I have to close my eyes to what's going on around me to simply survive, I always know the morning sky will scream my discontent to a world not listening. It's violently beautiful and echoes my heart."

I stop, realizing my words have struck a chord because Kevin is staring at me. Again. *A girl could get use to this*, I think a bit irreverently. I raise an eyebrow and look at him - waiting.

"You're doing it again," I say with a slight smirk playing on my lips.

"Doing what?" he replies, completely oblivious.

"Staring. Burning a hole into my cheek with your eyes. What gives?"

Kevin looks at me and pulls a stray hair between his fingers, watching the new sunlight make shades of iridescent gold patterns on my uncut layers.

"You sound like a poet," he says, smiling gently.

My insides quake and become a puddle at the bottom of my rib cage. If only he knew just what he was capable of with those blasted eyes, I think to myself as I try and focus on what he's saying. It seems important, judging by the intensity of his eyes and the set of his lips. I'm able to regain composure before he starts speaking again.

"When you speak...you sound like a poet. A broken, hurting, incomplete yet hopeful poet." He leans forward and whispers so softly I can barely hear him, "I sometimes hold it half a sin to put in words the grief I feel; For words, like Nature, half reveal and half conceal the soul within."

"Tennyson." I reply, my breath short with surprise at Kevin quoting one of my favorite poets.

He nodded, "Yeah. We read him the other day in English

and it reminded me of you. You always 'faintly trust the larger hope' in anything you do - it amazes me."

"It's the only thing I can do. My life - as you have witnessed first hand - isn't ideal. But I can hope, and I can dream, and I can look for moments that remind me I'm alive - because I am. Still alive, despite everything."

He glances at me out of the corner of his eye. "That reminds me of something I heard in church once. Something about God being able to restore the years all the locusts have eaten." He catches my frown and continues, "Yeah, I'm not very religious either. But it's kind of nice to think about the possibility of getting back some of the years you'd rather forget. Kind of like a new beginning, you know?"

I nod slowly.

"Yeah. A new beginning. Sounds almost too good to be true."

He leans towards me and rests his forehead against mine, "Just remember you have people who want to hope with you." I smile and shake my head, almost unwilling to believe him even though more and more, I find myself anxious to put my trust and belief in the fact that people are wrong - and Kevin is indeed good for me.

I step back from him and study his face, "Kevin - why are you with me?"

His eyebrows raise imperceptibly and he lets out a chuckle.

"What?" I can tell my question has unnerved him because he clears his throat and runs his fingers through his hair before looking at me again.

"I mean it. Why are you - the football star who everyone loves, with me? The screw-up?" My eyes grow thin and I place my hands on my hips, "This isn't one of those stupid pranks, is it? Like those lame teen movies where the jock has to go through with a bet to date the ugly girl?"

I can feel my heartbeat pick up as I'm asking him

questions that have been on my mind since we started talking. Regardless of what he says, it just doesn't make sense. We fit together - yes. But logically, how'd this even happen?

He starts shaking his head before I can even finish my questions, "Steph. Seriously? Listen to yourself." He pulls me close and wraps his arms around me. "Close your eyes for me. Breathe. Think about what you're asking." He lifts my head and pushes me hair back out of my eyes. "I'm with you because I care about you. I'm with you because ever since we bumped into each other at the coffee shop I haven't been able to get you out of my mind. I'm with you regardless of what others say and what others think because I know it's right. And your past - your family - the other ghosts in your closet - those mean nothing to me. Nothing. I'm in love with you Stephanie. All of you."

My heart keeps beating heavily, but in a different rhythm than the fear and dread she was playing a few minutes before.

"I don't deserve you," I whisper and he wipes a stray tear off my cheek.

"Yes you do. You deserve every good thing this world has to offer - including my love. And I'll spend my life proving to you that you won't ever have to worry about it being there."

I poke his chest as my stomach lets out an audible protest. "Really, Kevin? That seems a bit extreme." I cock and eyebrow and pull my hair back into a ponytail. "If there's one thing I've learned, it's that things don't last forever."

I look away from his gaze, hiding the emotions swirling and fighting for attention. Everything inside of me wants to believe him - wants to trust. But I just don't know if I can.

My stomach growls again and I grab his hand, "Look, I'm really sorry for my freak out. I just haven't had a lot of sleep lately and I tend to get emotional. Can we go eat now?" I nod my head towards the still-blinking sign, "I'm starving and I have yet to study. Not the greatest combination considering it's almost 6:30." I look at him and wrinkle my brows in disgust, "School starts in two hours, whether we like it or not."

Kevin reaches for my hood and pulls it over my head in a playful gesture, completely ignoring my second extreme mood-swing of the morning.

"Kevin!" I complain - but am stopped short by him leaning in to give me a quick peck on the lips.

"Race you," he whispers tauntingly and pulls away, my heart still shaking from the sudden and intimate contact.

He's off and running before I am able to comprehend what just happened. Looking over his shoulder he waves and hollers, "First one there gets the gooey center!"

I gape at his retreating figure and break into a full sprint, *there's no way I am going to catch him*, I think.

He reaches the door a split second before I do and I collapse into him, breathless from all of the running. Laughing, he opens the door and we walk in - instantly hit with the aromas of a diner come to life.

"Hey guys. How many?" The host smiles and hesitates for a few seconds on Kevin's face. I automatically step closer to him and grab his hand.

"Two," I say, daring her to match my gaze.

Her smile falters when she sees me and awkwardly turns to grab two menus.

"Follow me," suddenly her voice is a bit more subdued then before.

I try and hide a smile and glance at Kevin.

"What was that about?" he leans in, whispering in my ear.

"Nothing." I shrug and squeeze his arm before sliding into the booth. I smile sweetly and take the menu from the host - fighting the bubble of laughter rising in my throat. Her smile is less than friendly and laced with a jealousy I've never experienced.

Kevin notices and raises an eyebrow, "Okay. I saw that look. What did you do to her?"

I glance innocently at Kevin and point my spoon at him, "I told you. Nothing. I just saw her giving you the eye so I let her know you were taken."

He starts to blush, "Stephanie, she wasn't looking at me like that."

I glance out of the corner of my eye and catch her back at the host stand, stealing glances our way and whispering with the girl who just walked in from the kitchen. I sigh. Boys could be so blind sometimes. Refusing to spell it out for him, a grin creeps across my face and I meet his gaze.

"You're right. I was probably just reading too much into it." I stick my straw in my mouth and begin chewing as he creases his forehead and tries to keep up with my change in behavior.

"I'm...sorry. Did you just say I was right?"

I hesitate for a split second before smiling and rolling my eyes.

"Yes."

"Hmm," he goes quiet for a little while, a small smile playing on his lips. Looking at me from the top of his eyes, he pretends to intently study the menu, "So, uh...how'd that feel to admit?" I grab the nearest ketchup packet and throw it at his face - landing right in the center of his nose. He shouts with laughter. I'm not given any time to respond though, because our waitress walks up and hands us our coffee.

"What can I get you two today? You two gonna split one of our rolls?"

I watch her and and think of all the stereotypes of diner waitresses - because this one fits them all. She pulls her arm up to her mouth and coughs into the crease of her elbow - a low, choking smoker's cough.

"Well, Lord. Sorry about that. I haven't been able to take my break and these lungs are aching for some nicotine."

Her laughter is short and deep - her chest rising and falling, bouncing when she gets the giggles. I watch Kevin's nose turn up in just the slightest way at the mention of her cough and I rush in to break the silence before she sees the look of disgust crossing his face.

"We'll take the cinnamon roll, please."

She look at me and raises an eyebrow, writing everything down in her server notebook.

"Just one?"

I glance at Kevin and smile, "Yeah. Just one."

"Hmph. Alright. Would you like butter or brown sugar sprinkled on top?"

"Butter."

"Wise choice, hon." She gives me a once over for the second time and raises her eyebrows as she picks her teeth with the pen. "You need some meat on those bones anyway."

My cheeks turn rosy under her scrutiny and I clear my throat. Exhaling, she stabs her pocket with her notebook and grabs the pitcher of water off the near by counter.

"Your roll will be ready shortly."

And with a wink towards Kevin and a silent protest of me being, "just skin and bones" she walks off, her hips swaying to the rhythm of the Chuck Berry song blaring from the jukebox.

Kevin and I stare at each other, biting our lips until she is out of hearing range. As soon as she turns the corner, we burst out laughing.

"Kevin, please tell me you saw that one. Please tell me you saw her looking at you."

He wrinkles his nose, "I saw. She's like, twice my age." He shudders. "I'm so not into this whole cougar thing right now."

We laugh again and settle in to an easy flow of conversation.

I hear giggling over to my right and I glance at the two hosts, manning their station. One is mocking me and the other is joining in with laughter. I grab Kevin's hand from across the table. He glances up at me and smiles, rubbing my hand with his thumb. The giggling stops and I chance another look - catching one of the girl's eyes, I smile and wave.

Seven

I HEAR A SLIGHT COUGH AND TURN MY ATTENTION TO KEVIN. HE'S glancing at the waitress headed our way with breakfast. The cinnamon roll covers the entire plate and you can smell the butter melting all over the sides of the roll now, with only a small square left on top and seeping into the middle. She sets the plate in between us and gives him a slight wink before turning and walking to another table. I grab my fork and dig in, being careful not to drip sauce on my Physics book opened in front of me.

Kevin grabs his own mouthful and closes his eyes in satisfaction before looking at me.

"Have you been able to study much?"

I smile. I grabbed my book as soon as the girls at the host stand stopped staring at us and I knew we could eat in peace. But, since pulling the book out, I had done more studying of Kevin's face than the concepts of Planck's constant.

"A little."

I shrug my shoulders and stuff another piece of gooey dough in my mouth before he could ask me something else. He turns his head and looks at me from his right eye - and I almost spit buttery cinnamon all over myself. He looks like one of those cheesy actors from the popular forensic unit shows.

"Okay fine," I acquiesce. "I haven't studied much. I just can't focus." I motion my hand around the food, "Between this...deliciousness beckoning me and your face and my exhaustion, it's hard to focus."

"My face? What's wrong with my face?"

"Your face." I start to blush, "It's a distraction. I want to keep looking."

I know I'm being girly, and I know adults all across the universe would gag in their mouth hearing my reason, but it's true. I just can't focus when I have him to look at - he's absolutely gorgeous. I have to pinch myself to make sure I'm not dreaming. I can't help but wonder what he's thinking now that he knows what I've tried to hide for so long. I know he just answered some of my deepest questions, but I still wonder. Am I just second-hand goods? Does he still feel the same? I bite my lip and look out the window, fighting the thoughts screaming for attention.

He reaches over the table and grabs my book, being careful not to rake the pages through the messy leftovers on the plate. Opening it to where I started about thirty minutes ago, he starts quizzing me. When I get an answer wrong, he asks me again and explains away my confusion.

"I had no idea you were so good at Physics. Are you wanting to be an engineer or something?"

He laughs.

"No. Not at all. It just comes naturally to me for some reason." He shrugs his shoulders and looks at me, "I actually want to go to film school. Learn how to make movies."

I stare at him a full minute before responding. I wouldn't have pegged him as someone who enjoyed film. I guess I still had a lot to learn.

"What makes you interested in film?"

He doesn't even hesitate before responding, "Stories. Stories absolutely fascinate me. I love hearing people's stories and how they overcome obstacles and despite everything, still cling to hope." He clasps his hands together and leans forward, his eyes lit with excitement. "I don't know, Stephanie. It's just...there's so many opportunities out there to do good in the industry. You already have producers and directors who take advantage of their craft - aiming to scare people as much as possible or see just how much skin they can get away with showing before the ratings shoot sky high. I'm not into that. I believe stories can change the world - and I want to be on the positive side of that change."

"Look out, Angelina."

He starts laughing.

"I guess. I just think stories are incredibly important. An individual's story has the power to move others for change." He meets my gaze and holds it for while before continuing. "Even yours - especially yours. People need to hear what you've been through."

I look at him in mock horror, "You're going to create a film about my life?"

He shakes his head.

"No. But I see that journal you carry with you everywhere. I know you write." He leans back and rests his head against his hand. "I have a feeling you have a story inside that needs to get out just as much as I have ideas for film that need to be put into action."

I look at him and rub my finger across the plate between us, wiping the last bit of cinnamon and butter off the porcelain and into my mouth. Glancing around the diner, I begin to notice intricacies. The old couple laughing over a cup of coffee. The cook in the back yelling for some help. The girl sitting by herself and checking her watch every few seconds. Immediately scenes and conversations fill my head. I have to blink in order to calm the inner monologue to a dull roar.

"Yeah. I guess you can say I write."

"Have you ever thought about sharing your words?"

My head shoots up and I stare at him as though he has just offered the most ridiculous piece of advice. *Share my writing? No. Never.* I downplay my hesitancy and simply wrinkle my lips and look off in the distance, focusing again on the girl who seems to be waiting for someone.

"No," I answer simply, hoping for him to understand there really isn't much to discuss.

"I'd love to hear what you've written some time."

I look at him briefly before bringing my attention to the napkin in my hands. I've been shredding the paper into pieces. Throwing the mangled remains on the table I shoot him a look and shake my head.

"I've never shared my writing with anyone, Kevin. I don't think I'm going to start now."

"Try me. Take something from that book - anything - it could be a poem or a sentence or a paragraph about how Mrs. Peabody has a secret and disturbing crush on Shakespeare's corpse. I don't care. But try me - will you?"

I grab the book and flip through the pages, noting to myself certain passages I would never read to anyone. My journal is more than story ideas - it's a place to untangle knots and splatter thoughts. Mostly about my life. Sometimes I tackle my past. Every so often I'll write words picturing my future. I'm about to give up when my eyes rest on a poem I wrote two months ago, right after Kevin and I started dating. I blush at the memory and smile.

I guess I could read him this one.

He shifts in the booth, obviously catching on to my sudden openness, "Did you find something?"

I look at him and lower my gaze.

"Yeah. I did. But, I don't know if I will be able to look at you while I read this, so don't make fun of me or anything if I start to stutter or my voice cracks."

He throws his hand in the air and whispers, "Scout's honor," just like he had earlier that morning when I was begging for him to be quiet outside my house. Before my dad showed and everything shifted so quickly.

I avert my gaze and focus on the words before me on the page. Taking a deep breath, I begin to read - quietly.

Where did you come from angel of love
sent from above
and offering me hope
a belief
- or -
a prayer?
perhaps things aren't what they seem
perhaps one can truly find peace -
find a home
find someone who believes in you
I close my eyes and offer my hand
(even though the nightmares may come)
I close my eyes and offer my heart
(even though the scars may never heal)
and hope and pray and believe
you are my angel of love

I look up and Kevin is staring at me. *Oh great. I shouldn't have read the poem*, I think to myself, *now I've freaked him out and he's going to think I'm some crazy lunatic.* My heart sinks and I grab for the napkin on the table so my fingers can find something to latch on to. He grabs my hand as it clasps around the piece of cloth.

"Stephanie."

His voice is quiet. Endearing. I chance a look and catch my breath. He wasn't freaked out.

He drops his head for a split second, composing his thoughts.

"Stephanie," he repeated, "that was beautiful."

I start to shake my head and offer excuses, but he waves them away with his hand.

"No. I mean it. Do you only write poetry?"

I try and find my voice, lost somewhere in the pit of my stomach where my heart has formed into a puddle.

"No - I write stories. I have the beginning of about three novels written in this book - I'm just waiting for the opportunity to really focus on my writing before diving in completely...I uh, don't have a lot of time right now to focus on it like I would like."

I glance away for a brief moment before finding his gaze. He squeezes my hand and moves to get up. I look at him as he walks over to my side of the booth and motions for me to scoot over. I scoot, my eyes focused on his every move.

He looks at me very seriously and places his arm around my shoulder.

"Has anyone ever told you to pursue your writing?"

I fight the urge to laugh. I look at him, wondering where he's going with all of this, and simply respond, "Um. Mrs. Peabody likes my essays. She wrote "brilliant" on the last one I turned in for her. But, no one has ever said anything about me really focusing on writing."

He stares at me and leans closer. "Pursue your writing," he says it quietly and purposefully.

"What?"

"Pursue your writing. Listen. I don't know what you have

in that head of yours," he gently taps my forehead and continues, "but the world needs your writing. The world needs to see something as tragically beautiful as your story. They need to be reminded of hope."

I rub my neck and strain to leave his line of sight. His attention, his belief in me - it's making me feel strangely awkward. I'm not sure how to respond. I glance down and toy with the zipper on my jacket.

"Look at me."

I hesitate to meet his gaze and he grazes his finger on my chin, slowly lifting my line of sight until we see our reflection in the other's eyes.

"You need to know this. You need to know the power of your ability to wrap a story so fluently into the realm of believability and connection."

I nudge him with my shoulder.

"Thank you," I whisper, my voice threatening to crack under the weight of his words.

I pull my hair back away from my face and turn towards him, drawing the attention away from me for a little while.

"So, back to you wanting to do film. Have you thought about schools you want to go to?"

His eyes lit up for a brief second and a smile spreads across his face.

"Well, if I could get into the school, USC has an incredible program. They are pretty expensive, though and..."

"And far away," I finish for him.

He laughs. "

"Yeah, and far away. I'm not sure my parents would go for that, but it's a dream." He shrugs his shoulders and looks at me, "I've already sent in my application. I'm crossing my fingers for some type of scholarship."

"Do you have a back-up plan?"

His eyes light up for a split second.

"Yeah. I do, actually. I was doing some research online and found this film school in a slum in Nairobi, Kenya. They work with students who live in Kibera and tell stories about life in the slum. It's the largest in the world. I'd love to go and visit and work with them for a couple weeks - maybe even for the summer. I've always wanted to see Africa."

I wrinkle my brow, "But you wouldn't be actually...attending the school, would you?"

"I don't know. I mean, I'm sure I'd learn a lot from them. The guy who started it graduated from USC and moved back to Nairobi to start this program. It's pretty cool. As far as locally, if I don't get into USC I've looked into a few state schools. And, there's always the junior college if I get desperate. What about you? Have you thought about where you are wanting to go?"

I snort.

"Um. College isn't really a priority right now, Kevin. Do I want to go? Absolutely. Do I see the need? Heck yes. It's why I'm freaking out about this Physics test."

I motion to the open book sitting across the table, long forgotten in place of our conversation.

He smiles, recognizing the pitch in my voice changing due to the shift in topics - very easily we could start talking about my current situation and it was the last thing I wanted to rehash. Stretching his arms behind his head, he leans over and gives me a soft kiss on the cheek.

"Speaking of the test, it's 7:45. You wanna start heading over to the school? I don't want to make you late."

I glance at the clock on my phone and have a momentary shortness of breath when I realize just how soon the test will be placed in front of me.

"Stop stressing."

I look over and Kevin is standing next to the table, waiting for me to grab his hand. I throw him a look filled with chagrin and slide out of the booth.

"I'm sorry. I know I can be crazy when I get stressed about something. I'm just…really nervous about the test."

He squeezes my shoulder as we walk past the two hosts twirling their hair and giggling.

"You're going to be fine. I quizzed you, remember? You know the stuff. Don't second guess yourself."

I lean into his embrace and wrap my arm around his waist, taking comfort in his belief.

Eight

KEVIN AND I GET TO SCHOOL JUST AS THE FIRST BELL RINGS - SIGNALING
students to gulp down the last ounce of their energy drink
before settling into the routine of lectures, experiments, tests
and mindless busy work. Once the first bell rings it's absolutely chaos in the hallways. Kids hollering at each other,
couples sneaking kisses in unlit corners, boys posting up
against the wall attempting to discreetly pawn off whatever
"deal" they have on the latest Rx available in the school's
black market. It's always pretty impossible for anyone to walk
the halls unscathed, I'm always fondled at least once or twice
- however accidental it may be it still irritates the crap out of
me. I'm tired today - no - exhausted. I'm pretty sure if any
perv tries to touch me I may backhand him.

We make our way to my Physics class - making small talk
about how sticky our hands still are from the cinnamon rolls
and how we probably should have grabbed another coffee on
the way out of Cloud Nine.

"We can always sneak in to the teacher's lounge," Kevin says, "I know where they hide their coffee pot."

I make a face, "I'm not drinking that coffee - I may need energy, but I have higher standards when it comes to coffee goodness."

I let go of his hand long enough to pull my arms above my head and stretch, almost knocking out a small sophomore who could pass for a ten year old. I look his way as he passes me and mumble a half-hearted "sorry" before turning to Kevin.

I'm just about to speak when Marisol, the head cheerleader and a known partier, walks up to Kevin and places her hands on the zipper of his jacket.

"I see you're still settling with the left overs, Kev. Don't forget my offer. Call me when you come to your senses - remember - I'm cheap." And with that, she catches my eye and saunters off in the other direction.

"Um. What was that?"

Kevin blushes and closes his eyes for a split second before looking at me.

Clearing his throat, he leans toward me and whispers, "Some of the football players pay cheerleaders for certain.... favors. It's happened as long as I've been here." He looks sideways at me - measuring my reaction - and continues, "I don't have the best reputation and so they believe I'm an easy target."

I stare at him for a little while before finding words.

"They prostitute themselves?!"

"...yes."

My eyes grow wide and I breathe in sharp and quick, my hand finding the wall for balance. I take it all in - the truth of what's happening in my own school - and with a sinking realization know it's only a matter of time before my dad hears through the grapevine the lucrative opportunity happening within these walls.

Nothing is safe. Nothing is not touched.

Kevin steps over to where I'm collecting myself. Placing his hands on my shoulders, he waits until I find his eyes.

"You know I've never accepted an offer, right?"

"Of course. I just...I can't believe..."

"I know. Trust me. And to think they're choosing it - this objectification. It's mind bending. No guy here will ever see their worth if they keep throwing it around like it doesn't matter."

My mind is still reeling on the revelation - I honestly have no idea how to take it. I know it will haunt me for awhile and I can't help but wonder if there's some sort of connection, some sort of inner workings with Sam Tiller's name on it. It's just...too much of a coincidence. I check the clock on the wall and realize we're running short on time. Looking at Kevin, I attempt a smile.

"It's going to be a long day," I say - allowing my head to rest on his shoulder for a split second before we run into a freshman, wide eyed and timid and totally freaking out over the mass of hormonally charged students surrounding her.

She pushes up her glasses with the palm of her hand and I can't help but notice the finger printed smudge left behind on her lenses. That would drive me absolutely insane, I think to myself, fighting the urge to wipe them clean for her.

"I-I'm sorry," she stammers through a strikingly pronounced lisp, "I must have been looking everywhere but in front of me."

She rearranges her backpack and checks her watch. Cursing under her breath, she takes off running. Our near collision completely forgotten, her shoelaces trail behind her feet in dangerous circular motions - I half expect to see her trip. The warning bell rings and Kevin smiles and squeezes my hand.

"What's the symbol for Meter?" He asks.

"m"

"ampere?"

I look at him and wink, "A" I answer - growing more confident. "I'm going to do well on this test today," I shrug my shoulder and blush, "I had a great tutor."

"No flattery." He senses my confidences and responds - offering me a question that gave me problems while studying at breakfast, "What about the symbol for pascal?"

I scrunch my nose and avoid the herd of boys waddling to class wearing pants with waistlines around their knees. Kevin coughs to get my attention.

"Pa?" I answer, hesitantly. His smile of approval says it all.

"Relax." He kisses my forehead and makes his way to the exit across the hall - I secretly envy him having first period off before I hear him calling behind me, "You're going to do fine, Steph!" as I snake into the classroom right before the bell rings.

I smile and quickly glance around to see if anyone noticed him hollering, but everyone is too busy cramming or making tiny cheat sheets out of torn paper to even pay attention to the person next to them. As I make my way to my seat I can't help but think of Dante's warning - abandon hope all ye who enter here! - and how Mr. White could accurately hang that sign above his door because, well...let's face it. His class is hell. And honestly? My hands are already sweating and my pen is already tapping a nervous beat against the desk as the tests make their way through the rows. I look at the white paper filled with equations and multiple choice questions and close my eyes. Mind on Physics, Steph. Mind on Physics. The other stuff comes later, focus on passing. I open my eyes in enough time to see Mr. White looking my way as I give myself a little pep talk.

I smile and shrug my shoulder and whisper, "I'm a little

nervous."

He just continues to sit at his desk and stare - the smell of burnt coffee radiating from his cup that's obviously been through its fair share of beverages without a rinse. I fight the compulsion to gag at the scent radiating from the glass and attempt to focus once again on the questions in front of me. Glancing at the clock on the wall, I straighten my back and get to work, thoughts of newtons and coulombs and Planck's constant swirling around my head like balls lost in a pinball machine.

After the test, my mind feels like it has been replaced with a wad of cotton. I walk out of Mr. White's classroom disgruntled and sleepy and highly irritated at the additional homework he gave in preparation for tomorrow's lesson. Two nights of no rest has done me in and I feel a migraine coming - slowly crawling up the back of my neck. Dangit, I forgot to take my medicine, I realize as I massage my temples with my forefingers. I wrinkle my lips in disgust at a couple nearly copulating in the hallway and make my way to my locker to stash my backpack before English. I open the door and smile. Kevin left me a note - attached to a 20 oz Monster drink.

*Sorry for keeping you up so late thinking of you -
you're my beauty in a dark place*
Love, me

I blush and look around but again, no one notices my red face. I take out my cell phone to quickly send him a thank you text before grabbing the drink and popping the cap. I take my first sip and smile.

Now I can effectively make it through another one of Peabody's lectures on whether Shakespeare really wrote all of his plays, I think to myself. Passing by the couple still searching for each other's tonsils (among other things) I conveniently bump the girl with my shoulder. She looks at me between her dark eyeliner and starts cussing me out; I smile sweetly and glance at her boyfriend, which just infuriates her even more. I walk away before she can do anything, her threats still reverberating off of the walls. Looking behind me one more time, I wave and mouth, "sorry!" and put on a sincere face.

You can thank me later for saving you the embarrassment of losing your virginity in the hallways of a high school, I smile and take another sip of my energy drink and walk into English class.

"Stephanie! How wonderful to see you this morning!"

Mrs. Peabody announces and interrupts my mental dialogue with tonsil hockey girl as I walk in the door. I stop and look around before returning her gaze.

"Was I not supposed to be here?" I ask - confused by her overtly happy and welcoming manner.

Mrs. Peabody is probably the most eccentric teacher I have, but she's never been...perky. And right now, that's the only word I can use to describe her, and it's kind of annoying. Her smile gets wider and I notice for the first time just how white her teeth are - they shine.

"Why yes, of course dear. I just am excited to see your face is all." She reaches for my hand and gave it a squeeze, "I loved your latest essay about the price of untested virtue in Measure for Measure. Your writing showed such maturity!"

She walks toward me, her long jumper covering her bright red Keds - a staple in her wardrobe. I wince at the fashion mishap and focus again on her teeth. At least her teeth won't make me bite my lip to fight back images of What Not to Wear episodes.

I set my drink down on a desk and pull my bag off my shoulders, trying to avoid the awkwardness of the situation. I'm not use to praise of any kind, and even though I've accepted my ability in writing and literature, a compliment still leaves me at a bit of a loss of what to say.

"Um, thanks Mrs. Peabody." I look at her and smile - one of the first genuine smiles I've offered today. I glance down at my books and finger my Moleskine, "I worked really hard on that paper."

"Well, I most certainly noticed, and it isn't the first time you have excelled in your assignments. So. I took it upon myself to contact a few colleges heavy in the arts and I received a call back from USC. Stephanie, they are incredibly interested in you coming and pursuing a creative writing degree! They even spoke of scholarships available."

I stare at her lips, but am not sure what to think of the words coming out of her mouth. USC is in California. And expensive. My mind wanders to the possibility of scholarships and I can't help but maybe feel a pinch of excitement in my bones. Creative Writing. I immediately began building images in my mind of mornings spent writing on the beach or allowing the sun to warm my inherently cold blood - it seemed nice. Too nice. I politely listen and refuse to allow myself the comfort of building hope - not for this. Not now.

Wait. Instantly the conversation with Kevin at breakfast rushes through my mind and I begin to blush. USC. That's where he wants to go. I've never allowed myself the ability to think after graduation - I've never really considered what could or would happen between us. I certainly never thought we could end up at the same school.

Mrs. Peabody touches my arm and I blink back into focus.

"Here's their number. I went ahead and gave them your contact information and they mentioned they would be contacting you soon. I hope you pursue this. You are such a gifted writer and you have such a depth not many are able to see. You have stories the world needs to read. Write them. Share them."

She places her hand on my shoulder for a split second and moves on to greet the other students walking into the classroom. I slump into my chair, her words echoing in my head - and the only thing I can think of is I hope the admissions people don't call when my dad is home.

My eyes slip to my Moleskine sitting resolutely on the top of my textbooks. I grab it and hug it to my chest protectively. I need to spend some time writing, I think. Maybe I'll hit up the coffee shop on my way to Emma's, hole up in a corner somewhere and let loose on one of these empty pages. It's been way too long.

And with that, my mind has completely left the classroom and is in an altogether different world - one of peace and comfort and protection and mornings spent on beaches doing nothing but writing and watching the sun rise.

Nine

I GET TO EMMA'S AROUND SIX, COMPLETELY SPENT EMOTIONALLY FROM pouring everything I have onto pieces of paper. My hand is still cramping from the waterlogged words spilling out of my brain and into my heart - forever embedded on the pages of my journal. I open the front door and collapse on one of her couches, thinking that maybe, just maybe, the beginning of the story I just started to write may stick. I start to close my eyes before I hear his voice down the hallway.

"I'm telling you...you just need to be careful."

Jude's voice is abrupt and matter-of-fact. I'm still reeling over the other voice, though. At first I think I may have been hearing things, but I hear him again, countering Jude's warning.

"I'm fine, I promise. But we should probably look into it more is all I'm saying."

What is Kevin doing here? I crane my neck to look down the hallway and see Emma leave Benjamin's room. I close my eyes again to collect my thoughts and rub my temples in a circular motion - hoping for some kind of relief.

"Hey, you look like death."

I crack open one of my eyes and half-heartedly wave a finger in Emma's direction.

"Hey yourself. I had a long night, and no I don't want to talk about it. I just spent the past two hours writing at The Caffeine Drip. I'm on a severe crash from an espresso overdose and I have no emotion to share."

Emma places her hands on her hips and cocks an eyebrow, "So...if I told you Jude has Benjamin tonight for one of their bonding rituals as menfolk, you wouldn't be interested in going shopping with me?"

She has my attention now. If Jude has Benjamin, why did I just hear him talking with Kevin, and why was she coming out of Benjamin's room? I look at her and lower my eyebrows.

"Guys night? Is Kevin in on this?"

She snorts. "Kevin? What does Kevin have to do with guys' night?"

I shrug.

"I don't know. Am I crazy or did I hear him talking with Jude a minute ago?"

Emma looks toward the hallway and nods her head in understanding.

"Oh! Yeah. You did. Kevin called Jude earlier about some questions with his Government and Economics homework. He's been talking with him for the last thirty minutes about due processes and stock markets." She faked a yawn. "Boring if you ask me. But...that doesn't matter. What does matter is this shopping trip. You coming?"

She wags her eyebrows and pokes me in the side. I can't help but break a smile.

It's been forever since I've even been in a store - most of my clothes are hand-me-downs from my mother and even they don't fit correctly. I would never let anyone know this, but I've never been shopping just for fun. Fashion is one of my secret indulgences and I love looking at the magazines stashed in the check-out lines of grocery stores, imagining what I would wear had I the ability to buy whatever I want.

I sit up - slowly - and rub my eyes.

"Okay. Shopping. Let's do this. Can we stop and get something to perk me up? Food perhaps? I haven't eaten since Cloud Nine this morning."

Emma laughs and grabs her purse, "Come on. Let's go - I knew I could get you interested if I said we were going shopping."

I get up off the couch and grab my bag.

"What are we waiting for, then?"

I walk past her and out the door, looking behind me only once to stick out my tongue in protest. I hear the click on the Jeep and I open the door to get in from the cold. Emma isn't too far behind.

As soon as she climbs into her seat and starts the engine she looks at me and asks, "So what's this about USC?"

I stare at her and crinkle my brow.

"Seriously? How do you know about this? Were you in on it?"

She looks at me and smiles knowingly.

"Mrs. Peabody isn't as flighty as you think. She knows we are close and so when she found out they were interested in you she immediately e-mailed me letting me know. It's not that big of a deal, Steph - me knowing. But. You having an opportunity for USC is a big deal. Have you thought much about it today?"

"Yeah. For like a second. And then I remembered Pacey and Kevin and my dad and well...money." I tilt my head and twist my lips, "Is it an incredible opportunity? Absolutely. Is it realistic?" I shrug my shoulders, hiding my disappointment. "Probably not."

Emma looks at me for a brief second before turning a

corner into the local shopping center.

"Just promise me one thing, Stephanie."

"What's that?"

"You won't ever forget that impossibility is merely a dare."

I stare at her for a brief second before bursting into laughter.

"What are you, Hallmark?"

She grabs a toy from her backseat and throws it at me. Her words are ringing in my head, though. Emma knows me well - I can't ever say no to a dare. I continue laughing and look for Benjamin's chewing ring on the floorboard. No doubt he'll want it later.

"Okay. First stop is a haircut." She looks at me and smiles.

"Emma, I thought you just got your hair done a couple weeks ago." I glance at her short and trendy red hair and wonder what else she can do with it before she goes bald.

"This isn't a haircut for me. It's for you."

She grabs her purse and gets out of the Jeep, motioning for me to follow. I'm glued to my seat.

"What do you mean, for me?" I ask, still confused at what's happening.

Emma comes over to my side of the car and leans against the open door, pointing out my faded and torn jeans and shirt with sleeves two inches too short.

"Stephanie, when was the last time you went shopping?"

"Last week. Dad needed help with an anniversary gift for mom so I went with him to Walmart."

"No. When was the last time you went shopping for you."

I think for a moment before answering, suddenly realizing just how long it's been, "Um...it was in elementary school. First grade - before the first day. My mom took me to Goodwill to shop for shoes."

I keep my face planted firmly where my eyes are focused on the hole forming in my shoes passed down to me from my mother about two years ago. Emma attempts to hide the look of surprise but isn't very successful; she just grabs my hand and pulls me out of the SUV and stands in front of me until I look at her.

"Tonight is not about me. It's about you. You are going to get a haircut and some make-up and some clothes. Consider it an early Christmas present from Jude and me."

She looks at me in a no-nonsense stare and I know there's no fighting this. I roll my eyes and cross my arms over my chest, offering her a slight smile.

"Fine," I say.

I pull the rubber band out of my hair and let the brown mane fall below my shoulders. I obediently follow Emma into the salon and grimace. Am I excited? Yes, absolutely. But the thought of someone seeing these split ends and my mousy color is embarrassing. I take a deep breath and look around at the pink walls with pictures of Marilyn Monroe and Lucille Ball and begin to relax. The hairstylists in the middle of their work are funky and laugh while talking to their clients. A girl walks past me with hot pink hair and I can't help but stare.

Absentmindedly I touch my hair and Emma leans over and whispers in my ear.

"Don't even think about it."

I turn around and smile at her before sticking out my tongue in protest. I would never consider dying my hair that color - only in fear it would never return to normal. Or fall out. I'm deathly afraid of my hair falling out.

"Hey ladies! Would you like a drink? Water? Coke?"

My head turns to follow the voice and I see the girl with the bright pink hair smiling at us, her hands clasped in front of her.

"Oh, no - I'm fine," I say, content with just eavesdropping on conversations and morphing into a wallflower.

Emma speaks up - she complained of being thirsty in the car so I'm not surprised she takes advantage of the offer.

"I'd love some water, please."

Pink-haired girl nods her head.

"Water. Absolutely. Sparkling or tap?"

I fight from giggling and Emma just stares at the girl before answering, "Um, tap. Please."

I slowly begin to relax. I like the atmosphere. Everything - from the music to the furniture to the decor - has a vintage feel. As soon as I sit down on one of the leather couches, a girl comes from behind a curtained partition; I smile, focusing on her tattoo on her left arm - bright and colorful and vibrantly beautiful. It's just a bouquet of flowers - but they are delicate and strong and if you look closely enough, there's a little girl twirling her skirt. I make a mental note to ask where the inspiration came from to get it because it's absolutely mesmerizing. I stick my hands in my jacket pocket to keep from touching it.

"Hey, guys! Emma - it's so good to see you."

I move to look at whoever is talking and I see a girl giving Emma a hug.

She pushes Emma back so she can see her better.

"Look at you! You look amazing! And the hair - love it. I knew that cut would fit you."

Emma's hand immediately finds strands of hair and begins laughing, "I know. Whatever you did - it works. And thanks, I feel good. The best I've felt since Benjamin was born, really."

She turns and glances my way and, almost as if remembering she was here for me, blushes and catches the other girl's attention. I smile at Emma and wink - it's probably been weeks since she's been out of the house and in civilization so it doesn't bother me when she gets social.

The hairstylist sees me out of the corner of her eye and smiles. Holding out her hand, she introduces herself.

"Hi. I'm Ashlee. You must be who I'm working on today?"

I glance at Emma and nod.

"Yeah. I uh...my hair needs some work, I guess."

I giggle nervously and then cough to cover it up. *Smooth. Real smooth.*

Ashlee perks up and motions for me to come and sit in her chair.

"Perfect! I noticed your hair the minute you walked in - but probably not the way you think. I took one look and knew exactly what to do." I look at her reflection in the mirror as she plays with my hair. Looking at me, she asks, "You wanting a lot of length cut off?"

I find my voice amidst my embarrassment and give her a half smile, "Um...no, not really."

Ashlee smiles and nods her head. "Got it. I think I know the perfect cut to accentuate your high cheekbones and those stunning eyes."

Placing her hands on my shoulder she closes one of her eyes and loses herself in what my hair will look like. Once satisfied, she opens her eye and winks.

"This is going to be great..." She trails off - and looks at me questioningly, "I'm so sorry. I didn't get your name earlier."

"Oh, um...my name is Stephanie."

"Stephanie," Ashlee says, "this cut is going to completely change the way you look - but it will be easy to manage. Let's go get your hair washed and I can get started."

She shrugged her shoulders in excitement and motioned for me to follow her - I catch Emma smiling behind a magazine as I walk past her and hide a smile - the last thing I was expecting tonight was to be pampered, but honestly? Secretly

I love every minute of it.

We get back to her chair and she pulls out her scissors. I press my lips together and Ashlee catches my nervous glance towards the mirror.

"When's the last time you got your haircut, girl?"

I look at her and wrinkle my nose.

"Um - I honestly can't remember. My mom usually trims it before school every year, but not this year - so...maybe two years?"

I glance at my hair in her hands and I cough out an apology about how horrible it looks.

"Don't you worry about anything. Your hair is actually pretty healthy minus the split ends, and the color is spectacular. I have women constantly in my salon begging for me to match this with a hair dye - and you have it naturally! We're just going to lighten the roots a little with a slight blonde highlight to make your eyes pop."

She smiles at me and squeezes my shoulder with her hand. She then wraps my hair around her wrist and pulls through to make a low ponytail.

Eyes focused on her task, she whispers, "Now, don't freak out over what I am about to do."

She sticks a pin in her mouth and grabs her scissors again - this time cutting off an entire chunk of hair in one fell swoop. My heart falls with a thud in my chest and my hands start sweating.

She looks at my face going pale and smiles, "I told you not to freak," she says and turns my head away from the growing pile of hair on the floor.

"Sorry. It's a rule of mine. No peeking until I am finished - makes it easier for both of us. Sometimes it doesn't necessarily look like I want it to, you know? I would rather you see the finished product than the sketchy parts in between."

She touches my chin with her finger as she measures out

bangs and smiles.

"This is going to be fun, Stephanie. I can feel it in my bones."

Yeah. I can feel something - but it's something more akin to fear. Please don't make me bald.

I look at her through my hair and grimace. I'm trying to believe her, but the amount of hair on the floor below me freaks me out - regardless of her trying to comfort me. I try and keep my mind off of losing my hair - my eyes wandering to her tattoo.

"So, um...what's up with your tattoo?"

"What?" She looks at me - her eyes bent in concentration.

"The flowers and the girl. It's so...colorful."

"Oh! My tattoo."

She stops what she's doing and steps back, leaning on her counter and studying my hair for a brief second before grabbing another chunk and layering it with her razor. I try to ignore the sound it's making - like she's chopping away straight to my scalp - and hope she starts talking soon so I have something else to listen to.

"So a few years ago I heard about human trafficking for the first time. One of my friends runs an organization where they find girls who are at risk at being trafficked or who have been sex slaves in Honduras and they rehabilitate them. It's this beautiful picture of restoration. When I first heard about it, the guy who runs it said he got the idea of restoration and beauty in the midst of such chaos and horror from watching a little girl twirl her skirt. She was just so innocent...so mesmerizing...he couldn't get the image out of his mind. So he thinks of her every time he goes and rescues these girls. He calls the organization She Dances."

She catches my eye and smiles and I know from the core of who I am that she means every word she just said.

"Is this just in Honduras?" I whisper.

I already know the answer of course. I just need to know if she knows the answer. If my world isn't as invisible as I believe.

"Huh? Oh. Um...no. Not at all." She grimaces as if she doesn't want to share the information. "There's actually more slaves today than there ever have been in the history of the world - even during the Trans-Atlantic slave trade. And uh... America traffics thousands and thousands of girls a year." She's quiet for a moment as she focuses on my hair. "It's definitely not just in Honduras." She whispers this last piece - almost to where I can't hear her.

My vision starts to blur and my blood runs cold as I focus on Emma, sitting in the next room. I hone in on every little detail about her so I don't faint or go crazy. My heart starts hammering in my chest and I grab the armrests of my chair so tight my knuckles look porcelain. I know all too well this story. I can't help but flashback to the first time I felt the rough grasp of a man's hands. Most twelve year old girls spend their birthdays eating too much candy and giggling with friends while putting on make-up during sleepovers. Me? I spent my birthday trying to push a man three times my size off my small frame. I was always so curious about what my dad hid in his shed - secretly wishing it was some stash of Christmas presents or a hidden bicycle for my birthday. I use to even play spy games - sneaking around, trying to peek through cracks in the cement blocks.

After that night, I never wanted to go back. I never stepped within ten feet of his secret world - unless of course there was someone waiting and my dad watched me from the window, making sure I made it all the way to the shed. It wouldn't look good for his business if his main profit went running...

I blink and return to the present, Ashlee lowering her eyebrows for a brief second, "You okay?"

I choke out a response and ignore her question, "Is there

anything for girls here?"

"Absolutely. There are a few organizations who are worldwide. A few even focus on covert operations in order to rescue girls. Like this one organization named after a child prostitute in Asia - Love146. They raise awareness of human trafficking and sex slavery. The founder first saw the girl while on an undercover investigation. He sat in this waiting room, looking at these girls in an adjacent area, trying not to think of these men sitting with him. Men who were actually there waiting for these girls watching cartoons. He said these girls were...broken. Empty. Their eyes held no life."

"Where was 146?" I ask, my hands still shaking.

Ashlee smiles. "That's the thing. Apparently this girl was just standing there - staring at the men - almost as if she knew exactly what was going on."

She stops and wipes her nose; I notice for the first time tears streaming down her face. She laughs and brushes the back of her hand against her cheek.

"I'm sorry - this story just gets me every time. I mean, it's why I decided to get the tattoo - so I would have a reason to tell my story - her story - so people would know. It never loses its ability to break my heart when I think of this young girl, completely taken out of her family and stripped of any hope for a future, staring at these monsters just waiting to have their piece of her. What kind of men do these things? What kind of girls are able to live through it and still hope?"

"Those who have fight left in them."

"What?"

"The girls who are able to live through the hell and still have hope? They are the ones with the fight left in them. They are the ones who won't give up."

Ashlee stops cutting for a split second and moves back to look me in the eye.

"Yeah. I guess you're right." She takes a deep breath and

grabs another section of my hair, "That's why I have this tattoo though. It's so I never forget - and I always see those stuck in horrible situations as beautiful and not tainted by those who are stripping away their dignity."

I sit there silent, lost in my own thoughts of trying to convince myself there's still a shred of dignity left in me - that I still have a bit of fight left in my soul despite its constant rejection of worth.

Ten

SHE'S DONE WITH MY HAIR IN LESS THAN AN HOUR. I STARE AT THE mirror and at first, don't even recognize myself. What use to be long, mangy strands of hair hanging limp now sit on my shoulder in soft layers. The back is slightly shorter with highlights accentuating what I thought was an ugly brown. I bite my lip and hide a smile - I actually like my hair. I can't help it. I do a little hair toss and Ashlee laughs.

"There ya go, girl. I knew there was confidence hiding somewhere inside that head of yours..." She winks and teases my hair a little more before dousing me with the final set of hair spray. "You're good to go, beautiful. I'll throw in some of these products for free today." She stops and turns my chair to face her, "Oh, and...you look absolutely stunning." She turns to Emma and motions for her to join us. "I'm done with your girl, Em. Come take a look."

Emma walks into the room and freezes as soon as she sees me.

"Oh my gosh - you look incredible!"

She reaches out to play with my hair and turns me around

so she can see the entire cut. I try and keep from blushing and avoid her gaze. She's such the emoting machine she's probably already crying.

"Thanks." I smile as she squeezes my hand.

"How much do I owe you, Ashlee?" Emma asks as she pulls out her wallet.

Ashlee turns and looks at Emma and smiles, "You know what? You don't owe me anything."

She places her hand on Emma's arm and catches my surprised stare out of the corner of her eye. She winks at me.

Emma closes her wallet and looks at Ashlee again.

"Are you sure? I mean, you've done so much already, giving us free product and staying late..."

Ashlee looks at her and shrugs her shoulders, "What can I say, Emma?" She lowers her voice and I barely hear what she's saying. "You can never have too much love, Em - and I have a feeling Stephanie doesn't even know what that means."

Emma smiles and hangs her head - a motion of consent - and places her wallet back in her purse. Leaning forward she wraps Ashlee in a hug and whispers a quiet "thank you" before turning to me.

"You ready?" I see her brush her cheek with the back of her hand and smile at her amazing ability to feel when I spend my life trying to go numb.

"Yeah. I'm ready."

Taking a last glance in the mirror, I turn and smile at Ashlee. Getting off my chair I walk over to her and give her second hug of the night. I hear Emma's sharp intake of breath and chuckle inwardly at her surprise. I don't initiate physical intimacy. Like ever. I guess there's a first time for everything.

"Thank you - for everything," I say quietly.

Ashlee squeezes back and whispers in my ear, "Absolutely. If you ever need anything, let me know." Pulling away from the embrace she reaches over to her counter and grabs a card.

"Call me...anytime. I mean it."

I take her card and nod.

"Got it."

I can hear Emma talking on her phone and she calls my name from across the room, "We should probably get going. It's already 6:30 and we have an appointment about two minutes ago for your make-up."

I gather my stuff and walk out the door with Emma, mind still reeling on the splitting open of my world. Maybe there's hope, I think with no attempt to filter my words. Maybe someone will hear about my story and rescue me...

Emma looks at me as we walk down the sidewalk and bumps me lightly on the shoulder.

"So what did you think of Ashlee?"

I wait for a split second, allowing my thoughts to simmer before answering.

"She's pretty cool. How'd you find her?"

Emma is quiet for a moment before answering.

"She's a childhood friend."

I glance at her, waiting for more of the story. Realizing that she's not going to give me any more information, my curiosity is peaked.

"Have you ever seen her tattoo? Has she told you the story behind it?"

Emma smiles. "Yeah. Originally we planned on getting the same one - but I chickened out."

I smile and look at her, "You? Chickened out from a tattoo? Shocking."

Hiding a smile, she turns and looks at me and studies my face for a moment accepting my sarcasm.

"Wait. So you know about those organizations? The ones about trafficking?"

Emma nods her head and keeps walking, avoiding my gaze.

"Yeah. I know a little."

We walk for a few more minutes before she motions to a shop on my right - I notice the trendy models on huge posters on the windows and look at Emma.

"This looks expensive, are you sure you want us to go in here?"

Emma lifts her finger and shakes her head in her I'm-not-going-to-fight-with-you-about-this way and I shut up. I walk in the door and instantly the smell of citrus and self-tanning lotion assaults my senses. I inhale deeply - as much as I possibly can without ingesting chemicals - and find myself lost in the midst of colors I never knew existed. I pick up a package with blue blush inside and turn towards Emma and wrinkle my nose.

"Really? Blue? Is this for like, Halloween or something?"

I see Emma's eyes widen just enough for me to notice before I hear someone else joining our conversation.

"Or something."

I turn around to greet whoever felt the need to intrude when I notice the posh clothes and the name tag. The woman I am staring at is no shorter than six feet and one of the most beautiful humans I have ever seen. Her face is absolutely flawless. I smile and offer my hand as I sheepishly place the blue make-up back on the counter.

"Hi. I'm Stephanie."

"Yes. You have an appointment, no? My name is Eva. Follow me. You will be working with Nicole this evening. She is waiting."

Her words are short - void of any emotion and with a touch of Russian undertones.

I glance at Emma out of the corner of my eye and mouth a few phrases revealing my discomfort before she pushes me away to join Eva the ice queen.

"Thank you so much for waiting, Eva." Emma states

delicately, "I believe Nicole knows the package I signed up for."

Eva glances at Emma - sizing her up I'm sure - and curtly nods.

"Of course. Nicole is aware. You may wait here while Stephanie receives her makeover. Unless of course, you would like a makeover as well?"

Emma giggles and shakes her head, "Oh, no thank you, Eva. I am a new mom. Probably couldn't keep up with all the time it takes for toner and base and what-not - let alone blush and tanner. Oh and the eye shadow just isn't..."

I shake my head slightly at Emma, our standard signal for when we begin to talk too much. She does it more than I do - and usually I have to save her from embarrassing foot-enters-mouth episodes.

Her eyes widen and she clears her throat, "Anyway. Thanks for the offer. I'll just wait."

Eva regards her cooly before raising an eyebrow and letting out a sigh.

"Very well. You shall wait here then."

Does she even know how to smile?

And with that, Eva turns and begins walking towards the back of the store, I watch her for a split second before I realize she wants me to follow her. I sneak a glance at Emma and wrinkle my brow.

"Save me," I mouth.

She just smiles and motions for me to keep walking. I sign and turn around to find Eva already halfway down the hall. Almost tripping on my shoelaces in my haste to catch up, I wonder why Eva is responsible for greeting customers and hope my make up artist has a bit more...warmth than this woman in charge of hospitality.

"This is your room. Nicole will be with you shortly."

I look at Eva for the last time and muster up a smile,

"Thanks, Eva."

"Yes."

And with that, she walks away, her heels clicking menacingly on the tile floor. I scrunch my eyebrows in confusion and am startled by another voice calling my name.

"Stephanie! Oh dear. Look at those eyebrows." I turn and am met with a petite woman walking towards me with her arms outstretched.

She pulls me into a half embrace and frowning, rubs her fingers across my eyebrows, "Yes. We will certainly need to wax those." She looks at me and smiles, "Hello dear. My name is Nicole and I will be working with you today."

She ushers me into her room and sits me down in front of a mirror covered with lights.

She kneels down in front of me and clasps her hands in my lap, "So. Do you wear make-up often?"

I think about my drawer full of concealer, blush and one package of unopened eyeshadow.

"No." I reply.

"Perfect. This means you won't have as many bad habits to break. Let's get started, shall we?"

She moves to her counter and begins pulling out color charts and eyeliner and lipstick. I cringe when I see the wax heater being turned on - definitely something I'm not looking forward to experiencing. Nicole moves like a pro - I don't even have to talk, and it seems as though she would prefer the silence. She moves quickly and effectively, and before I know it, she's handing me a mirror and I am looking at someone I don't even recognize.

"What do you think? I didn't go for the dramatic look; I figured you would probably feel like a clown. What you see is a simple primer, base coat, concealer, blush, bronzer, eyeshadow, eyeliner, mascara and lipstick combination."

"That's simple?"

Nicole laughs, "Yeah. You'll be surprised how easy it is to effectively manage your make-up application once you get use to the steps. Just remember to clean your face every day so you aren't building up residue from previous applications." She grimaces. "That's just gross. Oh! And don't forget this."

She places another piece in my bag and I look at her questioningly, "It's what you put on after you finish your make-up. It makes sure everything stays on for longer periods of time." She smiles, "You look great, girl! Let's go show your mom."

I bite my lip and don't correct her. It's obvious tonight I am living in a fantasy world, and so I don't want to ruin it by reminding myself of reality. I follow Nicole out the door with one last look at myself in the mirror, wondering if she would mind writing me an instruction manual. There's no way I'm going to remember all of those steps. I raise an eyebrow and rush to meet up with Nicole.

When we enter the waiting room, Emma is on her phone looking out the window. I can hear her slight whisper and know by her tone she's probably talking with Jude and most likely it's something she doesn't want anyone hearing. I perk my ears - obviously. I'm nothing if not nosy.

"I know, honey. I just think we need to be mindful of our situation and the information we've been given. Are you absolutely positive that's what he said?"

She pauses for a brief second before her shoulders droop and her hand reaches for her hair. She twists and maneuvers a single strand into multiple pieces, braiding without realizing it. A sign of stress.

Nicole coughs quietly, but it's enough to make Emma jump and hang up without saying goodbye. I glance down at the floor as if breaking eye contact would help her adjust to the realization that we heard the end of the conversation - whatever it meant. I know Emma well enough to know she doesn't stress about a lot of things - except being a mom. I suddenly start to worry whether Benjamin was okay.

Once Emma notices the make-up, she freaks out as expected. She leaps from her chair and rushes over to where Nicole and I stand.

"You seriously took my breath away. You look...stunning!"

She smiles and I see the tears threatening themselves in the corners of her eyes. She shakes her head and laughs to cover up the emotion.

"These colors look perfect on her - thank you so much."

She pulls out her wallet to pay for the make-up and I make my way outside with my bags of hair product and the stuff Nicole gave me. The cool air cuts its way into my thin jacket and I shiver. Glancing at my phone I realize I got a text from Kevin.

> Hey. Thinking about u. Call if u need me - meet at r place 2morrow morning?

I smile at his text speak and send a quick response that I would see him bright and early and that I had a surprise waiting for him. I couldn't help but wonder what he would think of the hair. I'm still texting him when Emma walks up beside me and starts laughing.

"You would think that thing is attached to your thumbs permanently." I look up and she winks, "You ready? We have some more shopping to do!"

I return her smile and grab her jacket, "Hey, is Benjamin okay?"

She turns quickly and tilts her head, "What do you mean?"

Her eyes grow concerned and she checks her phone - as if she missed a text.

"Well I overheard the last part of your conversation and..."

"Oh! That!" Emma laughs nervously and waves her hair out of her eyes before grabbing my elbow and giving it a squeeze, "You don't need to worry about that - it's just house stuff." Her voice slowly grows quiet and I can't help but think she's not telling me everything, "You know...being an adult. It can be stressful at times." She shrugs her shoulders and places her hand on her hip, "Now, are you ready to shop or not? This is the important part - clothes."

I put my phone in my pocket and jump up to follow her into the nearby boutique. I glance around at the clothes and immediately start salivating, my mind completely forgetting the questions about Emma's conversation.

Oh yeah. I can do some serious damage in here.

I pick up a long-sleeve, snap button shirt. It's real cute - and I automatically picture wearing it all the time. A slow smile spreads across my face and I move to grab the price tag. Oh. Seventy five dollars.

I like it - but not that much. I place the shirt back on the rack and Emma grabs it from me.

"Oooh. This is cute." She catches my eye, "Do you like it?"

"Yeah, I guess....it's kind of expensive though."

Emma drops her arm and tilts her head.

"Stephanie. Do you like it? Would you wear it?"

I cross my arms across my chest and cock one of my hips. Here she goes again. The questions that require an answer. I sigh and give in to her line of reasoning.

"Yeah. I would."

"Alright then." She drapes it over her arm and grabs a necklace to go with it. "Listen, Stephanie. Jude and I can afford this, okay? He just got a bonus and I've been keeping tabs of what we spend. We've been saving up for quite awhile." She studies my face closely and grabs my hand. "Just have fun, okay? I know how much we have for this." Winking, she pats my shoulder and maneuvers past me.

I breathe deep and consider her words.

It's going to be pretty tough not looking at these price tags - but if I am going to get anything, I'm just going to have to ignore those pesky slips of paper. I resolve myself to have fun - to enjoy the incredible gift Emma and Jude have decided to give me. And I'm going to start with this white leather jacket that would look absolutely incredible with a pair of those skinny jeans and some red patent leather heels. I smile and scratch my eyebrow.

Yeah. Serious damage.

I'm looking over another pair of jeans when Emma pops up out of nowhere with three blouses and some leopard print flats. She hands them to me and points to the dressing room. The amount of clothes stashed on the chair inside the room she has already reserved takes my breath away. I nod my head and get to work.

This may take awhile.

While I am changing, she starts talking.

"So, I talked with Sheriff Goldsmith earlier today."

I freeze mid-leg of putting on the jeans and she sees my hesitancy - one foot hangs in mid air for about three seconds.

"No worries, Steph. I didn't mention the latest. I did however ask how the case from last time was coming along."

I thought of the last time I saw Sheriff Goldsmith - he was putting on his pants and avoiding my gaze at all costs as he finished his business and left me in my dad's shack - naked and violated. I shiver and force the jeans to hug my hips a bit quicker than normal.

"What did he say?" I manage to ask, and am pretty convinced at how casual I sound.

Emma sighs and I picture her running her hands through her hair and resting her chin on her palm.

"He's pretty frustrated with the whole situation, actually. It seems as though your father has some connections within the justice department here in town and they are forcing the case to remain stagnant." She got quiet for a split second before continuing, her voice definitely lower and more subdued than before, "He mentioned if something didn't happen within the next couple of weeks they would have to close the case."

Convenient for him, I think as I try to steady my breathing. I close my eyes and lean against the mirror for a split second to allow myself to regain composure. I understand what this means, and based on Emma's voice, so does she. I'm never going to get justice for what my dad has done. Emma has no idea the sheriff is involved, and much of the police force has made their way to my dad's backyard at some point within the last five years. It's a corrupt system, and I am certainly the victim. Of course they'd want the case to close. A closed case means an open door for their midnight rendezvous. A shiver runs through my body and I take deep breaths to even out my emotion.

"It got quiet in there. Are you okay?"

"Yeah. I'm fine."

I close my eyes for a few seconds and pull back the curtain. Walking over to her, I lean forward and give her a hug and am surprised to feel this time she is the one collapsing against me.

"There's nothing we can do about it right now," I say - hiding my emotion well under a mask of make-up and years of practicing, "So we might as well enjoy tonight as much as we can." I smile at her and she nods her head.

"I'm so sorry, Stephanie. I'm so sorry I can't do anything else."

"What do you mean? You've already done so much. I don't deserve you in my life yet you still love me. I don't really know why you do it, but I don't really want to know. It doesn't really matter, I guess. You've changed my life, you know. Because of you, I didn't give up - I kept trying - at life, at writing, at relationships. Thank you for reminding me of the importance of hope."

She sniffs and chokes on her tears and I start giggling. Seriously. How does she find all these tears?

Pointing at my outfit she responds, "Definitely a keeper. Place that in the yes pile. Those green shoes are a no."

She motions for me to continue trying on clothes and I oblige, running back into the room to tackle the pile of blouses and sweaters and jeans stacked on the chair. It's obvious that for now, the subject is closed. I honestly couldn't be any more relieved.

"I think I'm finally beginning to understand the advantages of having a son," I hear her calling from outside of my dressing room, I stifle a laugh and keep listening - knowing there's more coming. "I'm not sure if Jude could handle two females under the same roof with the emotions I have..," her voice trails off and I peek out from the curtain and give her a smile.

"You already have a daughter, Emma. Just not by blood."

Her eyes light up and she bites her lip to keep from crying again.

"You're right. Not by blood, but my daughter nonetheless."

I continue to hold her gaze and then close the curtain to try on the last of the clothes: a silk sundress perfect for summer evenings. It would be awhile before I could wear it, but we both decided it was too good of a deal to pass. I let it drape over my head and fall over my body before I allow myself to look in the mirror. Finally taking the risk of peeking, I gasp when I see a curvaceous woman in the place of what use to be me: skinny, no curves, long mousy hair with no make-up. I lean forward for a closer inspection before I let Emma in on the secret. Pulling back the curtain, I step out into the waiting room. I catch her attention from the book she's reading and she just places her hand on her chest and stares.

"Holy cow, woman! When did you grow up?"

I roll my eyes.

"Really? Let's not make a big deal out of this. Is it a yes or no?"

I have to fight from spinning in a circle because I love the dress so much. It's beautiful - and in it I feel graceful and delicate. Like a flower. I smile and reminisce about a little girl given a second chance at life, dancing with her skirt twirling around her. Beauty in darkness. It's what I want.

"What are you thinking about?"

Emma breaks through my reverie and I look up and notice her standing directly behind me. I'm watching her eyes threaten to spill over in tears - again - and I shrug my shoulders.

"I just like this dress."

She nodded. "I'd say so. You look absolutely beautiful." She places her hand on my shoulder and gives it a squeeze.

"Don't ever think you're anything less - I mean it."

I smile and respond, "With you and Kevin around, I don't think I have to worry about forgetting it anytime soon."

She gathers her purse and my bags and looks at her watch.

"They are about to close. Let's get all of these."

She sweeps her arm across the pile of clothes I have tried on - enough to last me for awhile - and turns to look at me,

"And we still need to find you a jacket."

"No we don't." I rush back into the dressing room and grab the white leather jacket I snatched from the rack before I came in, "I already found one."

Emma smiles. "Perfect," she says, pulling out her credit card. "Now let's go see just how much having a daughter costs."

It's almost ten o'clock when I get home. I have to put the bags down just to open the door, Emma's headlights illuminating the hallway for a brief second before I close the door. Out of everything I tried on and returned back to the rack, I've managed to come away with quite the wardrobe. I make a promise to myself to take Emma on a coffee date soon to thank her and clumsily maneuver myself through the hallway, trying to make it to my bedroom where I can stash the bags. I hear a chair creak in the kitchen and my heart sinks. I noticed my dad's truck in the driveway and was hoping I would be able to avoid seeing him tonight. I open my bedroom door and toss my bags inside on my bed. I can hear footsteps coming my way and I close my eyes in disgust when I smell the whiskey, yet again. Just one night. Just one night I wish he'd be able to say no. Dropping everything I have, I close the door and turn to walk towards the kitchen. Might as well get it over with - meet the enemy on the front lines, or something like that.

I turn the corner and find my dad, leaning against the wall - his head resting against his arm.

He hears me coming and looks up, "Well. Aren't we all gussied up this evening? Who put the whore paint on your face? You need to wash that crap off. Makes you look like your working the corner. Better yet, leave it on. Makes ya look purty. Kinda like your mom when she was your age."

He walks towards me, swaying and grabbing for the wall to steady himself. I fight the look of disdain threatening to overtake my face and push my sleeves off my wrists. I really don't like where this is headed. I bite my lip and shrug my shoulders, nervously twisting my hands - he never liked Emma, never liked hearing about her, but if he found out from someone else she was who took me shopping it would be worse than me telling him.

"Emma took me shopping today after school. It was her

Christmas present to me." I fingered the edges of my new hair, wondering if he even notices. "I got a haircut too - and she bought me some new clothes for the winter."

I'm not sure why I even bother. I see the change in his demeanor and sigh. Here it comes, I think to myself and brace for the inevitable.

He sneers and continues to lessen the distance between us, his boots striking the wood floor. Once he's close enough he grabs a handful of my hair, and pulls my head back so my eyes are focused on the wild motion of his own, "You are an ungrateful little snitch, you know that? That woman needs to stay out of our business. If it weren't for her we wouldn't have the police breathing down our necks every time we turn around."

"No, Dad...I believe I'm the one who is dealing with police breathing down my neck - not you."

He slaps me across the face, hard and fast. My jaw starts to throb and I taste the metal liquid oozing from his impact. I touch my lip and look at my hand. Blood. Perfect. At least I now have make-up to cover up the bruises.

He brings his face inches away from mine, a look of hatred emanating from every pore.

"You have no idea what I go through. You have no idea what I sacrifice making sure this family has a home and food on the table."

He grabs my cheeks with one hand and pushes me against the wall. I feel the tears start to come but I blink them away. I won't give him the benefit of knowing he's hurt me. I won't.

He looks at me and smirks, "First you get a shopping trip from some nice lady, and now I'm getting phone calls from some high-falootin' school in Cali-fornia wanting you to go to college there. What makes you think I'm going to let you leave, huh?"

He presses himself against me, the all-too-familiar feeling

of supper rising to greet me for the second time starts turning in my stomach. I turn away and he forces me to look at him.

I hate it when he gets to me like this, but I'm already whimpering against his hold.

"I didn't call them, Dad. One of my teachers called them." My voice breaks; I can only whisper as I see yet another dream fading away, "They like my writing and want to give me a scholarship."

A low chuckle burns deep in my dad's chest and he shakes his head, his hand still pulsating against my cheek. "They like your writing? You can barely speak full sentences, what makes them think you can write?" He finally lets go and turns around, facing the back door, "You are nothing, Stephanie. You think you can make it without me? You ain't good enough for some school in Cali-fornia. Besides. With you gone, how do you think I'd make my money?" His grin turns sinister and my heart stops for a split second before I know what's going on. He grabs my arms and pulls me close, "It's a good thing you put on make-up today, beautiful. The sheriff likes his women purty."

I let out a low moan and start crying, "Dad, please. Don't." My eyes focus out the back window and I see his shed illuminated with light from one of the lamps inside. Someone is waiting - waiting to take one more piece of me. I shake my head and start beating my hands against his chest, "Dad, no... no...please...don't make me."

My words are a broken record to his sick cycle of business. He pushes my small frame towards the door and makes his way outside, almost carrying me in my attempt to fight - to do anything but go in there. Memories start flooding my mind and I'm a lost twelve year old, all over again, broken and bleeding and crying out for some sort of rescue.

The door opens and my dad shoves me inside. Before he lets go, he grabs my neck and whispers in my ear, "Try anything stupid and I'll kill you."

My blood runs cold and I close my eyes in resignation. My dad takes the money from the man and slaps me on the rear on his way out, whispering under his breath, "Be good, punkin."

I shoot him a withering glance before allowing the tears to flow freely. The door slams and I am left alone.

"Please don't do this. Not again." My voice comes out in a hoarse whisper - blocked by the fear lodged in my throat.

My pleas are ignored for the second time. The man just sits there staring at me, anxious to get started. Smirking, he walks over to where I stand and brushes my hair behind my ear. I fight the feelings of despair closing around my lungs and breathe slowly.

"You look grown up - I like what you done to your hair."

A hand caresses my cheek and lands on my shoulder - inching lower and lower as the sobs keep escaping my mouth. There is no rescue this time. I hear the back door slam and a lock turns. I open my eyes and face the monster as he unbuckles his belt and pushes me on the bed. I focus on the gold wedding band glistening in the light as he grunts and works up a sweat to take every piece of dignity I have left. I brush a tear off my cheek and he grabs my hair.

"What? This doesn't feel good? You too used to other men?"

He snickers, his breath coming ragged and falling all over me. He rips off my shirt and comes close - kissing my neck and collarbone. I close my eyes and images of Ashlee's tattoo fills my head. I think of the little girl - alone. I think of the number 146 and how even in the most grotesque situation she is still seen as beautiful and lovely to those who recognize her worth. I think of the flowers and the little girl dancing, a picture of hope in the midst of hate. And then I pray. I pray for hope and fight and justice and innocence and rescue. I close my eyes tight against the tears and fight against my heart ripping in two, but it's too late. The monster is done and has all but collapsed on top of me in exhaustion. Every part of me hurts. He musters up enough energy to climb off of me and gets dressed without even looking my way. I am nothing to him - but he has become everything to me. I don't take my eyes off of him. I want him to see me - I want him to hurt - I want him to realize what he's done. I look again at his wedding ring.

"Does your wife know you like to rape teenage girls?"

He stops as he buttons up his shirt and looks at me. His eyes move into slits and his lip quivers with fear and disgust.

"You don't have the guts to say anything, little girl. You're nothing but a fifty dollar lay."

He looks me up and down and walks over to where I am still on the bed - too bruised to even move. He takes my clothes and puts them in his bag and turns to leave. I have no strength to call out or protest and I watch as he leaves with everything I was wearing - and my last shred of dignity turns to dust. I fall asleep to the sound of my own tears.

Eleven

I WAKE UP TO SUNLIGHT PIERCING THROUGH THE BLINDS OF MY DAD'S shed. It's hard for me to move because I'm so sore. I rub my eyes and old make-up from yesterday's shopping trip with Emma comes off. I'm sure after last night's crying my face looks like a drowned raccoon. I slowly maneuver myself to a sitting position - wincing at the shooting pain in my left hip. I glance down and a deep purple stain creeps across my skin - I frown and force myself to not think about how I could have gotten that bruise. It's not until I am standing up that I remember my clothes were stolen. I have nothing here - and I'm not about to wear the sheets out - at least I hope I won't have to. Glancing around, I wrinkle my nose at the dirty clothes strewn about haphazardly. I refuse to look through them - afraid most of them aren't even my father's. I curse under my breath and start looking in some of Dad's make-shift cabinets. Surely there is at least a shirt to cover myself. I stop cold when I see pictures in the far corner - behind his work boots and tool kit - just hidden enough for the regular snoop to completely miss them. Definitely hidden. I stretch to reach and finally grab hold of them. Pulling them out, I'm devastated.

They're of Valerie. Valerie with her mouth gagged - eyes puffy and red from crying. Valerie wearing one of my dad's shirts - buttoned only to where she is barely covered. Valerie in her underwear - her eyes void of hope. I wade through the pictures and grimace. There's more. And they aren't just of Valerie. I don't even know who these girls are - and they are so young!

My eyes rest on one picture - a girl with baby doll curls wearing a maid's outfit. The heels on her feet are too big, her eyes big and round. The sadness in her gaze penetrates my soul and I cry out in surprise. Her face is caked with make-up and her name is scrawled on the back - Zoe. I look closer at the scribble and read something else - upload to 'under 12' category. I fight the dizziness overtaking me and collapse back onto the mattress.

Under twelve? She's younger than twelve? I sit there for awhile, numb to what I am facing and lost at what to do. I don't even know where these girls are hiding - I don't even know if Valerie is caught as deep as I am or if it was just a one-time deal and my father decided to take advantage of the business opportunity looming before him. I'm suddenly reminded of Kevin telling me about the cheerleaders' business of passing out favors to the football players and it's just all too much. I begin to question again my father's involvement. It's just too coincidental. I wonder how he does it - how he convinces these girls to trust him - nothing about him leaks loyalty. I stare at the pictures a little longer and feel my heart's fissure grow more obsolete.

Everything I've been facing for the past week rises in one quick motion and I have no time to stop it. I throw up everything, right there on the floor, crying the whole time as I realize I am not the only one who has dealt with this... monster who claims to be my father. I grab a shirt off the shelf inside and wrap it around me, stuffing the pictures in the front pocket. I make a face as I grab the sheet off his mattress and wrap it around my waist. The hatred I feel for my father has just risen to a dangerous level, and I am hoping for my own sake I don't find him in the house because I just found another reason to fight. I open the door, blinded for a split second by the contrast of light, and make my way to the house - noting grimly how my father has given me a new definition for the walk of shame.

I don't care what it takes. I'm going to stop him. If no one will rescue me, I will find a way to rescue myself and these other girls who don't deserve the life they've been given.

I get to the back door and notice someone has left it unlocked for me - probably my father when he realized I didn't come back in last night. How thoughtful, sarcasm drips from my thoughts and I am still fighting the impulse to throw up again. I close my eyes and take deep breaths. Once I feel stable enough, I quietly walk to my room, hoping to not see Pacey or my mother because that would just be a whole lot of explanation I am not ready to give. I make it to my room just in time to hear Dad's truck pull out of the driveway; I pull out the pictures from the pocket of his shirt and stuff them underneath my mattress - there's no way I am going to lose those. I take off the sheet and shirt and put on my robe and head to the bathroom where I take a thirty minute shower - scrubbing everything I can of last night off of me. I finish - my skin red and raw but the scent finally has left me for the time being. I dry off, thankful for the new underwear waiting for me from shopping with Emma, and collapse on the bed. Pulling the sheets over my eyes, I drift off into a deep sleep, completely forgetting about meeting Kevin at the bleachers.

❋

I wake up a few hours later, my mom banging on my door. "Steph? Are you in there? Stephanie. Open the door. It's your mother. The school just called to tell me you missed another day."

I groan and throw a pillow over my face and hope she will give up sooner rather than later. When she opens the door, I shake my head and bury myself deeper into the covers.

"I'm sick, Mom. I couldn't go to school today."

She looks at me and places her hand on her hip, "But you were just fine yesterday."

She walks over and sits down on my bed and I can't help but think of the pictures burning themselves against the mattress underneath her. For once, I wish my mom would have a minor freak out and demand to search my room. She pulls the pillow off my head and moves to feel my forehead.

"You don't have a fever."

"It's my stomach," which isn't entirely a lie.

"Oh."

She leans forward and studies my face for what seems like forever. *What's going on in there? What are you thinking about, Mom?*

"Uh...I really need to rest, Mom. I'm exhausted and feel horrible."

Her eyes darken for a split second and she pats me on my hip. I try to hide the wince from her touching the bruise but I'm not successful. She looks worried.

"What's wrong?"

"Oh, Mom - it's nothing. Just my stomach. If I can fall asleep again it doesn't hurt as much."

She nods her head absentmindedly and I know then she's not really listening. She didn't come in here to check on me

- but she did come in to check something. She looks around briefly before her eyes rest on Dad's shirt and the sheet from outside. My heart stops but she says nothing. Her eyes grow cold and distant and she looks away from me out the window.

"Get some rest and I'll come check on you in a couple hours."

She turns around and shuts the door and I breathe a sigh of relief and snuggle deep into the covers again and hope to not be woken up again for quite awhile. Within what seems like seconds my mom slams open the door.

What the?

I'm jolted awake by her sharp nails on my arm.

"Mom? What's going on? What are you..."

"You think I don't notice? You are nothing but a slut. A whore."

She looks at me and I can't help but notice the smell of scotch on her lips that wasn't there before. I realize then she planned this whole thing - she just needed some liquid courage to find the rage to transfer on to my indiscretions.

"Notice what?"

I glare and try to wriggle free from her grasp but it's no use. She's got me locked down and her nails are digging into the skin of my forearm. I wince and try to ignore the pain.

"You. Trying to steal my man. You're father - you're such a sick little whore. Can't find anyone else? Can't find another man to try and steal you gotta steal my man? What's a matter with you? Don't you know no one wants you? Don't you know no one cares?"

Her lips wrinkle in disgust and she brings the cigarette up to her face to take a drag. Her eyes fall and focuses on the smoke dripping from the end of the cigarette. She pulls it from her mouth, closing her eyes as she breathes deep. I feel a sharp burning and glance down. She's burning my skin with her cigarette. The pain is immediate and intense.

"Mom! Mom. Stop. Please. Listen - I'm not trying to steal Dad. It's not me! It's not..."

Tears start rolling down my cheeks and I wrestle to get away from her and the burning tool she is using for punishment. I know she's not listening. I know with Dad's shirt and the sheet on the floor she will hear nothing and suspect everything. I finally manage to push her away and she straightens to her full height, fixing her robe and patting her hair.

"He's right you know. You're worthless. I wish I would have listened to him from the very beginning. You shoulda never been born. I shoulda aborted you when I had the chance. At least I wouldn't have had to worry about you stealing him with those chicken legs of yours."

She spits and I flinch, trying to get away from the wetness falling on my face.

"Oh - these fancy clothes?" She points to the bags from last night on the floor and begins rummaging through them - throwing them every where in her anger, "They won't find you another family. We're all you got - you hear that? We don't need no help from no one." Her lips curl into a snarl and she comes inches away from my face, her screaming now a whisper, "You're stuck with us."

She turns to walk out the door and leaves me there - still wondering where all of this came from and whether or not she would ever believe me about what really happens in the shed. And if she did, would she have the courage to walk out the door. Given her reaction to Dad's ultimatum about Tyler I doubted it. She'd fallen for Dad's schemes - like a lamb to her slaughter. Nothing I said would make her understand. Nothing I told her would make her believe that I was the victim here - not her. I thought about that irony for a second, about how stuck I felt.

And then I couldn't help but think of the girls. How many

were there? How long had this been going on? Were the police involved with all the dirty layers of Sam Tiller's business? Did they have any idea how deep his hands dipped into the innocence of girls in this community? Did they even care?

I lay there for what seems like hours, trying to fall back asleep to hide from the disaster of today, my thoughts careening around my head like a pinball lost in motion.

Twelve

BEFORE I AM ABLE TO ESCAPE TO COMPLETE UNCONSCIOUSNESS, I HEAR a knock on my window - soft and light. I know who it is before I even pull back the covers and throw on some clothes.

Crap! I was supposed to meet him at the bleachers this morning. Smooth, Stephanie. Smooth. He's going to know. He's going to ask questions.

I glance out the window, mentally preparing myself for the questions he will ask.

At least someone notices when I'm not around...

Kevin waits for me on the other side - a worried expression plastered on his face. I walk out the front door and he exhales deeply and walks towards me.

"Stephanie. What happened? I've been trying to get a hold of you..."

My phone. Last time I checked it was in the pocket of my jeans, which Casanova stole the night before. I rub my face and squint in the sunlight.

"I lost it yesterday while Emma and I were shopping." I lie, and he buys it - for now.

His eyes slowly start to register my hair and he smiles.

"Your hair...you cut it."

My hands move absentmindedly to rustle my layers and I look at him, "You like it?"

He moves closer and places his hand gently at the back of my neck.

"I love it. It's perfect."

He leans forward and kisses me lightly and for the first time notices my timidity. I have to fight from turning my face so he's left to kiss me on the cheek. He looks at me and burrows his brows.

"What's going on? What happened?"

I look at him closely and change the subject, "Kevin, aren't you supposed to be in class right now?"

I can't stop the sense of bitterness filling my voice.

"Aren't you? I noticed you didn't show and got worried. I decided to come check on you."

I fidget and move my hands around awkwardly, not making a great case for being calm or collected. I fight the tears but Kevin's scrutiny is too much. A single tear escapes and that's all it takes. The fear and anxiety and terror from the night before comes rushing back and I collapse against him - heaving sobs and drawing on him for strength. He has no idea what's going on - no idea what's caused this scene - and so he waits. It takes thirty minutes for me to calm down long enough to talk to him. I ask if we can go for a walk, not wanting to risk my dad coming home with me tear stained and standing in the middle of the lawn with some strange boy he doesn't know.

"Absolutely," he responds - choosing his words carefully - not wanting to prompt another outburst.

We walk down the street and turn on to the main drag

before cutting off into a side alley we sometimes find ourselves when we just need to be alone. I brace myself for his reaction and breathe a little easier just knowing I will be able to tell someone.

"So. Emma took me on this incredible shopping trip yesterday. I got my hair cut, and new make-up and tons of clothes. I've never been on a shopping trip like this before and I came home completely stoked and thankful. It was amazing, Kevin. I even met this incredible girl - Ashlee - who has this tattoo..." I stop myself before I get too caught up in side details and try and refocus myself, "That's another story, though."

I glance at him and he's focused only on me. I wish I wouldn't have to tell him this - tell him one more reason why I have such issues with trust and one more reason why humanity just really really sucks sometimes. Every time I'm with him I feel as though I take some of his innocence.

"Just tell me, Stephanie."

He notices my hesitancy and I smile to reassure him. I'm still me, I think to myself. No matter what I'm about to tell you - I'm still me. I promise.

I take a deep breath to center my thoughts and turn back to his eyes.

"My dad went crazy when I got home with everything. He hated the fact that Emma got involved and bought me stuff. He was already upset though - already drunk by the time I got home. He was waiting for me in the kitchen. Someone from USC called the house yesterday asking for me and..."

"Wait. USC? Why was USC calling you?"

I looked at him and noticed the confusion etched into his lips, one side crinkled in question. Oh. I remember. He doesn't know about that, either.

I wave my hand and dismiss it, "That's another story as well. Needless to say, Dad was upset because USC was calling and he thought I was going to try and leave and he said there was no way he was going to let me leave as long as I..."

My voice cracks and I suddenly realize just how hard this is going to be to tell Kevin. He squeezes my hand, encouraging me to continue. I look at him and complete my thought, "He isn't going to let me leave as long as I am bringing him business."

Kevin's face darkens and his knuckles go purple with rage. I stare at him hesitantly and finally break the gaze to study the frayed cuffs of my jeans. I'm not sure what kind of reaction I was expecting - but this is something new. I'm still getting use to someone getting upset on my behalf. And he doesn't even know the half of what happened.

He lets out a long breath and stabilizes himself before talking.

"Stephanie. Your dad is a douche."

He starts pacing up and down the alleyway and I wonder how long it will take for him to take off running. I've never seen anyone this worked up before - never seen what it looks like to be protected.

He continues his rant, beating his fist against his hand and shaking his head, "How can anyone...anyone....treat his daughter like that? I mean...how can anyone treat another human being like that?! You aren't something to just be sold...and besides, it hasn't happened in awhile. What makes him think business is going to slow down? It's been stagnant for years now."

I just look at him and he registers the tears beginning to form, cussing under his breath he places his hands on my shoulders.

"Stephanie...has your dad traded you since that night when you were twelve?"

I nod.

"When was the last time?"

I clear my throat and whisper - barely audible for either of us to hear - somehow, speaking it makes it more real.

"Last night."

Kevin closes his eyes for awhile and leans his forehead against mine. When he finally raises his head, he has tears running down his cheeks. He grabs me in a big bear hug and just holds me until I break - the tears flowing and my heart cracking and my body convulsing with grief and loss of something I didn't even know I owned.

"You have to tell Jude."

I ignore him and turn away, glancing around to see if we're being followed. I take his hand and keep walking - still unsure of where my dad's business partners take shop during the day. They could be anywhere - watching. They could be hiding out with other girls captive. The thought sends chills to the places most deadened by abuse and pain. I tighten my grip on Kevin's hand and he stops me, forcing me to look at him by placing his finger under my chin.

"Did you hear me?"

"Yes." I said. Not wanting to answer further.

"Well? Don't you agree? Don't you think we should get someone else involved?"

"There's more."

He looks at me, confused - as if the situation can get any more complicated.

"What do you mean? There's more? Like...more to the story?"

"I'm not the only one, Kevin."

"What?"

His voice raises an octave, I glance down at his fists - clenched and red at the knuckles. I debate for a split second on whether to tell him what I know before I decide to go ahead and do it. He's the only person I know who I can talk to about anything.

"I'm not the only one. I thought I was the only one my dad

traded. I'm not. There are more girls."

I study my fingernails for awhile, imagining the pictures still under my mattress. Closing my eyes, I fight to get Valerie's look out of my head. Lost. Hopeless. Despair.

"I found pictures today. Stuck in the back of my dad's cabinet in his shed."

Kevin cursed and kicks the ground. I raise an eyebrow and bite my lip - allowing him the time to process the information. Allowing myself time to swallow the tears threatening to make an appearance.

"Do you think..."

My voice trails off; I'm not sure I want to ask this question. I'm not sure I really want to know the answer.

"Do I think what?" His eyes look tired, older than his years.

I stumble through my words before steadying myself.

"Do you remember telling me about the football players paying the cheerleaders for sexual favors?"

Kevin hesitates, "...yes"

"Do you think there's any way these could be connected?"

"Are you serious?" He looks at me through squinted eyes, "Steph...you really believe your dad could pull something off that organized? Those favors have been going on for years. Everyone knows about 'em."

"But do the cheerleaders really want to be involved? Are you sure they're offering out of their own twisted need or do you think it's possible there's a deeper reason - something more sinister."

I can tell my questions made him uncomfortable. He's pacing now and running his hands through his hair.

"I can't believe this..," he mutters under his breath.

"Kev...I just know my dad. I know what he's capable of and the way his mind works. I also know how easy it is to pretend you're not bothered by something or that you even want what's coming simply because you wish to survive. I think they're connected, Kevin. I think it's all connected - I think this whole thing runs deeper than we could ever imagine."

He catches my eyes then - pauses his pacing long enough to see how serious I am - and hurries over to where I'm standing. Grabbing my arms with his hands, he looks at me and it's only then I notice the tears beginning to form.

"Stephanie, you have to tell someone about this. You can't let him keep doing this."

My hands fly to my face and I cover my eyes with frustration.

"Kevin - who do you suggest I tell? The police? We've been through this. My dad has them wrapped around his little finger. It would take nothing for them to turn it around on me in some twisted way."

Kevin looks at me and chews on his lip - thinking.

"You have to say something to Emma."

"Kev..."

"Stephanie." Kevin interrupts me and places his finger on my mouth to silence me from arguing any further. "I have said this and will say it again. You have to say something or it's going to continue to happen. This is not okay. People just don't sell other people. It's not...human. Not right. And if this whole thing is connected like you think - I mean...your dad needs to pay. People need to pay. We're talking hundreds of kids here - not just you."

My thoughts shift to the conversation with Ashlee and I begin to wonder just how many other girls are out there - alone and hurting with no one to talk to and no one to believe in them. I lean my head against Kevin's shoulder and sigh.

"What is it? Did that come across as too harsh?"

"No." I squeezed his knee in confirmation. "I was just

thinking. That girl named Ashlee? She had this huge bouquet of flowers tattooed on her arm, they were in the most beautiful and delicate and feminine shapes - it was absolutely breathtaking, and so I asked her about it. It's not every day you see someone walking around with such a striking tattoo."

I glanced at Kevin and he nodded, listening.

"Well, she started telling me this story about this brothel in southeast Asia that completely strips girls of everything they have - even their name - when they are brought to live and work there. There were these group of guys who went on a some type of undercover mission to expose human trafficking and they went to this brothel. As they were sitting in the waiting room, one girl, number 146, just stared at them through the window where the girls were held. All the other girls were completely lost in some mundane tv show, looking hopeless in their circumstance. 146 though - she had fight left in her." I stretch my neck and place my head in my hands and whisper, "Sometimes I wonder if I have enough fight left in me for this nightmare to end."

Kevin places his arm around me and kisses me on the shoulder and then grabs my hand to pull me up and follow him.

"Where are we going?" I ask.

"Away from here," he responds, "away from memories and away from thoughts." He turns and looks at me and places my hand in the crook of his arm, "At least for right now."

Thirteen

AWAY FROM HERE" TURNS OUT TO BE SPLITTING A BURGER AT THE DRIVE thru. Walking out of the restaurant, I notice the sky turning colors. I feel for my phone before remembering its demise.

"It's about 5:00," Kevin says, looking at me and sipping his chocolate shake.

I glance at him in surprise.

"Really?"

I think back to the day - collapsing on my bed, avoiding my mother, escaping with Kevin...and it begins to make sense.

"I guess today was a bit busier than I imagined."

Kevin wraps his arms around my shoulders and kisses my temple.

"No thoughts, Steph. Remember - those memories and issues can be dealt with later. Right now? You need to remember hope. Come on - I'm going to take you to one of my favorite spots."

I roll my eyes and follow as instructed, "Where are you taking me this time? It's too early for a midnight light show."

He turns around and waves his cup at me in a mocking gesture.

"Hope is a revolutionary patience, Stephanie. Remember that."

I snort and speed up to catch him. Swatting him on the arm I raise an eyebrow, "Don't even try and claim that as your own. Anne Lamott gets first dibs."

He looks at me and opens his mouth in shock, "You're an Anne Lamott junky? I pegged you as someone a little more brooding...Sylvia Plath maybe?"

I stare in mock horror and brush my hair out of my eyes, "Kind sir, even though yes - I do have daddy issues - my suicidal days are over."

I get quiet and dart a quick look towards his reaction to my last statement. I lift my sleeve and point to my wrists, outlining scars from my razor.

"See? Healed." I smile and grab his hand, "Besides. I like to think that all of my writings start in the same category as everyone else's. Even the brilliant ones."

Kevin looks at me, "What category is that?"

I glance at him halfheartedly, a bit disappointed he doesn't already know the answer.

"You aren't as much of a Lamott junky as you claim."

He raises an eyebrow and plays with his straw.

"What do you mean?"

"Well, if you would have read Lamott as much as you lead me to believe, you would know everyone - even the brilliant ones - start with absolutely horrible first drafts. Although those aren't necessarily the words she uses - I modify them for my own vocabulary."

He looks at me out of the corner of his eye, a smile playing on his lips.

"Your vocabulary, huh?"

"Yes. My vocabulary."

"Do you ever think about words? Like, how some words seem so foreign and others...natural?"

"Explain."

"Brouhaha. Megalomania. Chimichanga. Loofa. All of those words seem...weird. Foreign."

Megala-what? Where is he getting this stuff from? I smile and continue to listen - making a mental note to look up some of the words when I get home.

"So, if those words sound foreign...which sound natural to you?"

He thinks for a moment before answering. "Water. Phone. Ball. You know - normal, every day words."

"I think there's something to be said about the 'natural' words only having one syllable, but I'm not sure what it means."

Only we would be conversing about words - and enjoying ourselves.

Kevin chuckles and we turn the corner and walk through a lit path of trees and bushes - I notice the greenery becoming more prevalent and the pavement becoming more scarce. Kevin stops talking and focuses intently on his steps - leading me to believe we are almost at our destination. In less than two minutes we reach a clearing and Kevin freezes. I look at him, shielding my eyes from the setting sun, and press my lips together in confusion.

"Is uh...this our destination?"

Kevin smiles. "Nope. But that is."

He points off to the distance and I follow his gaze towards the town lake and the dam blocking the city from flood waters. He starts walking again and I follow - content to be away, if just for a little while, to forget about memories and thoughts and situations I will definitely have to figure out how to deal with later.

We reach the dam and climb the stairs leading to the

top - overlooking the lake and the city. Sitting down on the cement wall, I breathe deep and relax. The ball of pain still still sits square in my chest, but everything seems so distant for now - so other worldly. Smiling at Kevin, sitting down next to me, I lean over and kiss him quickly on the cheek.

"Thanks. I needed this."

He grabs an eyelash off my cheek and holds it in front of me to blow off his finger - I close my eyes and make a wish.

For new beginnings.

When I open my eyes, the eyelash is gone and Kevin grins.

"This is my haven. I come here whenever I need to get away."

I look at him and before thinking ask, "What do you need to get away from? You have a perfect family."

He lowers his head and examines a hole forming in his jeans before glancing back at me, a sad smile forming on his lips.

"My life isn't perfect, Stephanie. I don't deal with what you have to deal with; I don't have men buying me for sex against my will or a father who hits me with a fist, but I still have demons. There are still ghosts lurking around the corner threatening to take over again."

I turn to face him and rub his elbow, "What do you mean... demons?"

Kevin takes a deep breath and rubs his hands against his jeans. His eyes have that faraway look in them again - his thoughts somewhere completely different than where we are. I wait, knowing eventually he will start talking again once his words have formed themselves to his satisfaction.

He grabs my hand and looks at me.

"Did you ever hear about that party at the Williams' place?"

"The one like, two years ago? Where that girl was raped and no one would come forward to say they knew who did it because they didn't want to be known as someone who was there?"

Kevin winced. "Yeah. That's the one."

I'm not sure where this conversation is going, but my stomach starts doing flips in protest. I try to ignore it and focus my attention on Kevin - hoping he will rectify my thoughts and quickly - my nerves are already shot from months of hiding and screaming and yelling and fighting.

He picks up a nearby rock and throws it, grimacing at the distance. Probably buying time - forming his words. He always takes his time when there is something important he needs to tell me.

"I came forward. I came forward and talked to the police - letting them know I was there and even though I didn't know who did it, I could help them - tell them who I saw and try to get to the bottom of this. I know Jamie - she's a friend of mine. Hearing about her experience and how no one believed her and no one had the guts to talk...it infuriated me."

"What happened?"

Kevin sighed and looked off into the lake, focusing on a boat cruising before the last bits of sunlight escaped from the sky.

"I became the prime suspect."

My breath caught in my throat.

"Wait. Are you serious?"

"Yeah." He laughed. "Poetic justice? I don't know. I step forward - thinking I'm going to help a friend - and I end up getting screwed in the end."

"Well, couldn't Jamie vouch for you? I don't understand why she didn't say anything."

Kevin looked at me for awhile before responding, "She was too drunk to remember anything."

I close my eyes and let it register completely before opening them again and focusing on Kevin.

"So what happened? I mean, no one talks about that party anymore. It's old news. And isn't she at like, UConn or something, playing basketball?"

"Yeah. She is - and she's doing really well. I talk to her every once in awhile. The case closed due to lack of evidence, but her parents still believe it was me."

He shivers against the dropping temperatures and looks at me, scratching his forehead.

"The whole ordeal almost broke up my family. My dad started spending more time at work, my mom started taking these nerve pills...it was crazy. One minute I have everything in the palm of my hand, and the next minute my future hangs in the balance of this girl who can't even remember I was no where near her the night before."

I lean my head against his shoulder and move my hand into his jacket pocket for a second to warm up my stiffening hands. Everything makes so much sense now - at least, everything people have been telling me about Kevin. Even though they're still wrong, I understand now where they're coming from - for the longest time I thought they were just crazy or jealous or mistaken. They were mistaken - but the facts didn't help Kevin's reputation. Not in high school.

"That's why people tell me to watch out for you, isn't it?"

Kevin freezes before a split second before he bursts into a short chuckle, "People have really told you that?"

I nod, "Oh, you know...those kids at school. The ones who make it their job to spread rumors and warn others about impending doom. They cornered me after school one day and in no uncertain terms told me I was making a huge mistake." I start laughing, "They never bothered talking to me before. I don't think they've even glanced my way since then. But when the time was right, I was their primary target. They wanted me to see the light."

He shakes his head in disbelief, "That's unbelievable. What's crazier is that these are probably my friends - people I once thought had my back."

I lift my head to look at him and lean into him and smile, "They don't matter. Obviously. I didn't listen."

He grabs my hand and kisses my knuckle, "You're right. They don't matter. But that's why I brood sometimes. I have a past I haven't even lived - and sometimes I'm not even sure I'm going to get away from it. Small town rumors make for big town disasters, and I really need to get out of here for my sanity. My family may seem perfect, but my mom still struggles and I don't know if I'll ever get my dad's approval with anything I do. I still wonder if somewhere inside he questions whether I raped Jamie."

I turn my head toward him and study his face, "What do you mean?"

Kevin rubs his hands on his jeans and focuses on the sunset, "I'm pretty sure my mom still takes those pills. And if anyone found out she'd be devastated. She has this overwhelming desire to please everyone - to make it seem as though we are this perfect family who struggles with nothing. It's all about appearances - all about what makes the Matouse family worth envying. Every day though, I see her popping the pills - she thinks no one sees. What's even worse is that no one envies us. At least, no one my mother would want to envy us. Everyone sees the facade. Probably because they're living it too."

I wrinkle my nose, "Sounds like she's high strung."

He laughs and nods his head, "Yes. That would be an understatement. I think it's why my dad started working so much - he was trying to get away from my mom's scrutiny. So now, she's moved her focus to me and my dad has all but checked out emotionally. It's all about finding the perfect school and making the perfect grades and rectifying my reckless decisions..." He looks at me and gently nudges my shoulder, "Which is why I want out - away from everyone's blame and scrutiny."

I laugh. "Tell me about it."

He glances at me out of the corner of his eye and asks, "Speaking of getting out of here...what's this about USC?"

I raise an eyebrow and he just sits there - waiting for my reply. I pull my sweater closer to my chest and Kevin, noticing my shaking against the cold, pulls me closer and wraps me in his letter jacket.

"Okay. You're cozy. Now talk."

I giggle and look at him.

"I don't even know why it matters. My dad has pretty much refused to even think about letting me go."

Kevin looks at me incredulously.

"Seriously?" He shakes his head, "Your father is not the voice of reason. Don't ever let any of your decisions rest in what he thinks. Promise me."

I hear him in what sounds like an echo of Emma's words and my face softens.

"Fine. Whatever. He's not the voice of reason."

I give him a smile and make him wait for a little while before talking again.

"Mrs. Peabody sent USC some of my writing and they liked what they saw. They want me to come study Creative Writing and mentioned scholarships."

Kevin sits there for a few minutes before reacting. Suddenly he breaks into a huge grin and throws his head back, laughing.

"Stephanie. This is brilliant. USC! They want you. Do you understand how awesome this is?!" He leans forward and grabs my face in his hands and plants a firm kiss on my lips. "You need to promise me something else."

I stare at him hesitantly.

"I don't really like promises, Kevin."

He shrugs his shoulders, "Doesn't matter. Not here. Not now. Promise me something," he says, completely ignoring my concern.

People sure are asking me to make a lot of promises lately...

I hesitate at his persistence and nod.

"Fine. What is it?"

"Promise me you'll apply. Promise me you will at least pursue this. It's too good of an opportunity, Steph. You have to go for it. This is your ticket. For once, think of no one else except for you. What's best for you."

I'm lost in his eyes and words. I know what he's asking and it makes me nervous. It makes me nervous because it makes me excited and my heart has started to beat normally again. Thinking of beaches and nights smelling the ocean air leaves me with nothing but anticipation. I smile and look at his hands, clasped in front his chest in earnestness.

"Okay," I say, my heart jumping with hope at my agreement. I take notice of its message and grab Kevin's hand. "I'll do it. But I'm going to need your help."

He claps his hands and jumps up to do a little jig.

"Tonight's a night to feel alive, Stephanie - let's go find us an adventure."

His eyes sparkle as he reaches to pull me from my seat - my legs stiff from sitting so long in one position. Once I'm standing he wraps me in an embrace and holds me close. I breathe in his scent and for the moment rest against his chest - forgetting completely what brought us here and what's waiting for me back at the house. For the first time, I feel as though I have found my home.

Fourteen

WE MAKE OUR WAY DOWN THE LIT PATH AND FIND OURSELVES BACK AT the meadow. It's getting colder and I think I hear thunder in the distance, but I'm not sure. I pull my sweater closer around me and for the second time, Kevin notices my shivers.

"Here. Take my jacket. I have a hoodie underneath."

I turn and smile.

"Thanks."

I glance down at my hands - stiff with cold - and shove them in his pockets. I hide a grin when I feel lint, loose change, what feels like a stale Sour Patch Kid, and some crumpled pieces of paper.

He sees me fidgeting and laughs, "Oh. Um...sorry. My pockets can be a little messy, but they're still warm."

We keep walking, cutting across the meadow and meeting railroad tracks - Kevin looks at me.

"Wanna see where they lead?"

I shrug and take a look at the sky - knowing what borrowed

daylight we do have may not last for very long with the weather changing. The clouds have completely taken over the sun and are rolling with the prelude to a storm.

"Sure." I surprise myself at the spontaneity. "You wanted an adventure, right?"

Pointing at the sky, he follows my gaze and opens his mouth in surprise.

"Well, come on." He grabs my hand and once again helps me walk up the soggy embankment to the tracks. "This is something else I use to do when I was younger and needed to get away from everything." He smiles and focuses on the ground beneath us - looking for possible grooves which would cause me to trip. "However, when I was younger it was less of me getting away from a serious crisis and more me just wanting to get away from my overbearing parents."

I turn and nuzzle my hand in the crook of his arm.

"At least you have parents who worry about you."

He nods.

"Yeah. I know that now. Before, I saw it as something I hated - they just 'didn't get me' and only wanted to ruin my fun." He sniffs and wipes his cheek on his sleeve, "I know now - before the party, before everything got weird, they were simply trying to protect me."

"Do they know about me?"

Kevin smiles and continues to walk - measuring his words before he speaks.

"Yes. They do. They know you are someone I am seeing right now and am incredibly interested in getting to know more." He looks at me and puts his hand up as a promise, "They don't know anything else other than you being my girl-friend. I haven't said anything about...your situation."

I lower my head and focus on the ground before asking the next question burning in my chest.

"Do you think your mom would like me?"

He's quiet again - this time for a longer period of time. When he does begin talking, his words are quiet - measured, "I don't know. My mom has this tendency to take everything at face value. Because of this, she's already pinpointed girls she wants me to date. Girls who know how to put on a pretty face for the adults and usually turn around and party harder than anyone I know. Certainly girls who I would never dream of spending dinner with - let alone the rest of my life."

I notice the darkening clouds and their similarity to the growing storm inside me. Apparently I had been holding my breath, because I exhale slowly and press my lips together. His parents know about me. For some reason, this excites and terrifies me at the same time. *What if I screw something up? What if he realizes my situation is too much to handle? His mom already has girls picked out for him?! What hope do I have then? She'd take one look at me and say I was a disaster of a choice...*

I realize he's stopped and is pulling me toward him, his voice breaks through my downward spiral and I'm forced to watch his face - notice his emotion just beneath the surface of his eyes.

"Stephanie...I don't want you to worry about my mom. She doesn't matter. I've spent way too many moments worried about what they think and I forgot about what was important - what I needed to rely on wasn't them but something bigger - something more stable. It doesn't matter to me if she likes you or not. This won't change my feelings for you." His voice moves to a whisper and he comes close, "I know what I want, Stephanie," and he leans forward and kisses me - slow and kind.

"Come on, let's go," he whispers and I feel the heat radiating from my face - I can still feel the pressure of his lips against mine.

I stretch my shoulders and walk beside him a little more until we find ourselves getting ready to cross the bridge. I stop for a split second and Kevin looks at me.

"Everything okay?"

I stare down at the drop - nothing more than twenty feet - but my palms start to sweat and my knees start to shake.

I croak out, "I'm afraid of heights."

No, afraid isn't the word. It's more like terrified. Scared spitless. Horrified.

He throws his head back and roars with laughter, "Stephanie. I got you. Come on - you'll feel better once you cross this. Besides, it's quicker going this way than turning back and walking all the way through the meadow again." He shrugs his shoulders, "A shortcut."

I shoot accusatory glances his way and sigh, "Did you know this was here? Did you know we'd have to walk on this bridge? What if a train comes?"

"Impossible. This track is dead at night. I use to walk it all the time, remember?"

I take a deep breath and grab his outstretched hand, "Okay. Let's do this."

He leans over and kisses my cheek.

"That's my girl."

My heart nearly jumps out of my chest when I find my footing beside him, but I ignore the fear banging against my ribcage and look at Kevin.

"So, uh...I guess I don't get it. You said you would walk the tracks when you were younger to get away." I look around and try to not focus on what is below me. "What is it exactly about walking tracks that helps take your mind off the situation?"

"When was the last time you thought about why you were out here, Steph?"

I walk quietly for a moment before laughing.

"Point taken."

In the distance, a slight rumble fills the air and echoes around us.

"Looks like we may get rained on."

Kevin freezes mid step and turns to look at something to his right. The more I look at him the more I realize he's not trying to see something but hear something. I stop, a funny feeling in my chest.

"What is it, Kevin?"

"It's not rain."

"What?"

"The sound. It's not thunder."

He looks at me, hiding nervousness by twisting his lips and darting his gaze away from my face.

He's avoiding me - he's hiding something. What's going on?

"What is it then?" I start taking a few more steps before I feel the shaking.

The ground is shaking.

I put two and two together and don't have to strain my ears to hear the train's siren. I turn my head and see Kevin's figure - illuminated by the headlight. Even though I see the train and I know it's coming, it takes me a little while to process everything. The fear settles deep in my chest and I scream.

"Kevin! Kevin we have to run."

He snaps out of his trance and turns and rushes towards me, hurdling the grooves and crevices of the rails.

"Move," he whispers urgently, pushing me forward as he grabs my arms and pulls me with him down the track.

His eyes are wide and his breath is already labored, the fear and determination more evident with every step.

I look around wildly and know there's no possible way we can outrun this train. We can't jump, the riverbed has been dry for years now. The other side of the bridge is about 150 yards away, but at the rate we are running and dodging rails, we'll never make it. My heart pounds in my chest and I start heaving with fear. Kevin just continues to run - pulling me and yelling at me to watch my footing.

All of the sudden he stops and I charge in front of him from left over momentum. I turn around, the train's whistle getting louder and louder and the rumbling becoming more and more pronounced. My whole body is shaking now - and not just from fear.

"What...are...you...doing?" I ask him - furious now and ready to push him off the bridge for bringing me here.

I swear if I make it out of here alive I'm gonna kill him.

"Look." He points and I follow his gaze. We still have about 100 yards to go, but the other side of the hill juts out underneath the bridge - offering a makeshift overpass. We look at each other and hurriedly make our way to the edge where we can jump and hide from the oncoming train. We near the edge and I stop just as Kevin leaps for the hidden nook.

He has got to be kidding...

He lands hard and picks himself up, dusting off the dirt and grass. He looks around before realizing I have yet to jump.

"Seriously?! Do it! Come on - jump. It's not that bad. I'm here - I got you. Please, Steph. Hurry."

I toe the line and glance back at the train - closing in on me at breathtaking speed. I go to jump and freak out at the last minute, waving my arms around wildly before stepping back onto the track, gaining my composure and balance. I know I have less than seconds left, and I have to make a decision quickly. I don't know if I can watch, and I don't know if my heart will survive the adrenaline, but I close my eyes and step off the ledge, falling flat into Kevin as we tumble a few feet down the embankment. As soon as I land the train roars past - blaring it's horn. I seriously miss getting smashed by seconds. We lay there for a few minutes - collecting ourselves and recuperating from the jostle of the train flying over us. My heart is still beating at double time, but now it's not from fear. I feel...alive.

That was freaking amazing.

Slowly, I began to smile. A low chuckle starts in my belly and rises to a full blown snort of laughter. Kevin twists his head and looks at me incredulously.

"Wha...are you laughing? Have you absolutely lost all sense? I mean, really...what's so funny? We almost died. I almost killed you." He covers his face with his hands and groans. "Oh Stephanie, I'm so sorry. I made you walk the bridge. I made you do something you didn't want to do."

I can't help it. I try to stop laughing but I can't - it only makes it all worse. Trying to hold it all in, I fail and make a horrible noise with my mouth - I lose all control then. I turn and bury my face in his chest and laugh so hard my eyes start to water and my chest starts to hurt. I'm not laughing because anything is funny. Absolutely not. I'm laughing because of joy. Because, after the experience of running from a train and jumping and landing and feeling the vibrations even in my bones - I feel gloriously alive. Without even thinking, I jump up and start screaming at the top of my lungs - waving my arms in the air and twirling around. Once I stop, I hold out my hand and Kevin reaches for it - pulling me down on top of him. I push back his hoodie and look in his eyes.

"You are absolutely crazy," he whispers.

"Don't you feel alive right now?"

Kevin gazes into my eyes and grins.

"Yeah. I do. But mostly it's because of the girl leaning on me and not because I almost died from being run over by a train."

I hit him and he laughs. I sit back and place my arm across

his chest.

"You said you wanted an adventure."

He stops laughing and looks at me - pulling me close.

"I did didn't I?" he whispers, and then kisses me slowly and surely as the thunder roars in the distance and the night insects end their song.

✼

We stay that way for awhile - kissing and talking and kissing and laughing and kissing and well..kissing. It's wonderful. After about an hour, we've fully recovered from our brush with death and are now shivering from the coming storm.

"Let's get you home," he says, hugging me close and squeezing my shoulders.

I groan and make a face.

"I'd rather get drenched by those clouds then find out what waits for me at home."

Kevin stops for a split second and pulls me up towards him to cup my chin with his hands. He just sits there, staring, before saying anything.

"Promise me that no matter what happens you will always remember this night as something beautiful. Where instead of feeling worthless, you felt loved. Instead of hiding in fear, you fought and won. Instead of feeling hopeless, you remembered what it felt like to come alive."

I allow a slow tear to fall and he wipes it off my cheek.

"How did I even luck out with you, Kevin? I'm just waiting for you to come to your senses and realize I'm too much to deal with and I have too many issues."

He smiles and grabs my hand to keep walking.

"We all have issues, Stephanie. It's just up to us whether or not we make them the focus of our relationships."

We turn the corner of my street and the rain starts to fall - slow steady drops making their way down - for the first time I am anxious to get home to hear the rain falling gently against my window. I sigh with contentment and Kevin drops his head in agreement. We walk this way until we get to my house, where, out of habit, I look for dad's truck in the driveway. He's not there, but I'm not surprised. I take a deep breath and turn towards Kevin.

"Thanks for tonight."

He simply leans forward and gives me a peck on the cheek.

"Of course. Go inside and hang out with your brother. Write about our sordid adventure tonight."

He winks and I giggle, thinking again with butterflies of the train's headlight blinding me before I finally took the leap. I wrap my arms around his waist and lay my head on his chest for a little while before finally letting go and saying goodnight. I walk in the front door to a silent house, my mom crashed out on the couch with cough syrup on the table and a pill bottle in her hand. Walking over to her, I place a finger on her throat just to feel the pulse and once satisfied, walk towards the bathroom to take a shower and wash off the grime from tonight.

It's pretty sad when mom has to create her own cocktail in order to sleep through whatever may happen at night. I silently pray for a peaceful evening and turn on the shower, allowing the hot water to warm my frozen bones. I think of my time with Kevin and blush as the steams start rolling into the rest of the bathroom, fogging up the mirror. I know then, in the middle of another night spent with Kevin Matouse, I am desperately in love. It scares me to death.

Fifteen

I WALK INTO MY ROOM AND NOTICE ALL OF THE BAGS FROM YESTERDAY'S shopping trip still strewn all over my floor. I decide to empty them and place the clothes where they are supposed to be when I notice Pacey hanging out under my covers. My heart drops for a split second - he only comes to sleep with me when something is wrong. I walk over to the bed and sit down next to him, placing my hand on his face. He starts wiggling around and quietly moans.

"Hey Pace. What's going on? Why are you sleeping in my room?"

He opens his eyes and rubs the sleep out of them before talking. I glance at the clock on my nightstand and realize it's a little past one in the morning. When he realizes it's me he grabs my hand.

"Where've you been? I woke up the other day and you were gone and you weren't here last night."

I bite my lip and stare at him a little bit before answering,

"I just spent the night at a friend's house, bud. I'm back now."

I motion to pick him up to take him back into his room and he protests.

"No! Sisssssyyyy..." He stretches and rubs his eyes and I can see his lip begin to quiver, "Please let me sleep with you. I don't want to be by myself."

My arms drop and I watch him for a little while. Something else is going on - he's acting...different.

"Pace...what's going on?"

He pushes himself farther down the covers and peeks at me out of the corner of his eye, his head almost completely covered by my blankets. Slowly, he pulls out his arm and holds it up for me to see, his other hand resting underneath his elbow to give him support. I look closely - at first I have no idea what he's trying to show me. And then I see them - small dots on his upper arm - big enough for a cigarette butt. My blood turns electric and I fight to remain under control.

"Pacey, who did that to you?"

At first he just shakes his head, refusing to tattle, afraid something will happen if he gives up the name of his abuser. I have a good idea who it is - based on mom's cocktail of forgetfulness on the table outside in the living room and her outburst with me earlier this morning. He takes a deep breath and starts talking just loud enough for me to hear. His eyes are wide and tears are brimming thick against his lashes.

"Momma. She got mad at me tonight for not eating my bologna sandwich. Her and Tyler started playing connect the dots."

I look closer and see the lines connecting the burns - from a Sharpie, no less - and my eyes widen. I can handle being a punching bag. I can get over being bought and seen as an object. But I won't ever get use to seeing my little brother used as an ashtray. I close my eyes and lay down next to him, wrapping my arms around his small waist. He snuggles close to me and grabs my arms with his hands.

"I'm sorry, Pacey. I'm sorry I wasn't here to protect you."

He nuzzles his cheek against my neck and starts breathing evenly again. Within minutes, he's fast asleep and I'm lost in my own thoughts - knowing my apology means nothing to Pacey not because he won't forgive me, but because he's not even upset. He never finds blame in anyone but knows when something isn't right. And tonight, with painful burns dotting his arms, his four-year old heart knows something is definitely not right. There has to be something I can do. There has to be a way to get out of this mess, and the tears start to fall in frustration when nothing comes to mind. I fight to keep Kevin's words in my heart - that I am loved, and worthy; I fight to keep the feeling of coming alive in my bones - the exhilaration of the next breath and the wind rushing against my face as I jumped off the bridge - but it's not working.

It's just never going to end, is it? The question falls into my mind without any warning and I think about college next year and Pacey here by himself and Dad's threats to do whatever it takes to keep me home. Suddenly, the magic of my night with Kevin shifts and I'm reminded of my reality - the nightmare I face every day. And as I fall asleep with Pacey in my arms, I fight to keep the last piece of hope attached to my soul.

School the next day is a disaster. I can't focus because of the night before. Every two hours or so, Pacey would wake up screaming and crying - I had to calm him and talk him down from the nightmare. Of course, he would just fall back asleep, but it wasn't so easy for me. I didn't sleep at all, and it's showing in my lack of ability to stay awake.

These accidental all-nighters really need to stop.

I'm in history class now - specifically, Government. But somehow, the topic has shifted to the Trans-Atlantic slave trade. I'm only half listening. We've studied this every year it seems like since we were in elementary school. And we aren't even in U.S. History right now. It's Government class. Shouldn't we be discussing something like, I don't know - politics? I hear one of the students, Steven, ask my teacher a question and I roll my eyes. Steven is notorious for getting teachers off-track and trying to catch them in some type of trap.

"Hey Mr. Yeager, I heard somewhere that there's more slaves now than during the peak of the Trans-Atlantic slave trade. Is this true?"

I suddenly perk up and start to pay attention.

This could get interesting. Looking at Mr. Yeager, I wait for his reply.

He wrinkles his nose and waves his arms around for a few seconds before answering. He walks over and grabs his coffee off his desk and takes a sip.

He's totally stalling.

"Well, Steve - it depends on how you look at it. Many people will say there are more slaves nowadays, but these are people who truly aren't versed in history. We live in a time where people simply wouldn't stand for such injustice. Besides, if you look at it from an economics view, there's just no need for them anymore. The demand is gone."

Um...

"So what about these news reports and stuff? Weren't there two guys just executed in China for human trafficking? And aren't there rings busted all the time here in the U.S.?" Steven seems genuinely interested - I'll give him that.

"Yes. There were. But those are just two men. Two men can hardly do enough damage. And those rings you hear about on the news are often sensationalized. Most often, they are just prostitutes needing to turn tricks for money. They've chosen that life and so they will choose the consequence."

Suddenly my blood turns cold. Before I even realize, I'm joining the conversation.

"You're wrong."

All eyes turn towards me and Mr. Yeager widens his eyes in surprise.

"Excuse me?"

"I'm sorry, Mr. Yeager. But - that's not true. People have no problem standing against injustice when it comes to animal rights or..or the wasting of our resources, but when it comes to humanity? Actual human beings dealing with actual horror and the worst part of human nature? People tend to look the other way." I study engravings on my desk and lower my voice. "There are at least 27 million slaves in the world today. More than any other time in history. It's estimated that in a year, 1.2 million children are trafficked for sex. In fact, slavery and human trafficking have become such an investment it pulls in 32 billion dollars a year - more than Google, Nike and Starbucks' profits combined."

Mr. Yeager laughs and waves his hand, "Stephanie, those are pure speculations. There's no way slavery exists today. It just isn't possible."

I feel the tears start to form and I fight the feeling of despair rising in my chest.

"Pardon me for seeming rude, Mr. Yeager, but perhaps you simply aren't opening your eyes. Every minute, two children are trafficked for sexual exploitation. And, every single cent spent on or towards the pornography industry can somehow be traced back to human trafficking. So yes. Slavery exists. And it's a problem in your own backyard. The question for you is will you look long and hard enough to see it."

I can't stay in the room any longer. As I gather my belongings and move to leave, Mr. Yeager calls my name and I completely ignore him until I am at the door. I turn around, tears streaming down my face.

I'm sure I look so crazy right now...

"Mr. Yeager, I don't mean any disrespect. Really. I just need to leave before I make any more of a fool out of myself."

I shuffle through my bag and pull out one of Ashlee's cards with the website for Love146 scrawled on the back.

"Here. Take this. See that website on the back? Go check it out. Watch the videos. It's where I got all of my 'speculation' from - people who have first hand experience with the human trafficking industry. Oh and...two men can definitely do enough damage. All it takes is one person to completely tear a life apart. Trust me. I know."

I leave him there, holding the card and looking at his students, and walk out of the door.

❀

English class is only slightly better. Mrs. Peabody reserved the computer labs to give us a chance to work on our College Admissions project. I'm still fighting sleep and trying to forget about my outburst in Government when Mrs. Peabody walks over to where I'm sitting.

"Well hello, Stephanie."

She sits down next to me, her eyes wandering to the computer screen where I am looking at the local junior college's admissions page. For a split second, I consider closing the browser, but then I realize I just don't care. Some things don't change.

I aim high, Mrs. Peabody. You should know this by now.

"Have you checked out USC?"

I return her gaze and shrug, "They called a couple days ago, but my dad answered. He isn't too keen on me leaving and going to school so far away. Pretty much told me it wasn't going to happen."

"Why?"

I focus on the computer screen, giving me something to do, even if it's researching the incredibly boring and highly "intellectual" junior college just down the street from where I live. *Why does she have to stare at me like that? It's like she's trying to see into my soul or something...maybe she's been reading too many of those vampire books. Or Harry Potter. Wasn't there a teacher in Harry Potter that claimed to see the future?*

I hide a smile and glance back.

"Money, first of all." I notice her mouth opening in protest and I move to finish before she starts talking. "I know they are offering a possible scholarship, Mrs. Peabody. But what if I don't get it in time? Scholarships take time. And recommendations. I haven't necessarily been the world's best student lately. I don't know of many teachers who would vouch for my ability."

She leans her head on her hand and wrinkles her lip.

"Have you even taken a look at the site?"

I shake my head.

Motioning her hand towards the screen, she looks at me.

"Go to their webpage. It doesn't hurt to look. Just go - your dad never has to know."

I do as she says and she clicks her tongue with excitement.

"Go to the admissions page for undergraduates."

My breath catches when I see pictures of the campus and students laughing behind their computers. I know it's all advertising - and some of these students most likely posed - but the freedom shown in these pictures is enough to make me click on the "start your application now" button blinking every three or four seconds. I start doing research, and my heart rate starts to quicken.

"Do you think I could get into the Honors Program?"

Mrs. Peabody smiles at me and nods.

"Certainly. It seems as if the Culture and Values course as well as the Writing Seminar may be well suited to your interests."

She touches my arm and I turn my head from the screen.

They have annual research conferences. And a Narrative Study major. I could totally double major in Creative Writing and Narrative Study.

"Stephanie, what do you want to do with your life?"

Survive my father.

"I love to write. I love to tell stories and formulate problems of characters - digging them deep into a hole and watching them work their way out stronger than before."

She smiles.

"Sounds like you." She leans back in her chair and crosses her arms against her chest. "What do you think about USC so far? You haven't really researched extensively, but you know what you want."

I glance back at the computer for a split second - noticing again all of the programs offered.

"It's definitely captured my interest, I will say that. But, I have to be honest - I really see no way my father will let me go. It's just not possible. I mean, there's the money issue but...he's just overprotective. Can't imagine me living anywhere that isn't within a two mile radius."

Mrs. Peabody sighs and leans forward.

"You know I am the last person to encourage familial rebellion. But. Is it you or your father who is applying for college? Is it your life or your father's that will be forever impacted by the choice you make of where to go to school? Think about this, Stephanie. You have an incredible opportunity waiting for you here..."

I close my eyes and take a deep breath. I haven't been this excited about a possibility in a long time. I stare at the screen, wondering if I have what it takes. It wouldn't be hard to fill out the application. It would be even easier to somehow find some money to pay the application fee. But what if I were to get accepted? And what if my dad intercepted the acceptance letter before I had the chance to even see it? My pen starts tapping on the desk in nervousness and I look around - as if he's lurking in the corner, waiting for me to fill out the application so he can throw a fit and raise a scene.

I'm done. I'm through with him trying to run my life and succeeding. I click on the application page and create an account so I can come back later this afternoon or tomorrow morning and finish what I don't complete in class. I smile.

I'm really doing this. I'm really stepping out and making a decision on my own.

I spend the rest of class, filling out paperwork and thinking of nights spent writing on the beach and conferences focused on research and learning how to effectively craft a piece of narrative.

Once I get to Pre-Cal I throw my stuff on the ground under my desk and hide my face in my arms. It's been an emotional day. Between my argument with Mr. Yeager and the breakthrough in English, I'm praying for an easy class period - I'm not sure how much more I can handle. I'm spent emotionally and absolutely exhausted. I let the conversation fall around me and start breathing deep once the lecture starts on derivatives.

"What do you think, Stephanie?"

I jolt awake and glance up at the front of the classroom. Mrs. Houghton was waiting for an answer. Again. I lower my head and shrug my shoulders - I'm not even going to attempt to pretend to know the answer.

"I'm sorry, Mrs. Houghton. I have no idea."

She purses her lips and moves on to another student, but

I can sense her anger and frustration. I sigh - knowing I've screwed up again. I make an attempt for the rest of class to listen as closely as possible - hopefully rectifying her belief that I just don't care. It's no use. Again, it's too late. As the bell rings, she calls my name and asks me to stay behind for a little while.

I avoid the sly smiles of students passing me by on their way out the door and lean against a desk, inspecting a fingernail that seems ingrown.

"You know, Stephanie. Your attitude in my classroom is beginning to concern me."

I look up and meet her gaze and nod.

Remember - be polite. Don't get worked up. Smile. Agree with her.

"I understand, Mrs. Houghton. Things have just been a little rough lately. I have a lot on my mind, and I haven't been getting much sleep."

She crosses her arms and raises an eyebrow.

"Well. Sleep is certainly important; however, if I catch you nodding off again I will be forced to contact your parents. I'm sure they wouldn't be pleased to know you've missed another day of instruction because you're drooling on one of my desks."

I laugh.

"With all due respect, Mrs. Houghton, calling my parents will do nothing. Chances are, my mom would be punch drunk on cough syrup and pain pills if you got a hold of her. And if my dad answered? Well. Just be prepared for a verbal beating because you interrupted his midday poker game with his buddies. Heaven help you if you interrupt his nap."

Apparently, I've said the wrong thing. I wasn't even planning on getting personal; the words just kinda fell out of my mouth. She bristles and taps her papers on her desks before standing up and walking towards me, her heels clanging against the linoleum. I'm not gonna lie. I'm intimidated. I look around to see if any other students are left in the classroom. We're alone.

"Stephanie. I don't care where you come from. I don't care what your family situation is when you walk through your door at night. I don't care. But, when you walk into my classroom, you better show respect and an eagerness to learn. You will get nowhere in life with this woe is me attitude you give off everyday."

She thinks I have an attitude?

I tilt my head and glance at her out of the corner of my eye.

"I'm sorry...I know you probably don't really know where I'm coming from..."

"Don't be so quick to judge, Stephanie. I dropped out of high school chasing a drug addict boyfriend who abused me. I finally got my GED when I was 25 and fought my way through junior college so I could gain scholarships to study at a university. I know hardship. But I'm not going to make excuses."

I bite my lip to keep from exploding. Clenching my fists so tight my skin starts to crack underneath my nails, I fight to smile and gather my things.

"I won't be quick to judge, Mrs. Houghton. But you need to understand something. You have no idea the hell I live. You see the scars, but do nothing. You see me cry, but ask no questions. So, Mrs. Houghton, please forgive me if I fail to have any emotion when I'm in your class or if you feel I lack respect. The truth is, I know the answer to every question. I've aced every exam you've given. But you wouldn't know that because you don't know me. Here's the difference between you and me: you chose your hardship. You dropped out of high school. You chased the deadbeat drug addict. Me? There is no choice. I'm left with the mess and chaos and expected to survive. And in my world, I've learned to not trust those who don't take the time to know who I am, because chances are, they are only out to take something from me. And I'm sorry, I can't let it happen. I have nothing left to give."

I turn around to walk out the door before the tears begin to fall down my cheeks. I hear her try and follow me, but like every other time, she talks herself out of it and stops. I smirk at her predictability, and walk out the door, wiping my face of any evidence that what she said got to me.

Kevin is waiting for me outside.

"Hey, beautiful. What took so long?"

I shrug my shoulders and wave my hand as if to brush the thought away.

"Nothing. Mrs. Houghton just needed to talk to me about something."

Kevin studies me for a little while longer before clearing his throat and handing me the coffee in his hand. I smile. He always remembers to get me coffee if he stops by The Caffeine Drip for a grande mocha with an extra shot of espresso. I take a sip and exhale - the tension fading from my shoulders.

"So uh, I was talking to my parents this morning."

My heart stops for a split second. I breathe deep and force myself to not freak out.

Just because he's talking to his parents about me doesn't necessarily mean he's going to break up with me. It doesn't have to be negative. Just stay calm.

I glance at him and raise an eyebrow, "Yeah. About?"

He looks at me and grins.

"Are you freaking out?" Taking my hand, he pulls it to his lips and kisses my knuckle, "Relax, Stephanie. They just want to invite you over to Thanksgiving. Can you come?"

I try to hide my sigh of relief, but I'm not as inconspicuous as I want to be. I break into laughter and hit him on the arm for scaring me.

"Really? They want me to come over?"

"Yeah. I mean, they really want to meet you, and I told

them I didn't know if you would be doing anything for the holidays."

I chuckle and nod my head, "Yeah. Doubtful. Last year I spent Thanksgiving in my closet hiding from Mom and Dad's friends stumbling through our house in their drunken stupor."

I look at him and nudge his shoulder with my own. My voice drops an octave - I know how big of a deal this invitation into his family's traditions is to him.

"I'd love to come, Kevin. Please tell your parents I can't wait to meet them and I am so thankful they thought of me."

He kisses the side of my forehead and we continue to maze through the crowd and towards the office. Being an office aide was probably the most wasteful and useless class I had, but in an attempt to avoid having off periods, I had to fill my schedule. We walk into the front of the office, a wave of cinnamon and vanilla hitting our senses - a mixture of all of the air fresheners from secretaries' desks merging as one.

"You need a ride home today?"

I give him a hug and hear the head secretary clear her throat. Rolling my eyes, I step away and smile at him.

"Yeah. You wanna meet here or by your car?"

"I'll come pick you up here."

He looks at the lady staring at us under her bifocals and smiles.

"Have fun," he whispers - I just stick out my tongue and watch him walk out the door towards the gym.

As soon as the door closes, I turn around and stop cold at the look coming from the registrar.

"I'm uh...gonna go deliver these messages."

I grab the slips of paper with students' names on scrawled on top - beckoning them to certain assistant principals, most often for disciplinary reasons. Running out the door, I breathe

another sigh of relief.
Old people make me nervous.

Sixteen

It's an understood fact that the only students who sign up for office aide are the seniors who have no courses left to take. Because of this, it's a complete joke. Rarely do I ever actually "aide" the office in anyway. The ritual is pretty simple. I roam the halls for the majority of the period, trying my hardest to take as long as possible to deliver the passes to students. The longer I take the less likely I have to return to the office and either talk with the secretaries about their latest quilting party or clear another jam in the copier. Even more important: the longer I take out in the halls the less likely I am to run into the principal. In her mid-fifties and hair sticking out every which way, she barrels through the hallway like a German drill sergeant. This period though, she's always in her office. No one at this school intimidates me more than Mrs. Renthro. So I tend to walk real slow to the classrooms. Like I said, pretty simple and obvious.

I turn the corner and almost run into Marisol talking to

someone in whispers. I almost miss her hiding in one of the entry ways of an empty classroom, barely seeing her cheer-leading sneakers peeking out from the corner. But I hear her voice and listen quietly, taking my place behind some lockers. Even if she decided to leave and walk my way she wouldn't see me. I imagine she's talking with a football player or one of her friends. She's known to skip classes and find hideaways in the school - she's even been caught a few times and always seems to just laugh it off. As if her reputation doesn't even phase her. But I'm not listening for gossip. I'm not even sure why I'm stopping to hear what she's saying - and I definitely don't know why I'm hiding. It's just this unavoidable feeling of needing to know and needing no one to see me. I listen to my gut and hide behind the shadows. It's obvious whoever Marisol is talking to doesn't agree with her. An argument breaks out soon after I take my place between the lockers.

"I told you. I can't tomorrow. I have plans...I need to..." she stops short and her sniffs become louder. "Listen. I can get you the money. I promise. Just please don't make me go - it's not me."

Wait. Is she crying? Who is she talking to? I make an attempt to look but am too chicken to show my face so I sit tight and wait. I hear a throat clear and a low rumble of a voice respond. My heart stops.

"Why do you think I came? To just talk? There's no choice here. You're coming with me. I'll come pick you up tomorrow during third. You'll need to tell your parents your spending the night with a friend for a few days. Oh and bring your fake ID. We have out-of-state clients waiting."

I know the voice of the man she's talking to - the fear's completely gone now, I have nothing to lose if someone sees me. When I peek around the locker I see the leather jacket and torn jeans and I realize my initial thoughts were correct. This guy's been to my house. He plays poker with my dad.

Joey is his name...I'm pretty sure. I've never liked him - never liked the way he always seemed to look me over every time I'd walk in the room. My hand flies to my mouth and I stifle the gasp.

So it's true. All of this is connected!

"What was our deal?"

She's quiet and he repeats the question, a little firmer.

"What was our deal?"

"You-you told me all I needed to do was offer favors to the football players - give the money to you for my dad's debt from gambling. You got another guy to threaten the other cheerleaders to join in or else you'd show their parents pictures of them partying - pictures you guys doctored. I've paid you thousands of dollars! There can't be more...I've had to have paid you everything my dad owes..."

"Well that's the thing, sweetheart. Because you're dad gave you to me as collateral, I get to choose when I'm finished with you. And, I think I need more money. You're not performing as well as I'd hoped for someone like you. I mean, you're a cheerleader, right? Don't you know how to shake it a little better? Do I need to get Kristi to come in again as a cover? She could do a workshop or two with the cheerleaders - no one would even know." His laugh is throaty and vindictive and I fight the urge to walk over and kick him in the groin. I still can't believe I'm hearing this - and to think just a week ago I thought I was the only one who knew what it was like to be bound. Questions start flooding my mind and I file them for later - when I have time to process.

Who is Kristi? Does Marisol's dad play poker with dad? Did Dad suggest Marisol be used as collateral? It sounds like him..is this his new ploy? Beat a guy out of everything he owns and then buy his daughter off him?

"There's one way you could get out, you know."

Her breath catches, "How? I'd do anything...please. Just

let me know. Could I get another job? A real one? I'd give you every paycheck. I wouldn't take a cent."

He laughs again and clears his throat, "Really? Another job? Girl you're not gonna have enough time for another job. But, you could introduce me to one of your cheerleading friends. Or all of them, for that matter. Could you even imagine what we could do if we had them on our team of girls?"

"I don't understand...you already have all of us bribing the football players..."

"Oh honey. Football players are a far cry from who I have waiting for you. And they would jump at the chance for a night with multiple cheerleaders - it's every man's fantasy, really."

"You're sick, you know that?"

I smile at the tone in her voice and ignore the bitterness against Joey settling deep in my chest. She's a fighter, that's for sure. It makes me wonder how long this has been going on - how long she's dealt with last minute schedule changes and feeling like she's playing a game with reality. I hear footsteps and turn around. It's just a freshman, but I know this isn't a conversation he needs or wants to hear. He passes me, completely oblivious, pressing keys on his phone. He doesn't even see Marisol when he walks by her.

I feel a strange sense of regret - it's not until then I realize I wanted him to see. I wanted him to ask questions. Perhaps then it would be enough for someone to take a second look at what's going on because it seems like too many have turned a blind eye.

Marisol starts to cry and whispers, "Listen. I've never done anything like this before. I've just...you know ...gotten around the system by doing other things. I've even gotten my friends involved. One of them was even raped at a party...none of it would have happened if they didn't know me. Please don't make me do this."

She grows quiet and I hear shuffling. Chancing another look, I see the man pushed up against Marisol, her hands scratching at the wall and her eyes wild with fear. His hands cup her face and his mouth is inches from her ear.

"I've said it once and I'll say it again. You have no choice. Inexperienced just makes you more valuable, sweetheart. You have no idea how many men would fight for a chance with you. And once they find out you're fresh, well...there's no way I'm letting you go, now. Get it through your head. Now remember what we talked about: why am I picking you up?" Her voice is shaky, "You're my uncle. My dad's brother. You're picking me up because my dad's at work and my mom's sick and I have a doctor's appointment."

The man sniffs.

"Perfect. Now go back to class like the good girl you are - I'll be here tomorrow around 10:30. You better be here. Sam doesn't enjoy being stood up."

And with that, I hear his boots slap against the linoleum floor away from me, Marisol's tears echoing off the nearby walls.I could have walked away. I could have chosen to turn around the minute I saw them and I never would have known - never would have heard my father's name and understood that his obsession with young girls went deeper than trading his daughter for a good name with the police force. But I didn't, and as I walk over to where Marisol is sitting on the ground, her head resting on her arms, I wonder what pushes me to find out more - to sit next to one who understands. I have no idea how she's going to react, but I know I need to tell her. I need to look in her eyes and let her know there's more of us out there - and there has to be a way to stop it.

Her head flies up before I even reach her and she sneers.

"What do you want, Tiller?"

Well that's new. I've never been called by my last name and I'm half impressed she even knows it. I'm definitely invisible when it comes to the who's who at the high school, but I imagine a lot of the recent recognition has to do with dating Kevin. I ignore her tone and stuff the slips of paper with student's names long forgotten in my pocket. Sliding against the ground, I come to a rest sitting next to her. She just stares at me, an incredulous look on her face.

"Marisol...I heard everything."

Her eyes go dark and I see her retreat inward, "I have no idea what you're talking about."

She turns away from me and picks at a poster fallen to the bottom of the wall, it's edges brown from time.

I respond quietly, my voice steady for the first time in weeks.

"Yes you do. You know exactly what I'm talking about - who was that man you were talking to a minute ago? Who is Kristi? And who is Sam? Why does he expect you to lie to your parents and leave town?"

She looks at me surprised and I'm sure she didn't expect me to push back. I ask another question, the most important one: "Have you ever wondered who this Sam person is?"

She breaths in quick and wipes her cheeks, "I'm not talking to you about this."

She starts grabbing her stuff around her and I realize Joey must have found her in between passing periods - she probably hasn't even been to class.

"You don't have to, but I will say this - I know. I know more than you think. And...I think we could help each other."

She laughs then, a bitter and lonely laugh that eerily matches one that's fallen from my own lips on multiple occasions. I look around and am suddenly hit with a memory. I don't discount the fact that this situation - us sitting on the floor during school and me confessing my understanding

- isn't entirely unlike the mysterious girl I met just six months ago outside the front of the school. The memory enters and leaves my mind just as quickly as I breathe and I look again at Marisol. I know the bomb I'm about to drop on her will take awhile to process - and I know she may even be upset with me - with nowhere to place the blame it makes complete sense and I almost accept it as a guarantee.

"Marisol, listen for a second. I need you to hear me. Sam is my father. Sam Tiller. He traded me when I was twelve years old and he first got in trouble with the city police. I think he may be forming a trafficking ring of sorts through his gambling - maybe even a website. I'm not sure. There's not many people in this town I can trust. But I do know what you're feeling right now, and I do know you're not alone. I just don't know how to stop it."

She turns her head slowly toward me, her voice shaky.

"Don't ever come near me again - do you understand, Stephanie? This is your fault. I can't help that your father saw no use in you and decided to trade you for a good time and a clear name. But I can blame you for the fact that because of how it's worked for him, he's decided to find more girls - make them pay for your inability to be the daughter he wanted."

I start to speak but she interrupts, the tears falling freely. She points her finger in my face and I see the anger in her eyes. I know enough to understand the anger isn't directed at me but her situation.

"No. You don't get to talk right now. Do you know what they want me to do tomorrow night? They're taking me across state lines. Apparently there are clients waiting for me in three states and there's no way they can get here - so what does your dad and his posse decide to do? They're taking me to them. I'm a virgin, Stephanie. A virgin. Does that surprise you? Up until now, I've been able to fight for my innocence. I've been able to do just enough to satisfy the stupid teenage boys at this school. And my first time is going to be with some sicko who pays the highest price?" Her voice is getting stronger - louder. Grabbing her things and standing up, she turns around and looks at me again, "If this gets out...it could ruin me. You say anything and I'll make sure and let your daddy know. Would hate to have his rage pointed at you."

And then she smiles quickly - a detached attempt at sarcasm - and walks away.

I'm left there, sitting in the hallway, wondering about everything I heard in the past thirty minutes. I glance at the clock on the wall and realize I've effectively spent the entire period listening to Marisol. The conversation between her and Joey fresh on my mind, I head back to the office, trying to think of a reason why I didn't give out all the passes still stuck in my pocket.

Seventeen

KEVIN IS RIGHT ON TIME, WALKING THROUGH THE DOOR SECONDS AFTER the bell rings.

"Did coach let you guys out early or something? You never get here so soon after the bell."

I study his face and wonder if he's ready for what I'm about to tell him and if I'm even able to find the words to explain what I heard.

"Today was just lifting. And yeah, he let us hit the showers about five minutes before he normally does." He glances at the lady still staring from behind the bifocals and makes a face. "You ready?"

"Yes. Let's go. I promised Pacey I'd take him to the snow cone stand before it shuts down for the season."

"Snow cones? It's like...40 degrees outside."

I shrug my shoulders.

"My brother is four. His mind doesn't have any sort of reasoning when it comes to seasonal food or treats. He'd eat ice cream in freezing weather and drink hot chocolate during the summer."

Kevin grabs my hand and leads me outside, dodging young freshmen girls trying to stop and gain his attention. Once we get to his truck, he opens the door for me and I climb in, slide over to the driver's side and pop the lock before he reaches for his keys.

He opens his door and smiles, "You really are the only girl who has ever done that for me."

"What?"

"Unlock my door. I mean, everyone always yells at the guys for not opening doors for girls, you never hear or really see a girl talking about doing something for the guys. It's nice."

"Well, I actually never even considered it until I started going places with Emma and Jude. He always opens doors for her, but I noticed she did things for him. Unlocked his door, unwrapped his hamburger before handing it to him if we stopped at a drive-thru - little things. But he noticed." I look at him and smile, "I decided the least I could do was try and see if it really made that big of a difference."

He leans over and kisses my cheek.

"It does, Steph. Thank you for trying."

I grow quiet and he looks at me.

"Is everything okay?"

I turn and glance at him and chance a smile. Fidgeting with the zipper on my jacket, I wonder how I can even begin explaining everything.

"Um...not really. I overheard Marisol talking in the hall today during last period."

He makes a face and shrugs, "Let me guess. Was she with a guy?"

I nod.

"Yeah. He wasn't a student, though."

He is silent for a moment, waiting for me to continue.

"His name is Joey. Plays poker with my dad. Somehow he managed to sneak onto campus and catch her between passing periods."

I have his full attention now. He chokes on his coffee and looked at me in disbelief.

"What was he doing at the school?"

His question is deliberate - he knows very well where I am heading with the story. His eyes tell me as much.

"She owes him money. Well, she owes my dad money, really. Her father plays poker with the guys as well and he lost everything one night. I think my dad may have suggested Marisol as a token because he ended up trading her to Joey for collateral. He told Marisol he was coming to get her tomorrow during third - coming to pick her up from school as her "uncle" - and then she would be taken to some clients. She told me later they're taking her across state lines, Kevin."

He pulls the truck over to the side of the road and shifts into park. We sit there for a little while, completely quiet and taking in the gravity of the situation.

"Did you hear anything else?" Kevin whispers.

His knuckles are white, his hands wrapped tight around the steering wheel.

"Um...yeah. She mentioned that somehow they've gotten the entire cheerleading squad involved by threatening them with pictures the guys have doctored."

Kevin curses and hits his hands on the dashboard.

"You've got to be kidding me." He looks at me with an intensity I've never seen and grabs my hand. "Did she tell you what states? Think hard, Stephanie. Did she tell you what states they're taking her to tomorrow?"

I pause and wrinkle my brow, "I don't remember, Kevin - and what if I did? What would you do? Chase them down yourself? Not possible. I mean, obviously this isn't the most glamourous situation. Obviously something needs to be done - but what? How do we stop this? It's so above our heads - and I'm involved!"

Cooling down, he puts the truck back in drive and eases his way back into the lane of traffic.

"We just can't do nothing, Steph. I can't do nothing. It's hard enough for me not to say anything about what you deal with on a day to day basis and now it's like...the entire city is involved." He grows quiet and rubs his chin. "There just has to be a way..."

Pulling around the corner I notice a black car in my driveway. My dad's truck is missing. My eyes drop to slits and I wrinkle my lips in confusion.

"Who's here?" Kevin asks, pulling up to the curb and unbuckling his seatbelt.

My eyes suddenly focus in on a sticker on the back window and I pause.

"CPS," I whisper.

"CPS? What are they doing here?"

Kevin makes a move to open his door and I stop him - my hand on his knee.

"Kevin, you need to leave. I'm pretty sure my mom has already called my dad to let him know they are here, and if you are still here when he shows up, it could get pretty bad."

I drop my head and focus on my hands - my heart beating twice as fast as it was just five minutes ago. I can't believe this is happening. Again. I pray silently for Pacey - alone in the house - and I gather my bags and look at Kevin.

"You want to meet tomorrow morning? At the bleachers? It's been awhile since I've watched the sun rise and I have a feeling I'll need it."

He studies my face for a few seconds before answering,

"Are you sure you don't want me to stay?"

"Yes, Kevin. Go home. Don't hide - don't park down the

street and wait. Leave. Trust me."

My eyes plead with him to believe me and he finally accepts with a nod.

"Okay," he says. "Stephanie - be careful. Stay away from your father. Run away if you have to. You know where I live. You've made it to Emma's before." He pierces me with his eyes. "Be safe."

I smile - more for his benefit than mine - and step out of the truck.

"I'll see you tomorrow, Kevin."

I shut the door and wait on the sidewalk to make sure he turns the corner before making my way inside - hoping above all else that my home will appear somewhat normal to whoever is waiting for me.

"Mom? Pacey?" I holler as I walk in the door.

A woman steps around the corner. She's wearing jeans, a t-shirt and tennis shoes. Not necessarily the professional attire I'm accustomed to seeing on CPS workers who visit our house on a routine basis.

"Hi, Stephanie. My name is Rebecca Conway. I'm with CPS. Would you mind if we talk for a little while?"

"Where's my brother?"

I push past her and make my way into the living room and I see my mom leaning against the wall, her eyes puffy, mascara streaming down her cheeks. I walk up to her and am instantly hit with the stench of stale cough syrup.

"Mom. Where's Pacey?"

She looks at me with empty eyes and they narrow into slits - I step back, surprised at her breadth of emotion.

"They took him. You said something, didn't you? You just can't keep your blasted mouth shut, can you? You're a sorry excuse for a daughter, you know that? You keep spreading lies about our family, making it hard for us to do anything worthwhile for each other...was it the teacher again? Tell her to stop rubbing her nose in our business. Tell her if she knows what's good for her..."

I clench my fists to keep from slapping her and I take a deep breath and interrupt before she says something that makes it worse for all of us.

"Mom. What do you mean, 'they took Pacey' - who did? Where is he?"

And then I hear him, crying in the next room. I start to walk down the hallway before Rebecca steps in front of me.

"I'm sorry, Stephanie. You can't go in there. You will be able to see your brother in a minute but I would like to ask you a few questions first." She smiles and tilts her head, "You understand."

I rake my hands through my hair and start pacing, mentally preparing myself for the firestorm ahead. There's a lot I do understand. A lot Rebecca Conway couldn't even begin to wrap her brain around - but those are things left unsaid. What I don't understand is the chaos built around these visits. Interrupting our life, making it worse, leaving us in shambles to pick up after their exploration of our emotional rubble. Pacey by himself, answering questions he doesn't know how to handle, Dad coming home and finding these people prying into our lives again, the bruises that will most likely land on my skin later tonight once the blame is placed on my head....I fight the tears and force myself to calm down. *Do this for Pacey, Stephanie. Focus. Be calm. Be polite.*

I take a deep breath and try to smile.

"Where do you want me?"

Rebecca smooths her jeans with her hands and motions for us to sit on the couch. She focuses on the empty NyQuil bottle on the coffee table and writes something in her tablet.

"Someone sick?"

My eyes follow her gaze and I curse under my breath. No wonder my mom smells like cough syrup. The bottle that was half empty last night is now completely dry.

"Yeah. I've been having trouble sleeping with this cough...."

"I haven't heard you cough since you walked through the door?"

"That's because it's a lot better today - and it acts up mostly at night when I first lie down, you know - everything settles and stuff." I look her straight in the eye and hold her gaze.

I can do this all day, lady. You aren't taking my brother.

"Do you know why we are here, Stephanie?"

"Nope. Nothing has happened."

"Someone called in a report about abuse - both sexual and physical - have you experienced any of these?"

I blink and refocus myself. Normally they aren't so direct from the beginning of the interrogation. I can't help but think of Kevin. *Did he call? Did he tell someone? He's the only person who knows anything of what really goes on in this house...*

"I don't know what you are talking about, ma'am."

"Call me Rebecca"

"...Rebecca."

"How's your relationship with your parents?"

I fight a smile, and then think better of it. A smile would probably be beneficial.

"My parents and I are incredibly close. We've been through a lot and don't take family for granted."

I hear my mom snicker from the kitchen and close my eyes.

Really, mother? Now is not to the time to suddenly have an interest in what I say.

"What are you guys doing for Thanksgiving?"

"Spending time here. Eating. Watching football. Decorating for Christmas."

I start playing with my jacket hem and then pat it against my leg - reminding myself to make eye contact and engage in conversation.

"How often do your parents drink?"

"Alcohol?"

"Yes. Alcohol." Her eyes travel to the empty NyQuil bottle again and I speak up before she is able to make any correct assumptions.

"My mom has a glass of wine every night; my dad has a beer when he gets home from work."

"And that's all?"

"Yes ma'am."

For some reason my hands are shaking. I clasp them together and put them on my lap - bending my toes inward to keep from bouncing my legs up and down. I am a statue. Rebecca looks at me for awhile and smiles. Writing in her notebook, she glances back at me and continues her questioning.

"Stephanie, do you always have food in the house?"

"Of course."

"Would you mind if I look in the cupboards?"

"I think that's a question for my mom..."

"Or her father."

My heart sinks as I hear my dad's voice rumble through the hallway. I didn't even hear the truck pull into the driveway. I close my eyes and squeeze my fingers together - hoping Rebecca doesn't notice my change in demeanor. My dad walks around the corner and Rebecca stands to greet him.

"Good afternoon, Mr. Tiller."

My dad says nothing and glares at her, then looks at me.

"What's this about half-pint?"

"Dad, Ms. Conway just had a few questions for me. I believe she was almost done."

Rebecca looks from me to my dad and takes a deep breath. Holding my father's gaze, she reaches out to shake his hand and he continues to stand there - a pillar of intimidation.

"Stephanie's right, sir. I believe we are just about finished. My partner should be out any minute with Pacey."

Like clockwork, Pacey walks around the corner slowly, his hands over his mouth like he just got caught telling a secret. Big tears roll down his cheeks and he makes his way over to where I'm sitting on the couch. Climbing into my lap, he buries his head in my neck.

"I'm sorry, sissy." he whispers.

"Sorry for what?"

"I couldn't tell a lie. They asked me questions and I couldn't tell a lie."

My blood goes cold and I glance at my father who is studying us with intense focus.

"Pacey," I ask, "what do you mean? What did you say?"

I look toward Rebecca, and she's talking with her partner in hushed tones. My mom sits at the kitchen table with what looks like a shot of scotch and her cigarette. The women are comparing notes. I notice the partner motion to her arm and make tiny circles with her fingers - as if she's explaining something to Rebecca. I know with sudden clarity she's talking about the cigarette burns on his arm. I close my eyes and wait for the inevitable. Pacey doesn't have a chance to respond to my question, but by now, I already know what happened in the room. Rebecca walks over to the couch and kneels down eye-level with Pacey and myself.

"Hey Pacey. You're going to come with us for a little while, okay?"

Rebecca catches my eye and pauses for a split second when she sees the murderous look emanating from my face. I tighten my hold on my little brother and he moves his face away from the women threatening to remove him from my grasp. I hear his breath start to get heavier and small whimpers fall from his lips. They can't do this. They can't separate us. Please don't separate us.

"He's not going anywhere."

My mom starts choking back tears in the kitchen - away from everything, hiding, as usual. Her glass clinks on the table from her shaky hands trying to get a firm hold.

"No - no - no - no - no....not my baby." Her words are slurred and difficult to decipher. She never even looks our way - her eyes stay trained on her glass the entire time.

My dad starts yelling. Pointing fingers. Getting in the way of Rebecca and her partner who are threatening to rip my family apart and take the one person I love who shares my blood.

"Like hell you'll take my son! Like hell! You ladies better find your way to the door right now 'fore I get my gun - this is my property. He is my son! You can't take him - you can't."

His voice is echoing off the walls and it's hard to miss the way he slurs the words. Perfect addition to an already strong case against us.

Pacey holds on tighter and begins to cry.

"I'm sorry, Stephanie." Rebecca touches my knee and I flinch, moving away. She draws back, surprised at my reaction, and stands up to face my father. I hear police sirens in the distance and I beg someone - anyone - to wake me from this nightmare. Realizing she's not going to get any help from me, she focuses her attention on my father.

"Sir. This residence is not suited for the safety of Pacey. We will be taking him into the state's custody for the time being while we investigate further."

My dad's neck turns red and I automatically turn to hide from his wrath. His hands turn purple and he opens and shuts his mouth - unable to say anything.

Rebecca then leans over to grab Pacey and I fight for as long as I can before she looks me in the eye and whispers, "Please, Stephanie. Don't make this any harder."

Pacey is screaming. My heart is breaking. Rebecca holds him and carries him away and I watch his face, contorted and wet with tears. His arms are reaching out to me and he's begging and apologizing and kicking and screaming.

I can do nothing. There are no more pieces left to crack.

I am a statue.

Eighteen

THE NEXT FEW HOURS ARE A BLUR. A cop shows up and talks to Rebecca and her partner for a few minutes before turning to my father and explaining what will happen. I have to turn away when the cop looks at me. I've seen him before - he's one of the more violent clients my dad serves.

I sit there on the couch, head in my hands, when I hear the cop walk over to me and sit next to me, placing his arm around my shoulders like he's comforting me. I feel his hand squeeze my upper arm and I gag with the memories.

His breath is hot on my neck.

"I'll see you tonight...."

I close my eyes and wait for a reaction, but there is none. I just sit there. Numb. I feel the couch move with his weight as he stands and I glance up just in time to see him slip my dad some money. I shake my head at how obvious everything is - how no one seems to notice - or care, I'm not sure which one it is - right now, I don't even know if I care.

My dad shakes his hand and claps his shoulder. Business. I study his face. He continues to whisper with the cop and shoots glances at Mom, still sitting at the table, her face in her hands. He seems calm. He seems understanding of the situation and put-together. This is just surface level, though. I know my dad's undercurrent rages violently beneath his skin. It will be minutes before he bursts.

"I appreciate your willingness to cooperate again, Mr. Tiller. We'll see you around."

The cop turns around to walk out the door and throws me a wink as he motions for Rebecca. I turn away, unsure of how to react or even respond. The tension in the air is palpable and I'm still waiting for something - anything - to implode.

As soon as Rebecca and the cop leave my dad goes nuts. He and Mom start yelling in the kitchen; I hear glass breaking; I hear Mom weeping - and I just sit here.

My dad, in his rage, starts beating my mom senseless. I raise an eyebrow at the severity but can do nothing. I have lost all feeling - all reason - to fight. Pacey is gone and I don't know how to get him back.

"You are good for nothing you senseless wench. You just sit there, drunk on whatever you can find, and let our baby boy get taken away. My son! You are worth nothing."

He's leaning into her now, his fists cinched around the front of her shirt, her feet dangling six inches off the floor as he lifts her up and slams her against the wall. I flinch, but not because of the beating. Mostly it's because pictures are falling and shattering around them. I glance away, feeling as though I'm witnessing something intimate, and focus on the family pictures lining the hallway. Happier times. Those smiles seem completely foreign to me now.

I hear a thud and turn my head to look. My dad throws my mom across the room and starts barreling towards her - his fingers shaking. I study my mom - it looks as though she's passed out - either from pain or drinking, which one I don't know. I breath deep and close my eyes - still waiting for some kind of emotion, some kind of feeling, to well up inside of me. Still nothing. I just sit here. A statue. Pacey's screams and face etched into my memory like a horrible song that never ends.

My dad grabs my mother by her arms and starts dragging her towards the front door. She cries out in pain as her shoulder dislocates and then passes out. As he walks by me, I move my legs out of the way. I wouldn't put it past him to kick me in the legs or grab one of my arms to pull us both out of the house at the same time.

He looks at me and sneers, "Get ready, precious. You're next."

I stare at him and force my gaze to move to my mom, as soon as she's below me one of her eyes open and I freeze. Her look says it all.

She's given up. She doesn't care anymore. I really didn't mean anything to either of them - it was Pacey all along. Pacey. If I were younger, if the state decided to take me, they wouldn't have cared. The only thing they would be upset about is their live-in babysitter and prostitute would be gone.

I feel a tightness in my chest and then it disappears - my one moment of feeling vanished. Out of pure curiosity, I follow my parents outside, ignoring the small trail of blood my mom left behind on the floor. I walk outside and my dad is in the middle of the front yard, screaming and kicking my mother - and just as soon as he starts, he stops and stares at her for a split second before collapsing to the ground and covering her body with his arms. *You have GOT to be kidding me. Don't give in, mom. Don't. Don't buy into those lies he's whispering into your ear right now.* I cross my arms over my chest and wait.

"Oh baby, baby I'm sorry. I'm sorry, please forgive me."
He starts kissing her arm, her cheek, her hair. My mom
moves slightly and whispers something to him - I can't hear.
His back stiffens and I know what's coming. Slowly, he lifts
his head and looks at me - his eyes destitute, empty.

The second round is about to begin.

I brace myself for impact. Clinching my hands together,
my nails digging into the skin of my palm, I close my eyes.

He makes it over to where I'm standing within seconds. He
punches me in the face first. I fall to the cement, my breath
knocked out of me and my nose throbbing. My head bounces
against the concrete and I scream out in pain, lifting my hand
to touch my nose, he grabs my fingers in his own steel lock.
I try to ignore the popping sounds and the way my fingers
twist unnaturally. He rips me up from the ground and pulls
me inside.

"We don't want to entertain the neighbors, now do we?"

I hit the wall with my whole weight, my face running into
a picture of me in kindergarten, a fake bookshelf behind me
and an apple on the fake desk. I'm smiling in the picture.
Again - the smile looks foreign to me. The glass shatters and
I feel a piece break the skin on my cheek. I wince and feel my
hair pull from my scalp as he maneuvers my face so I have to
look at him.

"Why'd you do it, huh? Why'd you say something? Why'd
you open that pretty little mouth of yours? You just can't keep
quiet, can you? Was it that prissy little Emma? Huh? Did you
tell her what goes on in this house? Did you?"

With each question comes a hit, a pinch, a punch, a kick.
My body is just about to give out and then he stops. I crumble
to the floor and lay there in a fetal position, every muscle
aching. I feel him kick me and wetness fall on my cheek.

It's not tears. I haven't cried yet. I feel the pain; I do not
feel anything else. My heart is stone. No - I'm not crying. I

realize with slight revulsion my father is spitting on me.

I am nothing. I feel nothing.

I close my eyes and wait for everything to be over. I'm not sure how long I'm out. I'm not even sure what's happening. I feel someone pick me up and take me to the restroom where the cut on my cheek is cleaned. I cut in and out of consciousness but can't for the life of me open my eyes. I don't want to. I flinch against someone taking off my clothes - and notice new clothes being put on - I fight against the heaviness pushing against my eyelids and try to wake up, but I can't. I feel myself falling into a deep darkness, and I can do nothing. I finally quit trying and let go - floating into complete oblivion.

❅

I wake up in my dad's shed. His friend is already there - waiting for me to open my eyes.

"Ah. Sleeping Beauty. Glad you decided to join us."

Us. Plural. I look around and see four guys. All sitting around in anticipation. I only know the one - the cop - and my heart sinks with realization when I understand this has just become something a bit more than I ever imagined. This isn't just a simple trafficking ring where cops are able to get their kicks and go home to their wives. No. I think of Valerie and the other pictures of girls I don't even know. My head rings with the impact of what my dad is responsible for and a moan escapes my lips.

There's no way out. I'm stuck here. Someone...please come and rescue me.

My hand instinctually moves down my side and I frown at the fabric.

What am I wearing?

I look down - someone has changed my clothes. I'm wearing a pin-up costume, complete with high socks and...heels? My dress barely covers anything. The socks are thigh-highs and there is still about three inches in between them and my dress. Normally, I'm incredibly small chested. People have told me I look like a twelve year old boy rather than a teenage girl. Looking down, I'm surprised (and embarrassed) to see cleavage.

I feel like a two cent hooker.

I have no idea where the outfit came from, no idea who changed me, but I'm slightly nauseous at the thought of these guys' hands already on me while I had no inclination of what was going on. They notice my uneasiness and one speaks up.

"Don't worry. Your dad changed you before bringing you out to the shed." He lifts a camera and smiles, "We did take pictures, though." He walks over to me and caresses my leg, "With a body like that, you're going to be famous. We all are. These pictures are headed to the internet, honey. They're better than the ones already up. Here, let me show you."

He leans over and starts weaving through the pictures stored on his camera. Pictures of me, knocked out and completely clad in this...outfit. If you wouldn't know the circumstances, you would think I consented to all of these pictures - they had rearranged me in positions that made my stomach twist in knots. I notice it's all about hand placement - fixing my hair to cover my face in what seems like a seductive dare. And I had no idea they were doing this. I look away and feel my breath start to come out in gasps. He turns and laughs.

"These pictures excite you?! Oh boy. They excite me, too." He makes an obscene gesture, his eyes trailing down my body. I shiver.

"Oh...you're cold?" He turns and looks at the other three guys and nods. "I think our girl needs to warm up a bit, don't you think?"

They cheer, with perverted anxiousness, and my eyes move to slits in my face. I cower from his touch and lift my chin.

"Get away from me."

My voice is hoarse - my throat hurts and my body is sore when I move.

The guy straightens his back and his face darkens. A small, sinister smile snakes across his face.

"Ah. We got ourselves a feisty one, gentlemen. I think I kinda liked you better when you was knocked out. Less fight." His hands move to his belt and he unbuckles it slowly, raising his eyebrow. I watch his hands - they're shaking with desire. I turn my head toward the wall and refuse to look at him.

"Oh no you don't, pretty little thing. Eyes over here. You get to watch the show. Boys, don't forget to keep those cameras rolling. Men will pay good money to watch what I'm about to do to this delicious piece of heaven."

I ignore him - which seems to get him even more riled up. Grabbing my arms, he pulls me to my feet and presses me against him. I feel his heat and try not to gag. The men behind him start whistling and snapping pictures with their own cameras and something starts building in my chest. Indignation. Fight. Contempt. Hate.

I breathe deep and close my eyes, waiting for everything to reach a boiling point. I feel my face on fire and my own hands start to shake. Opening my eyes, a small tear falls and I shake my arms free from his grasp and push him as hard as I can.

"I said get away from me."

Stunned, he crashes against one of the chairs, his buddies try to catch him but are unsuccessful. All eyes are one me.

It seems I've wakened a monster. He springs up from the ground and leaps towards me, his hands instantly gripping my cheek. I taste the blood from the inside skin of my mouth being pushed against my teeth.

"Just who do you think you are? I paid good money for you. I traveled two hours because I saw pictures of your young, tight body and I wanted to have me some fun. And now you're going to try and take it away from me?"

He throws me on the bed and drops his pants. I've been here before, but every time the pain and disgust take my breath away. Suddenly, a small crack in the corner of my soul - the section I hid from everyone - tears open and I start to weep. I weep for my lost innocence and my brother and this hole I find myself in and everything I stuff deep inside. I can't stop. And apparently the men don't care. The crying makes them more excited. My pleas seem to them cries of pleasure. The cameras keep rolling and I can't help but think of those who will watch this - thinking nothing about whether or not I wanted this to happen. Whether or not I even had a choice. As if I wanted four men to have sex with me.

"No! Please. Stop. No!"

"That's right, precious. That's right. You like this, don't you?"

The voice is loud in my ear and I turn my head violently to keep the breath from rolling down my neck. My hands are tied behind me to a post above the mattress. The only reprieve I get from being tied down is when they get bored and move me to a different position - untying my hands to get me in a different spot. My wrists are raw; my eyes swollen; my hips tender from their weight.

I don't stop crying for the next two hours - but that doesn't stop the men. They keep coming. All four - multiple times. There isn't an inch of my body that hasn't felt the touch of these monsters, and when the last one shuts the door and I'm left alone, my body sags in relief.

"We got us some good footage, men. Sam will be excited to put these up on the site."

I grab one of the heels and throw it against the door with all my might, leaving a mark where the stiletto punctured the wood. I can't take it anymore. The pain - the grief - it's just all too much. I collapse against the mattress and close my eyes. *For now, it's over. For now. Close your eyes. Get some rest. Don't think about them. Don't think about the pain. Just...sleep.*

I keep crying though. I cry through the entire night - sobs wracking my body - tears continuing to wet the sheets tainted with the scent of men who are now at home, sleeping with their wives. Sorrow doesn't even begin to describe what I feel as a fresh wave of tears flow through me and I claw at my eyes to stop the pain.

As the sunlight starts peeking through the one window, I finally fall asleep - exhausted in my own anguish. I pull the covers around me in a protective measure - as if covering myself will erase what the men did. Where they touched and how I'm still shaking from the force they used. I know I have bruises on my legs because every time I move I feel pain shoot up from my calves to my upper thighs. I can't even kick off the other heel I'm so tired.

I close my eyes and dream of Pacey and sunrises and moments where I feel alive because right now, I feel nothing but death.

Nineteen

THIS IS HOW KEVIN FINDS ME: IN A FETAL POSITION, SHAKING AGAINST the cold, whimpering in my sleep. I don't even hear him open the shed door. He runs over to the mattress and curses. Touching my arm, he whispers my name.

"Stephanie? Stephanie? Ohmigod. Please...wake up."

I open my eyes slowly and moan. Realizing Kevin is sitting next to me, my eyes go wild and I reach for more covers. I can't let him see me like this. My heart leaps in my chest; my face turns crimson with intense embarrassment. I'm hardly clothed. I'm bruised.

Oh no - dad. He can't see Kevin here. He can't. He'd....kill him.

"Kevin...Kevin - what are you doing here?! Are you trying to get killed?! If my dad sees you..."

"He's gone. I checked. His truck isn't in the driveway." Kevin rolls back on his heels and shakes his head. "Stephanie..."

"You still didn't answer my question. Why are you here?

How did you find me?"

He looks at me and says quietly, "You stood me up for the second time. I sat there, on the bleachers, waiting for you. Once you hadn't shown by the time the sun hit the horizon, I was on my way over. I knew something happened. You don't ever miss the sunrise."

He kisses my shoulder and I sigh.

He just kissed my shoulder. My bare shoulder. I glance down and notice - for the umpteenth time - my lack of clothing and wrinkle my face in disgust. I look like a whore. I cover my head with my hands and try to fight the thoughts swirling in my head.

"Stephanie - why are you wearing..." he can't find the words.

Doesn't surprise me. The elastic of the thigh high socks cuts into my skin and I move my hand and stick my finger between my skin and the fabric, allowing my circulation a chance to flow freely. Slowly he backs away and finds himself sitting on a chair, his chin resting in his hands; his eyes fixed on mine.

My hands move from under the covers and I wipe my cheeks at the tears threatening to spill out again.

He notices the bruises on my arm and shakes his head.

"You look horrible. You need to see a doctor. There are... bruises everywhere." His eyes focus in on my face, "And I'm pretty sure your nose is broken."

I hadn't even thought of my nose since last night. I lift my hand to touch it and moan. Too much movement. Rolling myself in the fetal position again, I close my eyes against the sun and start to cry. I'm useless. Spent. Normally, I can take the thoughts captive and remember moments I've felt alive - remind myself there are people who still want me. After last night - after what the men did - I know I'm nothing more than second hand goods.

"I can't do this anymore, Kevin. I can't. I have nothing left to give. I sat there last night and watched my dad beat my mom to a pulp and did nothing. I didn't even fight until I was faced with four men staring at me like I'm a piece of meat. Who stands there and does nothing? Horrible people. I'm a horrible, miserable person."

He walks over to the mattress and sits next to me. "You are not horrible."

Looking me over, he curses again under his breath, his face forming a sense of resolve.

"I'm taking you to Emma's."

I cry out against the idea.

"Please...no. I don't want her to see my like this."

"Stephanie, I'm sorry. You don't have a choice." He places his hand gently on my cheek and leans in closely, "Listen. I love you. Do you hear that? I love you. And you don't let the people you love go through what you are going through. You just don't. I'm taking you to Emma's. If for nothing else than to get Jude involved. It's time."

I can't even comprehend what he just said because my heart refuses to believe it. *He can't love me. Can't. I'm a freakin' whore for crying out loud - my body isn't even my own anymore.* And then I remember - my brother.

"Pacey," I whisper, one more crack becoming more complete in my heart which seems more like a piece of stone than a living muscle.

Kevin stops and looks at me.

"What about Pacey?"

I open my eyes enough to find his gaze.

"They took him yesterday. I don't know where he is. I broke a promise, Kevin. I told him I'd always be there and now I'm not and I don't know where he is..." my voice breaks and I start weeping.

Again.

I thought by now the tears would have dried up. My head throbs from the night spent crying and begging for release.

Kevin sighs and runs his fingers through his hair.

"Okay. We'll get Emma to make some phone calls."

He leans over and slides his arms underneath me. I try not to cry out in pain but it's too hard. He stops for a split second and narrows his eyes.

"I swear. If I ever run into any of the bastards who did this to you…," his voice fades and I notice his eyes focused on something in the far corner of the room.

Freeing his arms, he walks over and stands by the window for about five minutes - frozen.

"Kevin?"

He turns; I notice tears running down his face. My heart jumps in my throat.

"Kevin - Kevin, what's wrong? What is it? No - no you don't want to see those pictures. Please."

He walks slowly back over to the mattress with what look like more pictures. He hands them over to me and I look with disbelief at the handful of photographs taken on this very bed. Photos of me. Photos from when I was knocked out. How'd they print them out so quickly?

Kevin clears his throat and wipes his eyes. He looks tired. Haggard. As if these past ten minutes has exhausted him.

"There was a sticky on the pile."

I look up at him - waiting for him to finish. I can hear his breath come out in short, hurried gasps.

"What did it say?"

"Upload to Daddy's Little Girls."

My vision goes blurry. I see multiple of Kevin and know I'm seconds from passing out. He has a website. The men weren't messing with me. He has a freakin' website with my picture to lure guys….I can't even finish my thought for fear of either passing out or throwing up. I hand the pictures back to Kevin and manage to squeak out a response.

"Can you uh...put these somewhere? We need them. Put them in your pocket or something."

Kevin nods and wipes his face again with his sleeve.

"Stephanie...."

I wave my hand and shake my head, "Please, Kevin - don't. Not right now. I can't...I don't want to...talk about anything. Just get me to Emma's. I need her."

He exhales deeply and slides his arms underneath my legs and shoulders again - and I fight the pain from his arms resting against bruises. I lift my hand and rest it on his shoulder and lean my head against his chest. He grabs a sheet to cover me and I wrap myself in it, finally feeling safe.

"We need to hurry, Kevin. My dad..."

"I know," he says and turns around, carrying me out the door and into the backyard and through the fence door.

❊

We get to Emma's in record time. Kevin pulls me out of his truck and carries me to the front door - banging with his foot until Jude cracks it open. When he sees us, he throws the door against the wall and yells for Emma.

"Emma! Oh god, Kevin - bring her in and take her to the guest room around the corner. Emma! Come here. Quick."

Emma comes running down the stairs, her eyes wild with fear and dread. Benjamin is in her arms, rubbing his eyes. She's still in her robe, her hair thrown into a high, messy ponytail.

"Jude, what in the world? What's going on?"

She knows something is wrong - Jude rarely yells, if at all. Her face rests on mine and she blanches - almost dropping her son in shock. Jude steps in to grab Benjamin and Emma comes running over to me, tears already flowing freely. She doesn't even know what's happened yet and she's already feeling. I realize then just how much I love her.

"Oh Stephanie....what did they do?"

"Jude said to put her in the guest bedroom."

She covers her face with her hands and nods. Breathing deep, she follows Kevin into the guest bedroom and begins talking as he gingerly sets me on the bed and pulls covers over me.

"Okay. We need to...we need to clean her. I'm going to run a bath for her and..."

"Wait."

Kevin and Emma turn to Jude standing in the door, his face grim.

"Stephanie, were you raped?"

"Jude..." Emma turns and glares at her husband. A few moments pass as they speak to each other silently - almost as if they knew it would come to this - he's the first to speak. I close my eyes and wish for better days - sitting at their table, eating dinner, helping Emma make cookies....it all seems so surreal now. So foreign.

"Emma. If she was raped, she has evidence. DNA. I mean, look at her. She's a wreck. She needs to clean up, but not before someone is able to gather evidence to make sure whoever did this is caught."

I open my eyes and focus on Jude, his face set in a protective glare.

"Jude. It wasn't just one man. There were...there were four of them..," I whisper.

All three curse under their breath and Kevin speaks up for the first time. He's looking Jude square in the eye. Emma just sits there - holding my hand.

"Stephanie's father runs a trafficking ring. Men travel from out of town just to have their chance with her - and some of her friends. Stephanie found pictures of Valerie in one of the cabinets in the shed and we just recently found out he's even blackmailed the cheerleading squad because of a gambling debt."

Kevin turns to look at me - his eyes asking for permission to continue. He knows I didn't want them to know about this. I nod my head slightly and he looks back at Jude.

"He even has a website posted with pictures. Daddy's Little Girls."

Kevin's face contorts with disgust when he says the name of the website. Emma gasps and her hands fly to her mouth again. Her eyes constrict with pain and she looks at me.

"It's true, Em," I whisper.

Jude stares at Kevin for a split second before storming off and grabbing the phone. Kevin follows him.

"Don't call the police, Jude."

"Like hell I'm not gonna call the police. That sick bastard..."

"...uses the police force as a cover." Kevin finishes his sentence and Jude hangs up the phone.

"What?"

"Stephanie told me many of the guys she's seen are from the police force. One of the guys last night was actually the cop who came over after CPS was called. He came over specifically to set an appointment. There's not even a report about CPS yet with the local police. I called on the way over to check. He did nothing except strike a deal with her father."

Emma's face crumples even more as she listens and grabs my hand. Jude and Kevin begin whispering in the living room. I can't tell anymore what they are saying but I'm sure Jude is trying to find a way to seek justice - even if it's his gun.

"Stephanie. Why didn't you tell me? We could have done something..."

Her voice is earnest. Quiet. Broken.

"What?" I look at her and raise an eyebrow. "What could

you have done, Emma? Honestly..."

She looks at me and drops her head, resting it on the pillow next to me she just lies there, holding me. We lay that way for awhile, Emma crying and me finding comfort in her embrace. Jude walks in about ten minutes later. I open my eyes once I hear footsteps on the wooden floor. Emma rolls over and places her hand on my hip.

"Where's Kevin?" I ask. I'm so used to having him refuse to leave my side, I'm a bit confused when I open my eyes and he's not there.

"He's uh...resting on the couch in the living room. He dozed off while I was on the phone." He chuckles a little and then looks at me, as if he isn't sure he can laugh in this situation without being completely inappropriate, "He...he seems a little tired. It didn't take him long."

I smile and rearrange myself as best as I can without hurting too many throbbing muscles. Jude seems relieved to see me smile, even if he knows it's tainted with pain. He focuses on his wife as they start talking about what to do.

"Em, I just got off the phone with my buddy at St. Joseph. We're going to need to take her to the hospital. Derrick will wait for us." He holds his hand up in protest when he sees my face form an argument, "Steph, you need to be looked at. And I wouldn't trust you with any other doctor. This is one of my best friends. I've known him forever."

He walks over and sits on the edge of the bed. Grabbing his wife's hand and placing his other hand on my cheek, he starts to cry.

"Stephanie - I really wish you would have said something earlier. I could have spoken to the DA; we could have kept you here; something...anything....to get you away from that monster."

I am so out of it I almost forgot about Pacey. I sit up; Emma places her hand on my back and sits up with me, guiding me and protecting my muscles from working too hard too soon. I'm grateful. I've never been this sore in my life.

"There's something else."

Emma and Jude look at each other and her shoulders slump.

"What do you mean? What else is there? What happened?"

"They took Pacey."

They look at each other again - this time with more confusion, "What do you mean? Who took him?"

"CPS was at the house yesterday when Kevin dropped me off. They separated us to ask us questions. Apparently whatever Pacey said was grounds enough to pull him from the house, because they took him. My dad was there. That's what instigated this." I motion my hands up and down my torso, "I don't even know where my brother is or how to find him."

Jude sighs.

"This is a disaster." He looks at me and points his finger, "And Stephanie, don't pretend you are having a hard time understanding why they took Pacey away. You live in that house. You see the bruises on your brother just like people see the bruises on your arms. He may not have had to say anything. And I doubt their visit sparked last night. If I know your dad like I think I do...he's had this planned for a long time." He looks down and rubs his temples, "We'll find him, Steph. We'll get him. I promise."

I remember the cigarette burns and grimace.

"I just want my brother back."

The tears start to form and Jude clears his throat. I suddenly find myself leaning against his chest. He places his hand on the back of my head and strokes my hair.

"It's going to be okay, Steph. You're dad can't get to you anymore. We won't let him. I won't let him. Just relax...you're protected now."

I close my eyes and let the tears fall against my will. I'm so sick of crying. I'm so sick of my heart feeling incomplete and broken and split wide open.

"Why do you guys insist on getting involved?"

I place my hands on Jude's chest and push away. Looking at Emma, still sitting on the bed - her hand now on my knee - I wipe my eyes and focus in on the two people who have meant the most to me.

"I mean, really. Why do you two insist on getting involved with me? I'm messy. A disaster. I can't let you guys see me like this. I'm so embarrassed."

I wave my hands around and stop at what I'm wearing. Pulling the sheet up I rest the fabric underneath my arms and begin rubbing a knot forming in my right arm. I sit there and wait for an answer - any answer - half expecting them to realize what a waste of time I am and walk away. I can't even look either of them in the eye anymore.

Ashamed doesn't even come close to what I feel right now.

Jude speaks first.

"It's simple, Stephanie. Someone told me once God is on the side of widows and orphans - and though I know you aren't a widow and I wouldn't qualify you as an orphan - I would assume your situation speaks very closely to the heart of God and his desire for justice."

His voice cracks. I see tears welling up in his eyes. He steps off the bed and pats his pockets for keys and a wallet - distracting himself from the conversation at hand. I'd seen him do this once before - when his brother was in an accident and he had to tell Emma. She studies him and turns to me, finishing his thought.

"Stephanie, no one should have to go through what you deal with on a day-to-day basis. No one. We decided a long time ago we didn't want to be the couple who closes our eyes to what's going on around us. And then you came along - hard to ignore and absolutely easy to love."

I start to smile and stop when the skin around my lip starts to crack open from the punch the day before. Emma frowns and glances at Jude before focusing her attention on me. She exhales and slaps her legs. The decision had been made - whatever it was - I've seen that look before.

"Stephanie. Come on, let's go to the hospital."

I place my head in my hands and groan. I know what's going to happen.

"How is this even going to work? You guys realize you aren't my legal guardians. The hospital is going to call my parents and then my dad is going to come up - pretending to be concerned but secretly seething and waiting for a moment to pay me back. And it will be worse. It's always worse when others get involved."

The fear starts pulsing then - the fear of my father finding me, of living in this life one more day, of seeing his eyes grow into slits behind the backs of those he's tricked into believing his charm. My hands start to shake and I take to wringing them so I don't start pulling out my hair.

Jude slips his arms underneath my legs, much like Kevin did earlier in the morning, and carries me out of the room.

"You don't have a choice, Stephanie. We're going whether you want to or not. Right now, your health is our priority. I'll deal with your father when the time comes."

I bury my head in his chest and sigh. There's not much I can do - he's right. I allow myself a brief moment of peace and rest in the fact I have people who care so much for my well being. And I believe Jude - for some reason I know if anyone can deal with my father it will be him.

"Hey Kevin," Jude calls as he walks into the living room carrying me.

Kevin starts and pops up and off the couch with a burst

of energy - rearranging his clothes and patting his hair and stuffing his cell phone in his pocket.

"What's up?" He notices Jude carrying me and rushes over. "Is everything okay? What's going on? Where are we taking her?"

Jude manages to get one of his hands free long enough to place it on Kevin's shoulder to stop his constant questions.

"She's fine, Kevin. I just wanted you to know we're taking her to the hospital. You're welcome to hitch a ride if you want."

My voice cracks as I try to fit in a question of my own, "Kevin, who were you texting?"

He glances at Jude and looks back at me with a smile, "My mom. She texted me because she got a call from the school about me missing classes. I told her I was on a job shadowing day with Jude."

Emma walks around the corner with Benjamin.

"Alright honey, I'm ready."

She opens the front door and shivers against the cold. Benjamin sits quietly playing with his hands in his bugaboo.

Jude turns and makes his way out the door, "Kevin, will you grab a blanket for Stephanie?"

I hear Kevin in the background and the swoosh of fabric before he crosses in front of Jude and places a warm fleece over my bare skin. I meet his gaze and give him a half-hearted smile.

"Thanks, Kev."

He brushes my hair out of my eyes and winks.

"No problem. Here. Let me open the door."

Jude places me delicately in the backseat of their Tahoe and Kevin runs around to the other side and slides in next to me, grabbing my hand as soon as he's able. Leaning over, he whispers in my ear.

"Don't worry. I'm not leaving your side any time soon."

I turn and look at him, my eyes holding all the response I can handle at the moment. Emma buckles Benjamin into his car seat and maneuvers herself into the front. With all of the commotion around me, I barely even notice how exhausted I am. Within minutes of Jude starting the car, I'm asleep.

Twenty

Five minutes before we take the exit, Jude turns to Emma.

"Hey Em, will you send Derrick a text and let him know we're almost there? He mentioned to let him know so he could wrap up whatever he was doing and meet us at the front."

Emma nods and pulls his phone from his pocket.

"Is there going to be a girl in the room with them? I trust Derrick, but these tests are pretty invasive."

Jude glances at me from the rearview mirror before answering.

"I believe so."

Kevin glances at me and squints his eyes, "What does he mean...invasive?"

"He's talking about a rape kit, Kevin."

I whisper, but the emotion is evident. Kevin leans back and rests his chin in his hand - propped up on the windowsill. He sits there for the rest of the trip, staring out the window.

Please don't leave me. Please don't change how you think

about me. I notice his hand resting on my knee and I wonder at the small miracle of it all - how his touch is so welcome when every other is feared.

We get to the hospital within record time thanks to Jude's speeding. As promised, his friend is waiting for him at the front desk. He takes one look at me and curses underneath his breath.

Hm. Makes me feel confident.

"When did this happen?" His gaze pierces through my eyes and I blink at the severity.

"Um...last night....and uh, early this morning."

He looks at me again and goes to grab a few instruments to perform a quick check where we are. Checking my vitals with his stethoscope and blood pressure gage, he looks at Jude and Emma. Kevin still holds on to my hand as Derrick leads me to a nearby wheelchair. My bad knee is throbbing.

"How come she didn't go straight to the ER? Has anyone checked for broken bones or cuts that need to be cleaned?"

I stifle a giggle tinged with bitterness - considering the circumstances, a broken bone or a cut seem pretty welcome. Emma looks at him and raises an eyebrow, echoing my thoughts. Kevin shoots me a glance, confused at what I could possibly find funny.

I need to let him know of my tendency to laugh at inappropriate times...

"Um, Derrick - when she first came to our house - bones and cuts weren't the first thing on our minds."

Emma crosses her arms over her chest and Jude clasps his hands behind his back. I love them. Seriously. If I could have chosen anyone in the world for parents, these two would be at the top of the list and the ones I was stuck with would be somewhere without any kids at all. A prison perhaps.

He nods in realization and walks over to one of his colleagues, whispering in her ear. She turns and looks my way before writing something in her notebook and walking quickly away. Derrick comes back over and places his hand on Jude's arm.

"We're working on getting her a room. But, Jude, because you guys aren't her biological parents you're unauthorized to receive any information. We're going to have to call her parents and notify them of the accident."

Like hell they will.

"Please don't."

Derrick turns and looks my way, surprise written across his face.

"Excuse me?"

"I have some say in this, right? It's my body?" At least... theoretically. I shake my head to quiet the thoughts and continue, "Please...don't call my parents." I twist around in the wheelchair until I am facing Derrick completely. "See my nose? My dad's fist. And this bruise?" I point to one on my upper thigh, "My dad's knee. And this?" I point to a cigarette burn on my left elbow. "That's my mom."

I look at him again and mimic Emma's slap on the legs for emphasis. For the first time in my life I'm standing up for myself by sharing the truth with someone in authority - someone who has power to change things. *Please listen to me. Believe me.*

"Don't call my parents. It will only make it worse."

Derrick's mouth opens in protest and I continue.

"I'm not asking for Jude and Emma to take their place. I understand if you can't give them any information. But I do know friends and family are allowed in rooms, and I consider everyone here my family - more so than those who claim my blood. And really - how would anyone know?" I point to him. "Technically, you are the only person who knows Emma and Jude are not my parents or legal guardians."

Kevin smiles and shakes his head and watches Derrick

contemplate what I just said. Emma shifts her weight to another foot and bounces Benjamin in her arms. I glance at the clock - 10:00 AM - she's probably going to have to feed him soon.

Derrick's pager goes off and he twists his lip.

"The room is ready. Jude - just wait out here for now. I'll hold off on calling her parents, for now."

"Derrick, thank you. We'll be out here until we get the clear. I'm not leaving her with the chance of her dad showing up."

My breath catches in my throat and I silently say a prayer of thanks and let Derrick wheel me away from the small crowd forming in the waiting room. I turn around and wave at Kevin and he waves back, mouthing words of comfort until I can't see him anymore.

❀

My room is cold. Bare. The gown is scratchy against my skin and rubs against some of the more tender spots where bruises are continually forming. I glance around and my eyes rest on the pile of clothes now sitting neatly in a plastic bag on a nearby table. Evidence. Goosebumps cover my arms and I close my eyes against the memories of last night and rest my head on the lumpy pillow. I wonder if I will ever be able get to sleep more than three hours at a time.

My thoughts wander as I wait for the next doctor to come and perform more tests. I study my fingernails and think back to beautiful sunrises, rich in color and bright with promise.

I need a new beginning. I've been stuck in this night for too long.

"Good morning, Stephanie. I would ask how you are doing, but I'm afraid I already know the answer."

I open my eyes and am met with an incredibly petite

woman smiling at me. Her blonde hair falls right beneath her shoulders; her fingers freshly manicured. She looks breakable. I raise an eyebrow.

"My name is Natalie. I'll be performing some tests on you here in a little bit, but first I wanted to ask you some questions."

"Hi," I whisper, not sure if I can trust this small frame to hold the weight of the burden I seem to have carried into the hospital room.

She tilts her head and studies me for a moment before walking around to check my monitor. As soon as I was brought into the room they hooked me up to this huge machine and started pumping pain medication into my system. I already knew I had three broken fingers, a broken nose, a sprained knee and two torn muscles in my right thigh. Oh and...I was coming down from someone slipping me Ecstasy. I cringe at the headache and glance at her fiddling with the machine and wrinkle my forehead. Natalie isn't here to check on my injuries. At least not the obvious ones.

"You're looking good. Stable. How do you feel?" " L i k e I'm floating."

She laughs, "Perfect." Her smile fades and she touches my arm, "You do know why I am here, right Stephanie?"

"Yeah. I know. You don't have to explain what you're about to do or anything...I do have a question though."

"What is it?"

"Where do these tests go once you finish them?"

She searches my face before answering, "We have some of the quickest turn arounds in terms of rape kits - if that's what you are worried about."

My laugh comes out a bit more cynical than I aim for and Natalie squints in surprise.

"It's not the clearing of the tests I'm concerned about. It's the hands these tests fall under - do they go to some generic county facility or the police department?"

"Well, right now they go to our lab. Until the authorities are able to talk with you and determine whether or not files should be charged, we safe keep all results."

She tilts her head, giving me a half smile before gathering her tools.

"Alright, Stephanie. When was your last period?"

I think back - it takes a few minutes. These past few weeks have been slightly overwhelming.

"Two and a half weeks ago."

She writes something in her notebook and looks at me again.

"How old are you, Stephanie?"

"17"

"How old was your assailant?"

"Um - I don't know. I only recognized one. I'd say mid-twenties to late forties?"

Natalie looks at me and then places her pen on the clipboard.

"What do you mean - 'you only recognized one'? There were multiple men?"

"There were four of them."

Her eyes study my face and she continues writing - I wish I knew what she was thinking.

"Where did the alleged assault take place?"

"In my dad's shed. Last night."

"Did they use any physical restraints?"

Her eyes focus in on my wrists. I follow her gaze and notice the skin rubbed raw - a wound that would be there for quite some time. A constant reminder I wasn't ready to face.

I pick at my IV and run my fingers through my hair.

"They uh...they me tied down."

Her pen stops mid-stride and she tries to hide the emotion clouding her face.

"You know, I'm not really supposed to say anything other than these questions - and even then - I'm not supposed to respond to how you answer. But I can't help this. For the record, this question is not on my list. How long has this been going on?"

I hold her gaze for a minute. *Can I trust you? Why do you want to know this?*

"Since I was twelve. My dad um..," I pause, studying my fingernails to avoid the reaction on her face.

I don't even know why I'm sharing this with her. I continue before I change my mind, before the courage runs out and I'm stuck scared.

"...my dad runs this trafficking ring with some local girls. Three of them are my childhood friends. He's even brought in the cheerleading squad at the school and I don't know the youngest girl - I've never seen her before in my life. She's so young. Nine? Ten, maybe?" I turn to look out the window. "He has a website. Daddy's Little Girls. It's how men find out about us. There's pictures and videos..."

Natalie starts coughing and I look towards her. She's wiping tears from her face and writing stuff down.

"I thought you said this was off the record."

She shakes her head. "If I could explain to you the rage I am feeling right now at the injustice of what's going on in my own town...you would understand." She looks at me and I'm taken aback at the intensity of her eyes. "We're going to find you justice, Stephanie. The men who did this? They're going to wish they never clicked on those pictures. They're going to wish they hadn't taken your innocence."

I clear my throat. How does this stranger care more about me than my own parents? She's brought to tears over what I go through - and my own flesh and blood want nothing more than to cause my pain.

She returns to the questions on the sheet of paper and

clears her throat.

"Do you use any contraceptives, Stephanie?"

"No."

Placing her clipboard down on the table next to my bed she gathers her equipment and stands by my feet.

"Okay - I'm going to begin the physical examination now. Are you ready?"

"Yeah."

She grabs a cotton swab and scrapes the inside of my mouth and then grabs an envelope to place the swab. She does this under my fingernails, as well. The exam lasts about thirty minutes, with the most invasive parts lasting only about ten. I glance at the stack of envelopes now on the table and then look back at the nurse.

"Did you get everything you need?"

She grabs her clipboard and nods, "I did. Thanks, Stephanie. I am a bit concerned at some tears I see, but we will examine those closely over the next few days and call you with any conclusions. Did Dr. Martin take x-rays already?"

"Yes."

"Perfect. Well, I will go and let your friends know you are open for visitors now and start working on your discharge papers."

She pats my arm and throws me a sympathetic smile.

"Um, Natalie, do you know if anyone got a hold of my parents?"

"No."

She brings the clipboard closer to her chest and then tilts her head.

"Your home phone came back as disconnected and the cell phone numbers we were able to find didn't work either."

I close my eyes and allow my head to collapse against the pillow behind me.

Maybe someone is on my side after all.

"Is everything alright?"

I open my eyes and smile. "Yeah. I'm fine. Just anxious to see my friends."

She studies me closely and then walks back over to the edge of the bed, touching my cheek with her hand. I look her and try to ignore the awkwardness of the situation. I mean, she's a great nurse and all, just a little...touchy.

"Stephanie, if you only knew how much the heart of God grieves for your situation. He knows. He cares. And he hurts right there with you. Justice is coming. Rescue is coming. Hold on - and remember hope."

Before I can even respond, she kisses me on the forehead and turns around to leave, placing the newspaper from yesterday on the table next to me. I turn my head and stare out the window at the sun peeking through rain clouds, shining against the drops forming on the glass pane, my thoughts lost in what she's said.

Is it true? Is rescue possible? Maybe...they don't know my dad, though.

Her voice calls from the door.

"Do you see those storm clouds? They don't stand a chance against the sun. Remember that, Stephanie, in moments of despair."

I turn to look at her and she's gone - a chill runs down my spine and I grab the blanket and pull it closer around my shoulders.

Twenty-One

I<small>T'S ONLY AFTER SHE LEAVES THAT</small> I <small>REMEMBER THE NEWSPAPER SHE</small> placed on my bedside table. I grimace as I reach for the stack of papers, curious why she left it and feeling as though there was something she wanted me to see. The headlines seem monotonous - winter weather advisories, education in-fighting and the latest political debacle all within inches from each other. I scan the paper, almost deciding to toss it, when a headline jumps out at me. My skin immediately feels on fire when I read the words:

Authorities Fail in Human Trafficking Bust

Authorities received an anonymous tip yes-terday evening in the case of a runaway, Marisol Venedez. The tip reported her to be taken across state lines for prostitution. After searching nearby border areas, authorities failed to relocate Marisol and turned to family and friends for more answers. Her father, Filipe Venedez, denied such claims and assured authorities she was with friends. "I don't know who would find this funny - it seems a prank," he told reporters. Venedez recently immigrated from Juarez and currently runs a construction business out of his home. He continued, "Marisol spends time practicing with cheer friends. This is where she go last night. Not other states."

Stacy Jethro, a freshman at the high school and a member of the cheerleading squad, vouched for Marisol as well. "She was with me the entire time - we were practicing for our competition we have soon. I don't understand why anyone would say she wasn't here. I mean, it's absolutely ridiculous."

Jethro's parents admitted to not seeing Marisol, but believe their daughter. "We were out of town on a business trip, but Stacy has never lied to us before and wouldn't start now. This has all been a colossal waste of the city's time and effort."

The authorities aren't so sure. Although they never found Marisol across state lines, the tip came from a reputable source stating that the cheerleading squad would most likely cover for Marisol because they were coerced into the ring earlier this year when Venedez lost his assets in gambling. The state of the claim, and the specifics given, are enough to cause the authorities to investigate further.

When asked about the cheerleaders' involvement, Isabel Wright, a senior, denied all connections to the prostitution ring. "This is absurd. How can anyone force someone into prostitution? Everyone knows those girls are whores - they choose their own lifestyle. Marisol would never do anything to compromise the reputation of herself as well as the squad."

The principal echoed Wright in disbelief, refusing to go on record but also implying the tip was an elaborate prank in order to muddy the name of the cheerleading squad and high school.

However, other students aren't as quick to deny the allegations.

"It's pretty much a known fact that the cheerleaders get paid for sexual favors. No one ever talks about it but everyone knows," says sophomore Haley Higdon. "There's private internet pages serving as some back door into their business they have going on. I've never heard about it being forced though - I always thought they were just trying to raise extra money." Whatever the real reason, authorities are overwhelmed with the implications and are seeking assistance from state and national government.

"We'll get to the bottom of this," says Steve Pruett, the local sheriff. "We'll find the perpetrators. Whether this be an elaborate prank or the weaving of a master-pimp, justice will be served."

I throw the newspaper down and cover my face with my hands. It is all too much - the article, the truth hiding in plain sight, the worst of the criminals painted as a hero - I rest my head against the pillow and wonder if it will ever end. I hear footsteps and glance up. Marisol is standing in the doorway.

"What are you doing here?" I whisper. "How - how'd you know I was here?"

I panic for a split second, wondering if my dad's out in the hall, waiting.

"Relax," she says. "Your dad isn't here. He's beside himself looking for you, though - you should know it's only a matter of time."

Her eyebrows raise and there's a smile playing at her lips.

"Please Marisol...please don't tell him. Please don't say anything."

"You know...it's funny."

She saunters over to my bed and leans over the railing, her long silky black hair falling in wisps around her face.

"To see you begging - to see the role reversal so soon after your own betrayal. It's kind of satisfying."

She looks around the room and her eyes land on the newspaper. Her face darkens and she shoots me a glance.   " I didn't say anything, Mari..."

"Like hell you didn't. Who else knew, huh?! No one. No one knew but you. You're such a snitch. And now all our lives are going to hell because you couldn't keep your little mouth shut."

Her words are darts - barely above a whisper but close enough to hit me in the center of my fear.

"Do you know what happened the other night? The guys got wind that someone was on their tail. They ended up driving me around for hours, until they decided to freakin' pimp me out through taxis. Taxis, Stephanie. There was this special sticker stuck to the windshield to let any guy know there was a girl he could screw just waiting for him inside. I made thousands and didn't even see a cent. My v-card lost on some fat guy from Arkansas who came to the city for a good time."

Her eyes are already dead. She doesn't even shed a tear when she tells me this - she's lost all will to fight on her behalf and in turn has focused her rage on me.

"I-I-I'm so sorry, Marisol. But I didn't..."

"No. You know what? I didn't come here for sympathy. I

didn't come to hear your excuses or for you to try and get all buddy-buddy with me cause you think you know my life. I use to be able to hold on to college. I use to have this image of me fleeing to some unknown city - enrolling in college and having no one find me. A true chance to start over, you know? Now? You think a college is going to take me now? With a rap of runaway and prostitute hanging on my forehead? Yeah honey...labels don't ever go away. And you're stupid if you think otherwise."

She leans back and I fight for breath, feeling the tears come again.

She smiles, her damage evident.

"You're always gonna be a whore, Stephanie Tiller. You're always gonna be a cheap lay that even the boys talk about to other women. I hear about you all the time - the shy one. The one who doesn't give back. And you know what? They like me more."

"That's hardly anything to brag about...."

She grabs my arm and I wince, the IV pricking my skin and pulling in ways it shouldn't.

"Don't you get it? This is our life now. There is no other side. There is no rescue. These guys are so infiltrated with cops and lawyers and supposed good guys that there's no one we can trust. Get over it, princess. Your life is over."

She lets go and steps away from my bed, looking out the window.

"You know what's sad? I remember the way your family used to be - before your dad got drunk and started gambling - before he pulled in all of our dads into that stupid poker game. I use to envy you in elementary school, the way he'd pick you up and carry you to the car. I never knew that - never will. My dad was always too busy driving back and forth to Juarez in order to build his company and gain citizenship. Now? It's all trash. Everything."

Her eyes grow cold.

"I said it once and I'll say it again - I hate you. I can't help that you weren't the daughter Sam wanted. But now we all have to pay - because of you."

She leans forward and whispers in my ear, my blood running cold.

"He's coming, by the way. It's only a matter of time until he finds you. And oh does he have a plan for you."

She laughs then, a deep throaty laugh that makes me shiver with dread. Walking out the door, she turns to look at me one more time.

"I would say I'll see you around, but I don't know if that's gonna be possible," and smiling, she turns to leave.

I stare at her figure turning the corner out of my room and through tears I try and find the sunlight peeking through the clouds - that last glimmer of hope I felt before Natalie left. My pulse is racing and I contemplate running away - somewhere, anywhere other than here. I'm suddenly terrified at the thought of my dad finding me and heartbroken at the complete transformation of Marisol. Not knowing what to do, I press the button for more morphine and a nurse comes in to administer a new dosage. She doesn't even check my paperwork to see I received a dose less than two hours ago. Within minutes, I feel the warmth crawling up my legs and reaching my neck, my face, my ears. I fall asleep the tears still falling, the fear a distant memory.

I open my eyes and notice Emma curled next to me on the bed. Her eyes were closed and I can hear her even breathing. I hesitate waking her up, but know she probably would want to know when I was awake.

"Hi," I whisper.

When did she get here?

Emma's eyelids slowly lift and she rubs her forehead - a groggy habit. Checking her watch she grimaces.

"I've been asleep for two hours." She places her hand on my arm and looks at me. "How do you feel?"

"Good."

My eyes wander to the window and I frown. Pitch black.

How long was I asleep? It seems like just a second ago Natalie was in here...

Natalie. Oh God, Marisol. I look at Emma and decide to tell her about Natalie first. Maybe only. I'm still not sure if she is able to handle my situation. I'm still afraid I may break her.

"Did you meet Natalie? She mentioned she was going to get you guys in the waiting room."

"Who's Natalie?"

"She did my rape kit. She was just in here. You know - Natalie. Small...blonde...looked like she could be easily broken."

Emma looks at me and smiles. "Steph, I have no idea who you are talking about. Dr. Martin came and told us you were ready for visitors. She did your pap smear and rape kit. Maybe you got them confused?"

I shake my head.

"No. Her name was Natalie. She asked me questions about what happened and got all upset - started crying - and then she was going to leave but came back and told me my rescue was coming or something like that. I didn't really understand her, but I liked her. She made me feel...safe." I glance at the IV still dripping fluids into my system and glance at Emma. "For the few minutes she was in here, I actually believed she was right. That rescue was coming."

Emma leans her head against her shoulder and focuses on the ceiling.

"He's ready to come to their rescue in bad times; in lean

times He keeps body and soul together."

I look at her and frown, "What?"

She smiles.

"When I was in high school, I had my own bathroom. My mom got this idea to write me notes with expo markers while I was at school. She never knew this, but those notes were the high light of my afternoon." Her face clouded over. "My senior year is when my dad started drinking heavily. His whole...personality changed. My mom always put that verse up to remind me - especially after my dad had one of his fits. It always gave me comfort - hope. It's nice to be reminded that rescue is possible."

I study her face.

"Sometimes I forget."

"Forget what?"

"About rescue. About hope. Even when I go and watch the sunrise, I still have the thought in the back of my head floating around, whispering my mistakes and what I've done and what I have waiting for me at home. Escape is almost impossible."

I remember what Marisol said and I shudder.

Her eyes burn and she squeezes my hand.

"You're getting out of there, Stephanie. I promise. Some how, some way, we're going to figure out a way to get you out of there."

I fight back responses filled with cynicism and attempt to change the subject.

"Have they gotten a hold of Dad?"

She shakes her head.

"No. Actually, they gave up a couple hours ago - but they are still working on paperwork to get you out of here."

I stretch and make a face at the wires preventing me from making any sudden movements. I just want to get out of here.

Emma notices my face.

"I'm going to go check on how things are going. Hopefully we'll be out of here before too long."

She leans over and kisses my cheek before getting off the bed and making her way to the door.

"I'll send Kevin in to see you. He's been pacing all day, patiently waiting for his chance to come and sit by you." She smiles. "He's good for you, Stephanie. He loves you. I can see it."

I casually ignore her comment and roll my eyes.

"Where's Jude?"

"He went downtown to work on a few things and check on Pacey. He should be back soon as well - if he isn't already."

My heart jumps at the thought of my brother and I take a few breaths to quiet it down.

Whoever you are, Natalie - I'm not the only one needing rescuing.

Emma stands at the door, smiling.

"I'll go get Kevin, Steph - you rest."

I laugh and look around at the beeping machines and needles and bright fluorescent lights. *Right. Rest. Got it.* I stick out my tongue at Emma, but she's already gone.

Twenty-Two

KEVIN COMES IN MINUTES LATER, WITH A HUGE BOUQUET OF FLOWERS.
I don't know the names of them, but they're absolutely beautiful. I blush.

"Kevin. That looks really expensive. You didn't have to do that for me."

"Nope, I didn't. But I did - so enjoy them."

He smiles at me and sits on the edge of the bed, cautious of the wires. He grimaces.

"How are you feeling?"

"Better. Not as sore. Could be the morphine though."

He looks at me and closes his eyes for a split second.

"The doctor told us what all happened - the broken bones and torn muscles..."

I place my finger over his lips.

"Can we not talk about it? I know it happened. I know I will have to deal with it at some point. Right now? I want to talk about something else."

"Like how I got a phone call from USC today?"

"You did? What did they say? I didn't know you already applied..."

"...it was for you." He looks at me and grabs my hand. "And even if it was for me they usually let you know of your acceptance through a letter - not a phone call."

"Oh. Then why'd they call me?"

He dodges my question.

"How did they get my number, Steph? I mean, they have it in their files - but it's for me - not you."

"I may have put your information as my own on my application."

His eyes widen and I keep talking in order to keep him from freaking out.

"For no other reason but to avoid my dad getting another phone call or intercepting letters in the mail." I shrug my shoulders. "You were the first person who came to mind."

"You didn't think of Emma?"

"Well...no. And even if it did it wouldn't have worked - they use a PO box."

I look at him.

"Do you want me to change the contact information? I can. I didn't know it would be this big of a deal." I start playing with the edge of my sheet and try to quiet the pounding of my heart - it's so loud I can hear it in my ears.

"It's not. It just surprised me."

"So what did they want? Did they tell you?"

"Yeah. They did, actually - they've been trying to get a hold of you because they are wanting you to look into a few writing programs this summer to hone your skills before you go to class. It's something they ask every freshman creative writing major to look into, at least - helps you focus in on your talent and all that."

"Hmm."

I pull at the string loose on the sheet and start dismantling the fabric, unaware of my destruction until Kevin places his hand on mine.

"Hmm what?"

"Am I ever going to get out of here, Kevin? I mean....look at me. I can't even think about college right now - let alone imagine writing classes for the summer." Tears threaten to spill and I swallow them back, forcing my emotions at bay. "I'm an absolute wreck. Did you know if something were to happen and someone found out about what was going on - someone who didn't know me - I could be arrested?"

"Impossible."

"No. Truth. Kevin - look at me. I'm a prostitute. A prostitute. Men come and pay my father to have sex with me. The fact that I refuse or don't want them makes no difference. I'm a criminal in the eyes of the law. I know you guys care for me - you and Emma and Jude. But...sometimes I can't help but ask why. I'm used. Broken. A mess. Even if I do get out of here - I will never be normal."

He smiles and squeezes my hand.

"It's a good thing it isn't your choice, then - I don't think we are going anywhere. And, who wants normal? I don't."

He winks and taps my nose with his finger.

Endearing.

My lip curls in a half grin and I close my eyes to rest. I know these are the moments he just won't listen to my questions, and so I take it for what it's worth and rest in the fact that there are people who care for me - for now. I still wonder how long it will last - even if they tell me it won't ever change. My mind drifts back to Marisol and I hear her words echo in my head. I fight them this time - choosing to believe rescue is possible.

There has to be a way. This isn't how it's supposed to be, I think and I hold on with my life to the thought of another world.

He leans over and kisses my forehead and Jude walks in the door with Emma. Something's up - I can tell - Emma is avoiding my gaze for now because she thinks that will help me not knowing. I know them well enough to not ask. They'll let me know when they're ready...or I am.

Jude smiles and catches my eye and walks over to my bed, waiting for Kevin to slide off so he can take his place. Kevin moves to the other side of the room to grab one of the chairs.

"Hey, kid. How are you feeling?"

"Better. Where's Benjamin?"

"Good. We dropped him off at his grandparents on the way here. We figured he had enough hospital for one day."

He looks at Emma as she leans against the doorframe of the room. She's still avoiding my gaze - focusing instead on the hallway and the doctors passing by. I can't take it anymore. Forget waiting.

"What's going on?"

Jude sets his head against the metal frame and looks at me.

"Your dad filed a missing child report."

I shake my head.

"What does that even mean? I haven't even been gone..."

"For 24 hours. We know. But, it means the police force is required to keep an eye out for you. You're this close to being classified as a runaway. With that article that just came out about Marisol, we need to get you back home - before you are taken into custody. With your dad's history and how he's using the police for his benefit, this isn't good for you. We need to get you home - we don't need them to have any reason to take you in to custody."

I grimace at Marisol's name and finger the blanket.

"Um...did you guys read the article?"

Jude and Kevin glance at each other. Jude, rocking back

on the balls of his feet, nods.

"Yeah. We read it. Seems the authorities are a little overwhelmed at the moment. And no - I haven't said anything, Steph."

I breathe a sigh of relief I didn't even know I was holding, "Thanks, Jude. Have they found Marisol?"

"Not yet. Everyone of her friends is playing mum's the word and her father is pretending to know nothing. No one can find her mom."

"She visited me."

Kevin jerks his head around, his eyes probing my own.

"What?! She was...she was here? In this room? Steph..." he glances again at Jude and then back to me, "Why didn't you say something?"

"I don't know...it just, it was weird. It didn't feel like I needed to until now."

"What did she say? Was anyone else here? How did she even get here?" Jude starts shooting questions at me and noticing my eyes starting to glaze over he starts over, "Sorry, Steph. I don't mean to overwhelm you. Did she say anything?"

"She just said there was some way the guys found out they were being followed by authorities and so they turned around - ended up finding a taxi-driver to make his car a portable brothel for the evening."

Jude's eyes widen and Kevin nearly falls off from the edge of my bed. Emma, quiet until now, stifles a sob and moves toward Jude, grabbing his arm for balance.

"What? A...a taxi?"

Kevin looks at Jude for explanation and he nods, trying to remain calm.

"I've uh...I've heard of this happening before. Usually in larger cities, mostly during big events like the Super Bowl or the Olympics. Sometimes though it's just commonplace."

He lowers his head and starts to pace, thinking out loud. Emma takes to sitting on a nearby chair, her head in her hands, sounds coming out of her mouth almost as if she's praying.

"Did she say where they were?"

"No."

"Did she tell you who took her specifically?"

"No. It wasn't Joey. It was someone else."

"Did she tell you anything else we should know?"

"Yeah. She said other guys talk about me. Tell her they like her more. She also said my dad has plans for when he finds me."

Kevin starts clinching his fists and avoids my gaze. I know he's upset. I know he's struggling to find the balance between defending me and being there for me. I reach for his hand and his fingers relax.

Jude looks at me and studies my face.

"You know we're going to get you out of this, right? You trust me, don't you?"

I nod and a lone tear escapes, running down my cheek, "I trust you, Jude. What are we going to do though? How am I going to get out of this?"

He walks over to me and Kevin moves so Jude can have room.

"I have no idea, Steph. But I'm going to do everything I can to make sure you're safe. I won't stop until I figure it out - you believe me, right?"

I glance at Kevin, now taking to pacing the hospital room and Emma who is still rocking in the chair, her anxiety peeked. I can still hear the quiet whispers coming from her mouth.

I nod again and force a smile, "I believe you."

Jude sniffs back tears and kisses me on the forehead.

"Good. Now let's talk about a plan."

Twenty-Three

I THINK ABOUT OUR EARLIER CONVERSATION, ABOUT THEM TAKING ME home, and I groan.

There's no way I can go home again. No way I can face my family.

"I can't even stay the night with you guys?"

"No."

"Not just one night?"

I hear Emma sniff and I move my eyes toward her - she's already turning and walking off into the hallway. I glance back at Jude and catch him looking at his wife.

"She's taking this really hard, Stephanie. And I am too. It feels like we are feeding you to the lion, but we're going to do everything we can to get you out of there - for good. You just have to trust us. We're working on it, okay? We're not giving up - not in the slightest. We may not know where to start, but we're doing something. We're figuring it out as we go along. And we're not giving up - you know this but you can't forget it. The fight has just begun."

His eyes are spitting fire - and I have no doubt he means what he says.

"Okay."

My voice is small. My breath is coming in quick gasps, memories once again flashing through my head like a broken film strip wheel. Blinking and broken and blurry...I fight for control of my thoughts.

"So no, you can't stay with us tonight - maybe not for a couple of nights. The authorities are wound up about this whole situation with Marisol, and they're on high alert. The good ones don't know about the corrupt cops feeding your father information and the corrupt cops are starting to get anxious."

I shake my head in confusion, "Are they planning on doing something?"

Jude shrugs.

"I have no idea. I haven't been able to get info from anyone in our local police force. I just know this from experience - usually, the good guys have no idea and the bad guys start to get a little crazy when information starts leaking. We need to be careful."

I nod and whisper.

"Why does it feel like it may get worse before it gets better?"

Jude and Kevin clear their throats.

"I don't know, Steph. I can't - I can't pretend to understand what you're going through."

Kevin comes over and grabs my hand and rubs his thumb over my own.

"You always have us. Always. And you know where we live if you have to make a run for it."

"We got you something, too. Hopefully something that will help us keep in communication with each other."

I look at him and crinkle my eyebrows.

"You got me something?"

He hands me a box and I open it to find a cell phone - nicer than anything I've had before.

"We added you to our plan, so you don't have to worry about minutes or texting or anything like that - our phone numbers are already saved and shortlisted on the speed dial. There should be no reason why you can't ever get a hold of us. Just uh...make sure your dad doesn't get a hold of it. Make sure to keep it on you at all times, okay?"

My head drops and I smile. I don't deserve these people - at all. And yet, they keep coming back. Keep helping me and believing in me. I look at him and wipe the tears from my eyes.

"Guys - thanks so much. You...you didn't have to do this, at all."

"Yes we did," Emma calls from the door.

She's finally come in - her cheeks blotchy from crying. I look up and notice her smiling and standing next to Dr. Martin. Her smile doesn't reach her eyes though - and her fingers are clenched together by her sides.

Not good. *Stop stressing for me, Emma.*

"Hey Stephanie. I have some good news for you. It looks like we were finally able to get a hold of your father - he's on his way to pick you up. He sounds pretty concerned. You should be able to leave in a few hours."

The doctor is elated. She has no idea what's really going on because in order to keep my confidentiality, Derrick didn't fill in the rest of the staff about my situation. She smiles at Emma like she's done us a favor and turns to walk away.

My face crumples; my head falling into my hands.

No. No - no - no - no - NO! My dad can't come. He can't.

I feel Kevin's arms around me and I collapse against him for strength - relying on the fierceness of his hold and his breath close to my ear. I can't help but compare his embrace to the ones I received the night before. One forced, the other welcomed. One dirty, the other pure.

"Stephanie - I promise, with everything inside of me - maybe not today, maybe not tomorrow - but rescue is coming. I know it...I feel it. I will do it myself if I have to, but you will not be living in your hell for very much longer."

I freeze at his words.

"What did you say?"

Emma and Jude turn and glance at us from their corner of the hospital room - Dr. Martin pulled them over their to give them a time estimate of when my dad would come so everyone would be gone by the time he got here.

Kevin looks at me.

"You're going to be okay."

"No - the exact words." My face is earnest; my hands wrapped around his arms.

"Rescue is coming."

My heart starts throbbing - seriously - throbbing with pain.

Is this some kind of joke? Really? Because...I can't handle this much longer. Please. Don't be a joke...

I look at Emma and her eyes go wide. She's heard what Kevin said and she smiles. She walks over to me, tears in her eyes, and whispers in my ear.

"I'd listen if I were you. Someone is trying to tell you something. Hang on to hope, my girl. Hang on to hope."

Kevin looks at me and raises an eyebrow.

"Did I say something wrong?"

I laugh and shake my head.

"Not in the least. I'm so thankful for you guys. All of you. Knowing you're fighting my battles for me and with me makes everything so much easier."

I lean my head against Emma's and we stay there for

awhile before Jude clears his throat.

"Um - Emma, we need to leave before her father shows." He looks at me and smiles. "Hang in there, Steph. We're working on it. Promise."

I watch them leave and finally meet Kevin's gaze before I hear the crashing of boots against the tile floor outside. My breath catches and he places his hand on my arm.

"Don't worry. I'm gone. And don't forget, Steph - I love you."

He kisses my cheek and slides out the door, placing his hoodie over his head as he throws a glance over his shoulder - probably trying to catch a look at my father. I pray he doesn't notice Kevin and wait for him to walk in the room.

Breath raspy, heart pounding and tears forming - I wait for the man who haunts my dreams.

Twenty-Four

HE WALKS IN WITH DR. MARTIN.

"She sustained some serious lacerations from forced contact, Mr. Tiller. She's very lucky her injuries aren't worse."

My father grunts and rubs his eyes with his hands - the picture of a father broken over his daughter's attack.

"Do you have any idea who did this?"

His voice sounds strained - like he's actually forcing back tears. I fight the laughter at his display of emotion and wait for her to fall in to his grasp. They always do when they haven't had any experience with him in the past.

Dr. Martin catches my eye and I shake my head slightly - begging her to not share what I confessed to any doctor who would listen.

Not that it matters. You didn't believe me anyway.

"No - although the extent of her abuse makes us wonder if more than one person was involved. She will need a few days of rest."

He nods his head and lowers his eyebrows. Walking over to the side of my bed he caresses my arm and leans over to kiss my cheek. I hide the disgust on my face when I feel his whiskers grate against my skin.

"Don't think I can't smell that cologne you whore. I saw the boy leave. You trying to have some fun on the side? Not gonna happen. Don't let me see him around you again unless he's got money in his hands and a condom in his pocket. I may not have seen his face but I can find him. I can always find him. You better let him know I'm watching." His hand squeezes around my arm and I flinch, his breath is hot and I hear him chuckle, "Besides. Odds are he wouldn't be able to say no to Marisol. She paid you a visit today, didn't she? Are you beginning to understand just how powerful your pops is? You think you're life is a mess now, don'tcha? Just wait, you little whore. Don't cross me. I gots more surprises up my sleeve."

Don't make a face, Stephanie. Don't make a face.

I close my eyes and breath deeply. My stomach lurching at the picture of Marisol trying to come on to Kevin - having already seen her at work in the hallway at school, I know her tactics.

"Thanks Dad,"

I use the standard script. Be thankful; act graceful; show love.

"And don't think you're getting away with this. What kind of crap are you trying to pull? Coming to the hospital?! What the hell, Stephanie?"

His breath is fire as he pats my shoulder and brings his head up away from my ear. He's done with the lecturing. For now. I watch his eyes and fight against the bile when I notice his pretend tears peeking out the side of his eyes. I look over at Dr. Martin and she's bought his role - hook, line and sinker.

"Mr. Tiller, I would like to give you a card for our child psychologist. In these cases we feel it's necessary the girls gain complete restoration. Stephanie's gone through quite the ordeal, it's important you know it will take her awhile to achieve normalcy. Even then - everything will be different."

She has no idea what my normal looks like. I cough and they both shoot me a glance. My dad's face creases into a scowl.

"Oh...I'm sorry. I just saw a clown walking down the hall and he made me laugh. He was uh...wearing some type of..."

I motion to my robe and hope they understand what I am attempting to say. My dad rolls his eyes and Dr. Martin smiles.

"Oh yes - that's Hank. He's our resident comedian. He works with the kids in the trauma unit. They love him! Such a talent." She straightens her jacket and places her pen in her pocket. "Please do not hesitate to call if you have any questions about Stephanie's recovery. And Stephanie..." she turns and looks at me, "take care of yourself. No more late walks?"

I nod.

"Yep."

She purses her lips and turns to give my father a grin.

"Here are her papers - you guys are free to leave."

She walks out the door and for a split second I consider calling after her, causing a scene in the middle of the hospital.

Really - what can he do to me here?

I remember the runaway status though - and the fact that technically I am the one who is breaking the law in prostitution. I grimace and glance at my clothes in the bag. Evidence.

"Um, Dad - did you happen to bring me any clothes?"

He looks at me incredulously, "Do I look like I did? What

- you try and get me arrested and now you want me to read your mind?"

I frown at his logic and shake my head,

"No...I just...don't have anything to wear."

"Guess you're just gonna have to wear the robe out, then."

"Dad..it's 20 degrees outside."

He cocks his hip and points his finger at me.

"You know what? You're an ungracious know-it-all. You think you're so high and mighty, with your...your friends who say they love you. Do they pay for your food? Huh? Do they make you feel pretty and loved and...and...keep a roof over your head? Do they? No. They don't."

He takes of his jacket and throws it at me - the cigarette box stuffed in the pocket hitting my cheek.

"Wear that. It should cover your frame anyway. You look like a freakin' twelve year old. Why men want you is lost on me."

I bite my tongue and move to get off the bed - my body screaming at me in protest. Now that I've rested and taken the time to process, my body is a lot more sore than I realized. I grimace and my dad notices.

"Stop acting like a baby." He reaches to grab my arm with his hand and pulls a little too hard - my legs, not ready for the pressure of my weight - crumple beneath me and I fall to the floor. Pain shoots from my bad knee and right thigh and tears start falling down my cheeks. My dad starts laughing.

"Oh this is just perfect. Go ahead. Play the freaking martyr. I'll be waiting outside."

He walks out of the door, muttering under his breath the whole way. *I'm not ready for this. Please. Somebody put me out of my misery - it would be so much easier being dead.*

My hands shake at the thought and grasp for my new phone. I discreetly place it in my dad's jacket pocket and force my body to work for me.

Your rescue is coming. Do not give up, My child.

I freeze - my arms hanging limply by my side and my knees slightly bent. Am I going crazy? I look around and see no one and frown. The voice I just heard was so distinct and... intimate...I know I just heard it. I shake my head and gingerly place my arms within my dad's jacket. I zip it up to hide my frame and for the first time, look in the mirror.

Shoulders slumped, hair matted, bruises everywhere - I really do look like a two-cent hooker who's had her last trick. Dark circles surround my eyes and my cheeks sink against my face. I hear my dad talking in the hallway to the nurse and my eyes move to slits. I hate his voice. I look down at my hands - still shaking from the slight exertion. My eyes close for a split second and I say a silent prayer - to anyone, really.

Just let me get through this? Let me be free. And please stop me from grabbing one of those scalpels and stabbing my father.

I take a deep breath and walk out the door, my dad leaning against the wall.

"You finally ready?" He snorts. "You look horrible, Steph. Like someone ran you over with an 18 wheeler."

I imagine shooting daggers into his face with my eyes and smile.

"Thanks, Dad. I appreciate the compliment. Can we check out now?"

"Someone already checked us out. And paid too."

I pause for a split second before responding.

"Really?"

He looks at me from the corner of his eye.

"You think I don't know who did it? You think I'm stupid? I know it was that ragtag couple you can't seem to get away from. And that boy? The one who was in your room? I'll say it again. He steps foot on my property and I'll shoot him. I have half a mind to go looking for him right now. Don't test me. You're mine, now. This little stunt showed me I can't let you out of my sight."

"You can't keep me in your sight forever, Dad. What about school? What about your work?"

"Already got it figured out. I talked to some friends for ideas - you know one of 'em, Marisol." Her name falls of his lips with a sneer, "I'm locking your bedroom door from the outside. You'll be coming with me to work. I have a room in the back I can use for business during the day - maybe give some type of happy hour special or somethin' to interested customers."

He smiles and I don't even recognize him, the pure evil pouring from every inch of his skin. My heart sinks. Rescue? Forget it. I can feel hope slipping from my grasp.

"You wouldn't. Dad. You can't take me out of school."

"Oh sweetheart. I already did. Told your school you need a break for psych-iatric reasons. You just aren't safe, you see. That's all they really needed to know. No one wants a fire-cracker. Too risky." He wipes the stray chew juice off his mouth and smiles again, "It's okay though. You'll be plenty busy. You have two appointments tomorrow."

He turns and starts walking down the hall towards the exit and I stare after him for a split second before hardening. It's over. The dark tunnel beckons me, and my heart just can't take any more fight. I welcome the relief of giving into the despair, and forget any promise of rescue or hope. Marisol was right. My life? It just doesn't belong to me anymore. I follow my father out the double doors, away from the light and into the pitch black of night. The metaphor or irony wasn't lost on me.

The next few days are a blur. Every morning, I wake up in

my own bed to my father grabbing my arms and shaking me.

"Wake up, slut. It's time to work."

His words are the same. Short. To the point. Filled with hate and a gleam in his eye only described as monstrous. He's not my father anymore - he's my slave driver. But just like his words are repetitive, so is my reaction. I crawl out of bed as best I can, closing my mind to the bruises and sharp pain radiating from my body.

One more day, Stephanie. Last for one more day.

My mantra has changed in the past week. I haven't seen anyone in five days. I still have the phone Jude and Emma gave me; it's my lifeline. I thought I was talented during class - sneaking texts incognito with my hands in my purse and my eyes on my teacher. Whatever. That's juvenile, now. I sneak texts to those who breathe life into me while others try to snuff it out.

Today is no different. Five minutes after he leaves me still in bed and groggy-eyed, he barrels into my room again, yelling at me to hurry. With minutes (and fraction of my dad's patience) to spare, I quietly walk out of my room and past his glare. I never speak. I have no words to say. We drive to his work in silence - my forehead pressed against the icy glass.

I miss my classes. I miss my teachers and friends and trying to fight the crowd of students in the hallway. I miss Mrs. Peabody and her eccentric way of letting me know she believes in me. I even miss Mr. Yeager and the debates in Government.

I miss Kevin.

I feel my back pocket vibrate and risk a glance at my father to see if he noticed and roll my eyes at his oblivious nature. My head sinks against the glass again and I close my eyes. Just five more minutes...

My dad slaps me out of my reverie - literally.

"We're almost there."

I scowl at him and rub my sore cheek as we pull into his work and my blood runs cold at the sight of my prison - a dilapidated shed home to drug busts and rats. He pulls up next to it and shoots a glance around the road to make sure we have no other curious bystanders. I see a fancy car parked to the side of the field - far enough away from the road so no one notices. It's where my dad's customers are instructed to park. There's already an indention in the field where cars have kept running in anticipation of us showing up.

"This guy paid me almost a thousand dollars for you after watching that video I just posted on the website." He looks at me and raises and eyebrow. "Don't disappoint." Shoving me out the door, he guns the gas and hollers out the window, "I'll be back later tonight!"

Just like every other day, I search for a half a second for a plan of escape. I still hear the quiet reassurance of rescue - but I'm cynical. I close my eyes, allowing myself that brief fantasy of what it would feel like to have someone come rescue me.

I'm stuck in some room - with a guy. He's trying to talk to me and make himself feel better about what's he's about to do. Just as he's about to walk over to me the door bursts open, the sun shining through and illuminating the dust and dirt and grime in the corners...

I'm cut short by a cough and I turn around. A man is standing haphazardly on the staircase leading up to the shed. My head drops and I nod for a couple seconds in self-realization.

Sighing, I push out my shoulders and lift my head to greet the customer. He's older. Close to his forties, it looks like. Of course, his wedding ring glistens in the sun and I shake my head at the predictability.

If I had a dollar for every married man who started with the website and decided to make his way down here to "meet" me....I just don't understand.

I lose myself to the thoughts as he grabs my hand and leads me inside.

"I've waited awhile to see you in person, Violet."

I smile at my fake name and shrug my shoulders. I wince at the door shutting behind me - still a sound that makes me cringe. I play with the tips of my hair and look at my own personal nightmare.

My rescue won't be coming any time soon.

Twenty-Five

THE MAN LEAVES IN LESS THAN THIRTY MINUTES, AND I KNOW I HAVE A few moments to recollect myself and use the restroom before another one shows. I wait until I hear the screech of his tires peel out of the gravel before I wrap the sheet around me and run to the bathroom to clean off his scent. After my shower I don't even bother with make-up. Grabbing the cranberry pills, I pop two with as much water as possible. Last thing I need is an infection on top of what I deal with on a day-to-day basis. I walk over to the bed and collapse against the mattress. I glance at the clock on the wall and notice I have a few minutes of freedom. I pull out my phone to check if anyone has sent me a message.

I scroll down and my heart jumps at the new message from Kevin.

> "morning, beautiful. u still
> comin 2mrrw?"

I stare at the message for awhile before it registers. Tomorrow. I'm supposed to be going over to his house tomorrow.

You've got to be kidding me. Tomorrow is Thanksgiving?!
I think about meeting his parents and my blood churns. Before it was a bit more realistic - even though I lived a sordid past the haunting was really the only issue. But now? When I'm the other woman to so many families the thought makes me sick. I still struggle with even being a girlfriend. Whatever that means. I haven't seen Kevin in weeks and I still have no idea why he's with me. Why he chose me - the prostitute.

My head pops up at the sound of gravel crunching beneath tires and my heart starts to pump. I quickly type out a message letting him know I would try and think of something to get away before I see the shadow of a man walking up the stairs. Throwing my phone in my purse, I turn in time to hear a nervous shuffle and the doorknob turn.

I cross my legs and close my eyes and focus on the task at hand.

Just make it through today, Stephanie. Just make it through today....

I lift my head and smirk.

"Another cop? Perfect. Welcome to the ring of brotherly misconduct. My name is Stephanie, but the men like to call me Violet - prevents them from having to attach me to an actual person."

He looks at me and raises an eyebrow.

"Hi," he mutters, his face white.

I stare at him and bite my lip. Something's wrong. Something's...different. He's different. Normally, men are clamoring over their clothes to get to me and get out on their lunch break - their one fling for the day before they return to their normally scheduled lives of families and jobs and contributions to the community. Him? He's...just sitting there. Bouncing back and forth on the balls of his feet. Hands in his pockets. Eyes anywhere but me.

"Um...I've been uh...sent to..."

He turns around and faces the other wall. The one opposite from where I'm sitting.

You've GOT to be kidding me. Who is this kid?!

I jump up from the bed and walk over to where he's standing. I tap him on the shoulder and he turns around - crying.

"I'm sorry. I'm...I was just sent here by Jude. I'm a lawyer in his firm and he was telling me your story...I didn't believe him."

He rubs his hands over his face and looks at me from in between his fingers.

"What the hell is going on here?" He whispers. "You're like...twelve."

"I'm 17."

"Oh."

His voice is small. Defeated.

"So it's true? You're a...a prostitute? At 17?"

He sniffs and wipes his eyes on his sleeves.

"Where are your parents? Isn't prostitution....illegal?"

I watch his face for a little while before answering. I guess I could trust him - he seems legitimately concerned. I turn around and make my way towards the bed, grabbing the sheet to wrap my self for his benefit - he's obviously never seen a woman scantily clad, let alone naked.

"What's your name?"

"Chad." "And Jude sent you?"

"Yeah. He wanted to see how the system worked. He uh... reserved an hour with you under a pseudonym and told me the directions."

My heart jumped at the actions taken by Jude to get me out of here. I fingered the gold necklace he gave me that night a couple months ago while eating dinner with him and Emma. We'll always be here he said when he gave it to me.

"I'm not sure how much Jude has told you, but I'm not a

prostitute. Well. Not in the typical way most people assume. My dad is down the street working. He's who set this up. He's my pimp. I don't get any money." I look out the window and notice some storm clouds rolling in - "This whole thing started small - a little ring within the police force to keep them quiet about his abuse and neglect. Then, they started taping. My dad got a website. Downloaded pictures. Worked so well with just me they thought to add more girls. Some young - some my age. All against their will. Decided I didn't need school if it meant him making more cash, so he withdrew me last week."

"How'd he manage that?"

"Told them I would be homeschooling. The administration knew I had been hospitalized. My father forged a doctor's note and told them it was for health reasons. Psychiatric rehabilitation."

I play with the edge of the sheet and bite my lip. Looking at him, I realize I haven't even asked some basic questions. I fight the fear and lack of trust and take a deep breath.

How do I know he's really with Jude? What if he's a plant from my dad to see how much information I'd give up if asked?

My blood runs cold and I grip the sheet tighter.

"He's trying."

I look at Chad, my eyes shifting and disconnecting my thoughts for a brief second. I wasn't even able to get out a question.

"What?"

"Jude. He's trying. He and Emma both are. People think they're crazy, you know. I was one of them. I think that's why he sent me out here instead of coming himself. Well, that and the risk of your dad finding out."

I shudder at the thought of my dad walking in to find Jude sitting casually on one of the chairs - having a conversation with me. Or worse yet - what would happen if Jude would actually try to rescue me or something.

"Just remind him this isn't a movie, okay? This is my life. I appreciate him trying to help me. Really. I do. But, I can't have him trying anything stupid - the risk of a bad ending is still very possible and with my luck, a given. I can't imagine what would happen if I lost Emma or Jude. They are my life-line."

Chad wrinkles his face and shakes his head.

"Believe me. I've been watching Jude these past few days. Something has gotten into him. He's on the phone non-stop, calling reporters and checking up on leads given to him and running himself ragged." He pierces me with his eyes and I lean back. "He's not resting until you're free."

I blink and try to find the words to respond, but there's nothing. How do you respond to such a claim? I look around the shed and see the dwindling daylight dancing across the inches of dust. The wind's picking up now - blowing debris every which way. Thunder roars in the distance. How I ache for freedom. I want to have hope. I want to buy in to what this man is saying - that Jude and Emma are working hard to get me out - but it's just so hard. Suddenly, it's just all too much. I've managed to hide my tears for days, but the threat of their return comes to me like a dagger to the heart. I gasp for breath and begin weeping.

It never gets old, this crying. I always think I'm over it - always think I've spilled the last tear. And then another reminder - another wrench in the wound - and everything opens up fresh. Chad grabs my hand and we sit like that for awhile - me, clinging to his hand like a life line - as if I'm afraid every ounce of life inside of my heart is seeping away between the tears. I finally catch my breath and he hands me a hankie out of his breast pocket.

"Are you okay?"

"I will be. I always am. I just close my eyes and hope for a new sunrise...I just take one more breath and one more step and keep thinking today is a new day." I pause and look at him, my eyes bent into a permanent question. "I want so badly to be able to be done with this. To look at this moment as a brief glimpse of my history. Why is yesterday still haunting? Why isn't the past letting go? Why are these burdens so terrifying? I feel as though even if I do get rescued - even if I am freed - the process of recovery and just getting my life back will be impossible. How am I supposed to love when I've been through nothing but hate? How am I supposed to trust when I've known nothing but fear?"

I have no idea what it is about Chad that allows me to open up, but I'm taking it. Perhaps it's human contact - another human being looking at me as if I'm worth something - that's allowing me to feel again.

Chad looks at me for a moment and dips his head.

"You know, Stephanie. Life doesn't have to be the absence of good and Holy. It can be enriching and beautiful and glorious and memorable and reckless and intoxicating. It can be love. And I have faith in Emma and Jude's love for you. It's pure and absolutely reckless with protection. You will be free one day, and you will be restored. I have no doubt."

I blow my nose and look at him from between the crease in the hanky.

"You sound like them. Emma and Jude. They always say stuff like that."

"Like...."

"Like....hope stuff. They're who got me to start hoping in a better life in the first place. I won't lie. Sometimes I wonder if it's made everything worse - sometimes living numb is so much easier, you know? I can forget. I can not think about the fact that my life isn't normal - that it shouldn't be like this." I look at him and smile. "Thank you. I needed you coming."

He sighs and looks at his watch.

"I guess I better be going now, huh?"

Standing up, he runs his hands over the pleats of his slacks and glances at me.

"Take care of yourself, Steph."

"I always do."

"That's what I'm afraid of," and grabbing his jacket, he walks out the door.

I stare at the blank space where he left for awhile before resting my head against the pillow and allowing myself to relax. I think back over the day's events. My broken resolve and hopeless outlook quickly changed directions once Chad came to visit - giving me proof people in the outside world were fighting for my freedom. I needed the intervention more than I care to admit.

No more giving up, Stephanie. You've come too far. There is hope.

I hear my dad's boots colliding with the gravel and take a deep breath. I wonder if he saw Chad leaving - if they ran into each other. Would Chad have the ability to make something up on the fly? I start freaking out for a split second before I hear Chad's car roar to life and I know he missed my dad by seconds. My mind reverts back to before Chad - when I remembered I was supposed to be at Kevin's tomorrow. I had been forming this plan all afternoon - a way to get out of his scrutiny and sneak over to Kevin's house for Thanksgiving. I close my eyes and focus. My performance needs to be absolutely flawless in order for me to pull off the deception. I dismiss the disgust lurking in the corner of my mind at what I have to do and listen for my dad's arrival. I hear the squeak of the wooden stairs before the door caves in with his frame.

"You already done?"

"Well, yes. It looks that way."

"That was kinda quick, don't you think? Did you give them what they want? Were they satisfied? I'm not gonna receive no bad reviews, am I?"

He squints at me and shifts his weight, almost as if he's preparing himself to pounce at a moment's notice. A nervous cat - that's what he looks like.

I shrug and raise an eyebrow.

"I mean, they did drive all the way out here, didn't they? I assume they knew what they wanted...and got it. I don't really have much say, Dad."

He snorts and I wrinkle my nose at the chew beginning to leak from his mouth. Again. It's just gross.

"Fine then. Be ready in about ten minutes. We're headed home." He turns around to leave and I make my move - this is my chance.

"Hey, Dad?"

He turns and looks at me.

"What?"

"Um, I was wondering if I could go shopping tomorrow."

Please don't realize it's a holiday.

"Why you wanna go shopping? Didn't you just go with that woman? Emma? Did she not buy you enough clothes?"

I bite the retort forming on my lips - I haven't really been able to wear any of the clothes - or the make-up she bought me. Trapped in this hell hole it's a little hard for me to wear anything but what my dad chooses. Which is the base of this plan I have forming.

"I do have enough clothes. I don't need to buy anything. I was actually thinking about helping you out - giving myself a break but bringing in more revenue for you."

He crosses his arms across his chest and bounces on the balls of his feet.

"What are you talkin' about, Steph? Reve-what?"

He starts flossing with a toothpick he finds in the pocket of his jeans - throwing the lint and leftover chew box on the floor.

I smile at his horrible vocabulary and think of a way to spell it out for him.

"I want to go to the mall. Walk around. Window shop. Maybe meet a few people. Make some friends. Girl friends. And then, when the time is right, you can take them like you always do..."

I glance at him out of the corner of my eye, drawing on every acting skill I never knew I had. I lower my voice and turn away, looking at him over my shoulder.

"You know the drill. More girls - more money. Filipe's mistake in gambling bought you the cheerleading squad, but think of what could happen if we found more girls? Marisol is the only one besides me reaching men outside of the high school. Right?"

He clears his throat.

"I hadn't thought of that."

I shrug my shoulders and sit down on the bed, placing a pillow in my lap as a barrier between me and the monster standing within inches of one wrong move resulting in more bruises. I need to tread carefully here.

"It makes perfect sense. The girls will trust me - I'm their friend. But, unlike the other times where you thought I had no idea you were taking them to your shed, this time I will be the one orchestrating it."

He stands there, watching me, chewing on his toothpick and swaying side to side.

"I like it."

I smile and raise an eyebrow and attempt to not jump up in glee. My dad doesn't know, but he just signed my ticket out of here.

Twenty-Six

I WAKE UP THE NEXT MORNING CURLED UNDERNEATH MY BLANKETS. I know before I even step out of my bed that it's going to be a cold one, so I reach for my robe draped over the chair next to me, the cold air crawling its way up my arms and settling deep in my chest.

"Holy cow it's freezing out here..." I jump up and down, fighting to get the blood moving in my arms and legs, and opt for a hot shower instead. My parents must have conveniently forgotten to turn on the heat last night. It's not until I'm in the shower and the water is thawing out my frozen limbs that I realize this is the first morning in quite awhile my dad didn't wake me. I smile to myself. My plan actually worked. I'm free today - walking out of the house will be no problem at all.

Maybe I will even go see Pacey.

At the thought of my brother my heart sinks against my rib cage and I rub my chest against the spasm. I miss him. And even though I know he's in a safe place - at least - as safe as a make-shift group home can be, I still fear what could happen. I say a silent prayer for his heart and hope he hasn't grown bitter towards me.

I'm coming, Pacey. I haven't forgotten.

I turn the water off as soon as it starts to cool and dry myself off before throwing on my robe. I open the bathroom door and gasp.

"Mom! W-what are you doing? You scared me! That's kind of weird - just standing outside a door..."

Her eyes are glassy. She grabs the door frame with her hand to stay balanced. I watch as her head lulls left to right and she tries to slur words out of her limp mouth.

"You ru-ined ever-thing."

I drop the towel from my head and gently move past her into my room, recognizing her outburst as one I've seen before. I brace for the assumptions thrown my way.

"What are you talking about - you're not making sense."

Her voice rose to a shriek - her eyes wild.

"You!"

She comes barreling towards me and out of pure defense I move out of her way and watch her fall into my dresser, cutting herself on a sharp edge. I go to help her but realize she doesn't even feel it. Looking at me with pure hatred, she picks herself up and walks over to where I am - stuck between the wall and my bed. I contemplate jumping on the bed and maneuvering out of my room, but where would I go then? The last thing I want to do is wake up Dad - remind him of what I could be doing. She starts poking me in the chest with her pointy nails and I flinch every time she breaks skin. I know she's smaller than me. I know I can simply push her down - but I just can't. She's my mom, and she's inebriated, and for some reason...I recognize her hopelessness. I grab her by the shoulders and look her in the eye.

"Mom."

I snap my fingers and force her to look at me. Her lip curls and she tries to fight my embrace, hollering about me ruining everything. Again.

"You took my man from me...you slut. He's your father. What do you guys do all day? Huh? What's in the shed out back? You think I'm stupid? You think I don't see those men coming and going? Whore. I don't even see any of the money. Whatdya do with all that money, slut?! It's because of you he's gone. You took my baby. I miss him...Pacey."

Her voice breaks and we collapse on the floor - her head in my lap and my heart threatening to burst. I close my eyes and begin rocking her back and forth - just like she used to do for me before she lost her job. Before she started drinking. Before she hated me because of what Dad was doing. I sit there for about thirty minutes before she falls asleep - drooling and flinching at imaginary dreamworlds. I quietly move out from under her and get dressed. I want nothing to do with this house right now. I don't want to think about the fact that my mom - who I thought had been completely oblivious to it all - knows exactly what's been going on....and she still chooses to do nothing. She blames me, instead.

I need out - desperately. I throw on the nearest pair of jeans and a hoodie and grab my scarf and gloves on my way out the door. I hear my mother protest but I think nothing of it. For today - I'm through. Just for a little while, I want to pretend to be someone else entirely. I walk out the door and into the brisk morning air and make my way to Kevin's house.

It doesn't take me long. Although his neighborhood looks completely different from mine, it's only on the other side of the street. I walk up to his front door - shaking. It's been awhile since I've seen him. I close my eyes against the nerves and knock on the door - noticing the Happy Thanksgiving!

decor hanging on the wooden beams.

His mom answers wearing a white cashmere sweater and grey leggings. She looks no older than thirty - although I know she has to be at least forty. I smile and hold out my hand.

"Hi, Mrs. Matouse. I'm Stephanie. It's so nice to meet you."

She glances me over and leaves my hand hanging in mid-air. Turning around, she calls for Kevin and glances back at me - her eyebrow raised - before walking back into what I assume is the kitchen.

Well, that was awkward.

I brush off my misgivings and peek in around the door for Kevin - I hear him running down the stairs and I smile. He jerks open the door and greets me with a huge hug and a peck on the cheek. Pulling me into the house, I am hit instantly with the delicious smells of cooking turkey and fresh pies. My stomach rumbles and I realize it's been days since I last ate.

"I didn't know if you were going to make it or not."

I push against his chest so I can look in his eyes.

"I know - I'm sorry I didn't respond to your texts. I've been...busy."

His face clouds over and he shakes his head. Whispering, he leans in and looks me in they eye.

"You can always run away, Stephanie. You can always..."

I cut him off.

"I'm not that person today, okay? I'm someone different... someone who doesn't deal with her worst nightmare or who has problems trusting." I smile. "I'm normal. No baggage. At least for today. I need to be normal."

He smiles and places his hand behind my head, drawing me back into his embrace.

"Absolutely. For today, you are normal. Which reminds me of something. I wanna take you somewhere."

His eyes glint mischievously and I back up, raising my

hand as a warning.

"Um...last time I remember you taking me somewhere resulted in us running for our lives against a train." I quiet my voice at his earnest glance towards his mom in the kitchen and I lean forward so he can hear me. "Not too keen on surprises right now."

"Trust me - this one is a good one." He raises his eyebrows and chuckles. "Come on - it will be..."

"...let me guess - an adventure?"

I finish his sentence and his mom clears her throat in the kitchen. I follow the sound and find her standing behind the counter, hands on her hips - staring at us.

"Where are you planning on going, Kevin? Dinner will be ready soon."

He walks over to her and places his arms around her shoulders, pulling her close to him.

"I know, Mom - it won't take long at all. We'll be gone for about an hour."

She smiles at him and turns her gaze towards me - her eyes resolute. I can't help but feel as though she is casting judgment my way. Almost as if she's already made a decision. I think back to the conversation with Kevin at the dam and wrap my arms around my chest protectively and turn away.

"I'll wait for you outside, Kevin."

I call out to the mother and son - still standing in the same spot, conversing with their eyes. I see Kevin nod and follow me.

"I'm right behind you, Steph."

"Please be careful, Kevin. I'll see you guys when you get home."

His mom hollers after us and I hear Kevin chuckle again as he meets up with me, wrapping a scarf around his neck and rubbing his hands together for warmth. He looks over at me and winks.

"I've missed you."

He grabs my hand and kisses the knuckle. My heart sings at the simple and unexpected touch.

"I've missed you. Where are we going?"

I notice he turns toward Emma's house and I look at him questioningly. He curls his lips conspiratorially and taps a few keys on his cell phone.

"Huh? What was that?"

He looks at me as if he's heard nothing. I hit his arm.

"Don't play dumb with me. You've got something up your sleeve. Why are we headed to Emma's?"

"Just wait."

He grabs my hand again and places it between the crook of his arm.

"Have you been okay, Stephanie? I know you wanna feel normal today - but I need to know. Have you been okay? Every one at school is worried about you. Your dad said you withdrew for medical reasons?"

I nod my head.

"Yeah. He did. Psychiatric. Said I would be homebound for the rest of the year. And it was a lie - obviously. I haven't seen anyone from the school come to the house with assignments or news from my teachers."

I stare straight ahead and notice the sky begin to change colors, the line of iridescent clouds growing more vibrant and alive by the minute. I take a deep breath and let the beauty and warmth seep into my chest. It's been awhile since I've seen anything worth inspiration. I make a mental note of words collapsing against the walls of my mind and glance again at Kevin.

"I've been okay. I'm surviving - that's pretty much all I can hope for right now."

"Hope is a powerful thing."

I smile as he squeezes my hand.

"I know, Kevin. It's just remembering that power. Knowing how to tap into it. That's the hard part. And I had a visitor the other day that reminded me of everything worth fighting for - reminded me that there are others fighting on my behalf."

He turns his head and looks at me,

"A visitor? Who? How did anyone manage to get past your father?"

I smile at the memory.

"Jude sent someone. Bought an hour through the website and sent a lawyer who didn't believe him when he tried to tell him my story. Told me I needed to remember hope - that there was good in the world. And then he told me that Jude was fighting to get me out of there."

"It's true. Everything he said is true. Emma and Jude have been working nonstop. I've been over there watching Benjamin while they talk on the phone and meet with local representatives. You can't forget that we're over here fighting for you, trying to figure out ways to catch your dad."

We walk in silence the rest of the way - each lost in our own thoughts. My mind wanders back to Kevin's mom and I wonder if I've finally said too much - if my authenticity has moved its way toward her in their conversations. I can't help but think she sees me as second-rate. Used. Tarnished. Second best. I glance up at Emma's house and a slow grin spreads across my face. I had forgotten just how much I missed them. My pace quickens as I run up the stairs and burst through the door.

"Emma? Jude? Where are you guys?"

I turn circles in the living room looking for them, listening for sounds of where they could be. As I'm turning, I notice a remote control airplane stashed in the corner. I walk up to it and pick it up, inspecting the handiwork. It's one of those fancy ones - where you have to put it together before you are even able to fly the thing. It reminds me of Pacey.

"Pacey wanted one of these for Christmas."

Kevin clears his throat and I turn around - Emma is standing there, her arms around Kevin and tears threatening to spill down her cheeks. I laugh.

"Good grief, woman. I'm here, okay? I'm alive. Don't be so dramatic."

I run over to her and throw my arms around her waist. I smell a mixture of fresh cookie dough, baby lotion and turkey stuffing. It smells like home would smell.

"I have something to show you, Steph."

Emma glances at Kevin and grabs my hand. She walks me up the stairs and stops in front of a door at the back of the hall - it's always been Jude's office so I've stayed away. I look at Emma and then Kevin for some kind of clue and reach for the door handle. Emma stops me.

"Wait. Before you go in there - I need you to know something."

I look at her confused, my heart starting to race at the seriousness etched in Emma's eyes. I've seen her intent on something - but never this cautious.

"What is it?"

I feel Jude's hands on my shoulders and I look at him - tears welling up in his eyes.

"Hey, Steph. Good to see you."

My eyes light up and I lean against him for a split second before looking back towards Emma. I hear Jude clear his throat and Emma catch his eye. Looking back towards Jude I see him whisper something to Emma but I can't catch the words. Kevin tightens his grasp on my hand.

"Okay guys - seriously. What's going on?! Are you just going to stand here whispering code words to each other or are you going to fill me in?"

I snatch my hand from Kevin's hold and cross my arms

for emphasis. I stare at Emma until she folds. I know she can't ever keep anything from me - it's one of the things I love about our relationship. No secrets.

"Before you open the door, Stephanie - just remember there was no way for us to let you know. We definitely didn't want to do it through a text message. And, this doesn't change anything about us trying to get you out of your situation or the fact that we love you."

"Okay."

I say, hesitantly. I'm really not sure what to expect when I open the door. I glance back at Kevin and he smiles reassuringly. Jude squeezes my shoulder and I move to turn the knob. I hear the click of the lock and the door swings open against my weight. I wrinkle my forehead at the change. What use to be Jude's office is now a bedroom. Blue paint lines the walls and someone painted a mural of airplanes flying in between huge clouds. A bookshelf leans against the opposite wall and books already lay on the shelves - I see the complete set of Harry Potter before anything else. And then my head moves towards the bed. It's small. Twin size. But big enough for a little boy. My breath catches as a head peaks out of the covers.

"Sissy?"

I've lost all control of my emotions. I run towards the bed and grab Pacey and pull him close to me as he buries his head in my chest.

"Sissy, I've missed you! Where you been?"

His voice is raspy - thick with sleep. My tears fall on his hair and I just sit there - rocking him. Emma comes and sits next to me, wrapping her arms around me.

"As soon as we heard the news, Jude made a few phone calls and we set ourselves up as his foster parents. We couldn't imagine you two being separated. More importantly, we couldn't imagine him dealing with some of the people he would have had he stayed in the system."

She places her hand on my face and turns me toward her - forcing me to look her in the eyes.

"Please say something."

I lean my cheek against Pacey's forehead and marvel at how relaxed he is - how comfortable he seems here in Emma and Jude's house. Almost like he belongs. He's already fallen back asleep against my shoulder.

"Emma...I don't even know where to begin. I mean, he's my brother. I've been so worried about him and where he'd end up - I thought he was in some home all this time."

I glance at her again and notice the fear falling into her gaze and I smile to ease the tension.

"But honestly? I can't imagine him anywhere else. You guys are incredible..."

I kiss his head again and lay him down with no protest. He snuggles against a huge stuffed animal propped up against him and starts to snore. I lean in to Emma and give her a huge hug.

"Thank you."

She sniffs and rests her chin on my head - the roles reversed from when I was holding Pacey a few seconds ago.

"You're welcome, but we have you to thank."

I lean back and stare at her like she's crazy.

"What?"

"Stephanie, if it weren't for you coming into our life like a freight train, none of this would have happened. We have you to thank. Because of you - we're reminded of the beautiful moments of life. We're reminded of hope. We're reminded of strength within tragedy. You're an inspiration to us. To me."

I stare at her - my mouth open but no words coming out. There's nothing to say. In the space of an hour, these people have once again shattered all of my expectations. I glance at my brother again, sleeping peacefully for the first time in who knows how long, and I catch Kevin's eye.

"I love you guys. All of you. I don't deserve what you do for me."

Emma smiles and kisses my cheek, and Jude and Kevin join us in a family embrace - all of the people who bring me life reviving me in a way none of them realize. For those few moments, I feel alive again.

Twenty-Seven

WE MAKE OUR WAY DOWNSTAIRS AND EMMA PULLS OUT SOME FRESHLY made cookies. I smile and take one from the bowl.

"You are so predictable." I tease.

She laughs and shrugs her shoulders.

"What can I say? Sometimes you need predictability."

Winking, she motions for us to sit at the table and glances at her husband with a smile.

"So, tell me. How did you guys manage to find Pacey? I want to know everything."

Jude rests his elbows on the counter and looks at me.

"It was relatively easy for us to find and request Pacey. We were licensed last year in foster care but hadn't accepted any kids because of Benjamin. I want you to know - your brother is considered a legal risk foster care child. We're in this to adopt and in all likelihood your brother will be available for adoption, but there are still a few things that could happen that would prevent it. CPS is first and foremost for the reunification of a family."

I laugh.

"Even ours? Doubtful."

He smiles and nods his head.

"Yes, Steph. Even yours. The good news is that Pacey will be with us until anything else happens. He is on track to become permanently adopted within our family. They won't take him out for another placement. You are another story though, girl."

I look at him in between bites and lower my eyebrows.

"What do you mean?"

"Well, you're 17. That's old in the foster care system. It's why they didn't take you from the house the night CPS showed up. Not knowing there was a family ready and willing, they opted to keep you within your own biological setting. Better for a child to stay with his or her parents then age out of the system with nothing."

I roll my eyes.

"So glad they want to protect us."

Jude and Emma chuckle and Kevin hides a smirk. Emma rests her hand on my arm and tilts her head towards me.

"Regardless, Steph. You are welcome here. We've said this before and we will say it again. As far as we are concerned, this is your home."

I squeeze her hand and fight back tears for the second time in less than an hour.

"Thank you guys. Really. You have no idea how worried I've been about Pacey and where he's been and who was taking care of him..."

I sigh and let the worry visibly leave my face. I shake my head and look at both Emma and Jude - my real life angels.

"I love you two. Pacey couldn't be in better hands."

Our visit is cut short when Kevin's phone rings. His smile shifts as soon as he answers and he catches my eye.

"It's my mom" he whispers and I nod.

A strange misgiving making its home in the pit of my stomach. I try and listen as Emma and Jude catch me up on everything that's happened, but I'm distracted by Kevin. His voice is...different.

"Mom, Mom...I know...I know..," his voice is short and quiet - at the point of frustration.

He turns and winks at me before walking out of the room to continue talking. Before I can even focus again he's back, and holding the phone out for me.

"You didn't tell me this. I can't believe you didn't let me know. Mom, it's doesn't matter. I don't care wha -" his voice catches and he hands me the phone with an apologetic turn of his lips, "Uh, Steph...my mom wants to talk to you."

My eyes grow wide and I shake my head.

"Kevin...no! What? Why?"

My whispers are urgent. Talking to his mom? My mind shoots back to earlier in the day - her cold stare and refusal to shake my hand. Suddenly I am very, very nervous. He shrugs his shoulder and mouths, "sorry" before motioning with the phone again. I wipe my hands on my jeans and glance at Kevin before taking the phone. His eyes tell me nothing and he shakes his head against Emma and Jude's questioning stares.

"Hello?"

"Ah. Yes. Hello, Stephanie. I hope I don't ruin a surprise, but Kevin was going to take you ice-skating at the local pond. Of course, he took you to Emma and Jude's first - but that was his choice. I need him home. His father has some last minute guests for dinner and we need Kevin to help prepare. I know you will understand."

My eyes shift towards Kevin and I smile, "Not at all, Mrs. Matouse. We can come back now. We'll be there in less than ten minutes."

I squeeze his hand and reach to give Emma a hug good-bye while finishing my conversation with Kevin's mom. Jude waves as we make our way to the door. Bracing myself against the cold wind, I snuggle into Kevin's embrace and walk the sidewalk, staying away from frozen puddles. Mrs. Matouse's voice took on a different chord - almost protective - and I pause.

"That's another thing. Well...." she pauses and I sense a shift. I stop walking completely and wait for the rest, the cell phone hot against my ear.

"When we invited you over we didn't really know about your situation. Kevin always had such an incredible taste in girls, we trust him implicitly when he says he's found some-one special. We have no doubt you are indeed someone spe-cial, but unfortunately, not for my son. I mean, you two are so different. So different - don't you see?" She clears her throat and continues while I fight for balance against my world crashing around me, "I worry about Kevin getting involved with someone like you because he likes to think he can save people. He likes to think he rescue them from circumstances. I just want more for him. Again. I know you will understand."

My heart crashes against itself and I stumble to the curb to sit down.

"I'm sorry...what did you say?"

I glance at Kevin and he reads my expression. Concerned, he walks over and sits next to me, watching my face and wait-ing for me to say something. I hold up my hand and motion for him to wait just a second - the walls already beginning to form in my heart - his mom breaks in and starts talking again.

"Let me put it this way, Stephanie. The company coming over are long-time family friends. They have a daughter. She's going to Princeton in the fall. Don't worry, you wouldn't know her, she goes to a local private school. What I'm trying to say here is this is the type of girl Kevin needs to get involved with

- you're seniors. Almost graduated. It's time to get serious, now. Time to stop playing games. This is life - this is my son's life. And to be brutally honest, I question whether he has feelings for you or whether he just feels sorry for your lot in life."

I close my eyes against the whirlwind. I hang up the phone without even responding and pass it back to Kevin. His eyebrows shift in confusion as I move myself to stand directly in front of him. I grab his hands and bring them to my lips - kissing his knuckles and fighting the tears. The thoughts fight themselves in my mind.

I should have known. I should have known it would end this way. There are a handful of people who love me - but everyone else sees what's really there. Trash.

"What just happened there? What did she say? Whatever it was - whatever made you this upset - Steph, just don't worry about her. We'll go brave the dinner together."

I ignore his words and sniff back the tears already forming.

"Kevin, there are no words for all you have done these past few months. No words. You have shown me love, protection, adventure and life. You've made me believe there's a world out there where I can exist as a normal person and not some shell of what I could be - but it's not reality."

I place my finger on his lips to stop him from speaking.

"I'm not good enough for you, Kevin. I never will be. You deserve someone pure and beautiful and talented - someone not ripe with baggage from her abusive father. I'm not going to hold you back. I won't." I tilt my face towards his and standing on my tiptoes, kiss his forehead. "Please don't follow me. I know what I'm doing. Your mom thinks you're on your way home - alone. She made it clear I wasn't to be with you and I can't help but agree."

I step away and wipe the tears falling from off my cheek, and avoiding his gaze I turn around and walk away from love. It's not until I turn the corner down the street that I chance a glance back in his direction. He's still standing there, hands in his pockets, frozen to the ground. I close my eyes against the memories of the past few months and hold my hand against my chest as if to keep my heart from falling out of its socket. Behind him the sun blazes pink against the storm clouds moving in from the west. I suddenly think of Natalie back at the hospital and laugh.

What about these storm clouds, huh? Is the sun enough for these storm clouds? Because really...this rescue I'm promised is looking pretty grim.

Rain starts falling frozen from the sky. I lift my face and accept the sharpness of the rain scraping against my skin like broken glass.

I walk through my front door soaking wet and shivering. The house is dark and quiet - but I know this means nothing. Quietly making my way through the living room, I eye my surroundings before turning down the hallway towards the bathroom. I shut the door behind me and turn on the shower - letting the steam overtake my senses. Only then, under the warmth of the water caressing my skin, do I let myself cry. My body shakes with force as I realize what I've just done. My mind battles lies deeply embedded into the cracks of my soul.

You are worth nothing. No one will ever want you.

I collapse into a heap in the corner of the bathtub and let the water rinse off any hope I feel. Just like I do after any guy who pays to see me, I scrub and rinse and wash some more until there is no trace left of Kevin. My skin turns red and raw from the heat, but I just stay there - right now, it's my only protection against the war raging in my heart.

I stay until the water turns cold. Grabbing my robe, I

shelter myself against the frigid air and shudder when my feet hit the icy tile. Slowly I open the bathroom door, half expecting my mom to be waiting for me again. Once I realize the path is clear, I make my way to my room, shut the door and get under the covers. My eyes grow heavy and I refuse to fight against the exhaustion. I close my eyes and images of the day come rushing back, but I have nothing left to fight them. Small tears run down my cheeks and I say a silent prayer for Kevin. The only solace I have is knowing Pacey is safe.

Twenty-Eight

I WAKE TO MY DAD'S ROAR ECHOING AGAINST THE WALLS. I SLOWLY OPEN my eyes and squint at the sun shining between the blinds. Again, I search my mind to figure out what my dad could be hollering about, but find nothing. It's Friday, which typically means a late start. I reach for my phone to see the time and come up with empty space on my nightstand. My heart drops.

Where's my phone?

As if on cue, the thunder of my dad's voice grows closer. His words fall on me with clarity. My phone - it was in my pocket of my jeans, which I left in the bathroom last night after my shower. Text messages, Emma and Jude's personal number - everything. My dad would know everything. I wait for his wrath - his footsteps growing closer by the second. Memories of hiding underneath blankets resurface as I find myself inching further and further underneath the covers. I contemplate escaping out my window but know there's no way I could find clothes in time and he'd only catch me.

The only thing I can do is wait. I hear his cussing. I hear him crashing through the hall. I shudder at what may happen when he gets to my room...

It doesn't take long for me to find out. He kicks through my door and rips my covers off the bed. I curl up in a ball, protecting myself with my arms and trying to shield my body from the blows I know will come. Even with the preparation, my body never knows what hit her. Stunned with pain and instant smashing of skin against skin, everything is a blur. He pulls me from my bed and climbs on top of me, his breathing ragged and hands shaking with overdose. I catch a glimpse of his eyes for a brief second and see not a human, but a monster.

"Thought you could get away with this, huh? Thought you could go behind my back and still talk to those good-for-nothin' people who can't keep their nose out of our business? I told you. I told you to leave them be. I'll show them. Just wait. Just. You. Wait."

Each sentence is capped with a fist, each breath taken with a swing. My left eye, swollen shut from his elbow, throbs. It wasn't until the phone rings that he stops, breathless with rage. A slow smile spread across his face as he looked at the screen.

"Well lookie who it is."

I gingerly raise one of my hands - trying to get him to not answer - to maybe grab the phone from his grasp. He just laughs and slaps my hand hard against the floor. As he walks out the door into the hallway I can hear him taunting Emma. She probably called because Kevin let them know about me breaking up with him last night. I'm sure she's shocked and wondering what really happened. *Reality is what happened, Emma.*

"Hello? Yeah that's right. This is Steph's father. And I know who you are without needing to ask. And I'll tell ya another thing - you're gonna stay the hell away from her."

The curse words start flowing then, and I can hear the hate ricocheting off the four walls of my room. With the drums pounding in my head, I whisper a prayer for strength but receive nothing. For the first time, I know - my rescue isn't coming.

Welcome to your life, Stephanie. Get use to the hell.

I don't know when I fell back asleep, but I wake up to a kick in the ribs.

"Get up. You have work to do."

I rub my eyes and slowly gain my surroundings. Still on the floor, I notice the scene from a few hours before totally trashed my room. I grimace at the thought of cleaning and then moan at the protest of my muscles trying to move. My dad stands within inches from my face and leaning down, he pulls me to a sitting position by my hair. My eyes water with pain and I avoid his gaze. My voice cracks with the dryness in my throat.

"Work? Dad...you're not even going in today."

He leans over and grabs the back of my hair and twists my face so I'm eye-to-eye with him. It looks like he hasn't slept in ages. Dark circles etch deep into his cheekbones. His eyes are blood shot from the drugs he took earlier. He curls his lip in disgust as he looks me up and down.

"Since you didn't go to the mall yesterday, we're going to take a little trip today. It's the perfect day anyway - everyone'll be shopping for Christmas." He tosses a ***Day after Thanksgiving!*** sale ad and it hit my face before I can grab it to take a look. "You'll be finding me some girls whether you like it or not, ya hear?"

My heart sinks and I fight for words. My eyes focus on the ad and I remember yesterday. Kevin - his mom - seeing Emma and Jude and then having my father find my phone given to me by them only to have them call. Trying to speak, my throat constricts and I start coughing. Gasping for air, I push my way to the bathroom. I stagger like a fawn newly born breaking in its legs. Crashing against the doorframe, I wince and notice a black and blue bruise forming along my shoulder and upper arm. Something inside clicks and I remember my father's strong hands gripping me with a brutality I've never experienced. I almost make it to the toilet before dry-heaving from the memories.

"Oh don't try and play sick. It don't matter anyways - you're comin' whether you're upchucking or rosy faced." He walks in next to me and a towel falls at my feet. "Clean yourself up while you're in here. You look disgusting."

I cringe when he touches my cheek - running his finger along my jawline. "You know, you use to be a pretty girl. Worth somethin' - worth paying attention to and worth someone's time." He smiles and shakes his head. "You're nothin' but a whore now."

It's not until he retreats and shuts the door that the tears find their way down my cheeks. I stumble back into the room and notice the paper strewn haphazardly across my floor. The front page faces upward and once again I'm struck cold by a headline. I walk in slow motion and pick it up, my heart already beating an unsteady rhythm against my ribs.

Body of Local Girl Found, Authorities Believe Suicide

Late last evening, authorities found the body of Marisol Venedez in an abandoned hotel room. She returned home a few weeks ago after running away, silencing reports that she may have been forced to cross state lines in a prostitution ring. She disappeared again this past Monday and authorities have been looking for her ever since.

Due to the empty pill bottles and liquor found in the hotel room, authorities are limiting foul play. No suicide note was found. Venedez' father has remained surprisingly quiet since finding the body and her friends, those interviewed for the article about her last disappearance, opted out of being questioned.

Counselors have been meeting with students at the high school and are able to make appointments with parents if requested. Services will be held at St. Mary's on Tuesday.

The article is short - most of the space taken up with pictures of her cheering, the hotel where she was found and one of her returning home a few weeks ago, wearing the same outfit as when she came to visit me in the hospital.

My body goes weak as I think of the implications of what I just read. Without a doubt, I know Marisol didn't kill herself. Without a doubt, I know my dad was somehow involved. A hot brick settles in the back of my throat and refuses to budge. I can't help but wonder what she did to provoke this anger. I scan the article again to look for any news of a coroner's report, but find nothing. I wouldn't be surprised if Dad paid off the journalist to conveniently leave out the truth.

There really is no stopping what he'll do in order to get what he wants, I think. And as the reality of this hits me square in the chest, I feel an iciness to my veins - the blood running cold in terror and fear.

I startle when I hear footsteps behind me. Turning around I see my dad, leaning against the doorframe of my room. His face is wrapped in a smile revealing the sickest of emotions.

"I see you found the article. It's such a shame, really. Marisol was such a pretty girl. I had no idea she was so troubled."

I look at him and my eyes darken. The words fall out of my mouth before I can hold them in.

"What did you do to her?"

His eyebrows raise and he pushes himself off toward me. I swallow and wonder what I just started. If I even want to know the answer to my own question. I think back to all the times I've opened my mouth when I shouldn't - the marks and the bruises I suffered. I raise my chin in defiance. *If he does beat me, I'll take it for Marisol. For all the other girls he's used.*

It may seem naive, but it's my logic in the moment it takes for me to realize I've pushed a button. With my father? You have to be ready for anything. I brace myself for the worst and hold his gaze. He walks over and sits on the edge of my bed.

"Me? Oh. I didn't do anything. You read the article. She committed suicide. Took pills."

The glint in his eyes tells me more than I ever wanted to know. I wrinkle my lips and fight from spitting.

"I don't believe you."

"Well. Perhaps you'd believe Joey? I could always call him over to have him explain. He's always loved you the most, you know. Always watches you." He studies me and the smile wavers for a split second before he continues, "Anyways. I know Marisol always had difficulty believing things I said. Always needed to get Joey to help her understand. That's what he was doing for me before she offed herself. I sent him to let her know the cheerleaders would no longer be servicing just football players. They'd had enough practice and I needed them for...other projects. She seemed to want to fight me on it - seemed as if she was trying to protect those whores or somethin' - as if wearing those short skirts weren't enough of an invitation."

He laughs and chokes on his chew. I freeze and blink my

eyes in surprise, not sure where to go from here. I think back on my morning and realize this is why Emma called. She'd read the paper and called to warn me. Probably to tell me to run.

My dad leans over and grabs the back of my hair, pulling me up with him to a standing position. His breath is ragged and the stench of alcohol and tobacco washes over me.

"So I'll say it again. Get dressed, sweetheart. We got business to do today. We're shy a girl and I need a replacement."

We get to the mall less than an hour later and before we can even walk through the doors I feel hands on my arms.

"Stephanie?"

I turn to catch the voice and force a smile.

"Hi, Mrs. Peabody. How are you? How was your Thanksgiving?"

She hesitates and smiles while glancing toward my dad. He notices and reaches his hand to grab my own - squeezing it unnaturally in the process. I bite my lip to keep from reacting while trying to avoid the people rushing into the store to grab their last minute deals. I look around before settling on a spot a few feet away from the entrance and attached to my father, make my way with Mrs. Peabody away from the crowd. I mentally run through reminders on how to act normal - smile, look her in the eye, ask questions...

"My Thanksgiving was wonderful; I spent it with family. But, dear - how are you? We've missed you in English. The rumor is you're sick? I've been giving the home-bound teacher papers to send to you but haven't gotten anything back."

I open my mouth but my dad interjects before I can say anything, "Excuse me miss - it was nice of you to stop and chat but we're on a schedule." He smiles and lets go of my hand just long enough to reach it out for Mrs. Peabody to introduce herself. "We're trying to get some Christmas shopping done and this is the only time we can escape our house without her mom suspecting anything."

Mrs. Peabody lifts her chin with understanding and catches my gaze before allowing my dad a smile in return.

"Well, sir - it's a pleasure to meet you." Turning to me she winks, "Hope to hear some good news from you soon, young lady. I hear USC just sent out their letters of intent." And with that, she turns and walks towards her car.

My father squeezes my arm while muttering under his breath, "Why would you be expectin' a letter of intent?"

I stutter from the pain of him squeezing my bruise and force myself to look in his eyes and shrug.

"I-I-I have no idea. It's Mrs. Peabody, Dad. She's crazy sometimes."

"Well, apparently." He snorts and spits some chew dangerously close to my shoe. "I mean, she thought you'd be able to get into college. She's gotta be crazy."

I fight the resentment building - the loss of dreams and the beach scene falling away with the winter wind slapping my face. I shrug my shoulders and act nonchalant.

"It's whatever," I say as I push around him and into the store, hoping he won't immediately follow.

Attached to my father isn't my best idea of a day at the mall.

He catches up to me midway through Dillard's and I throw him a withering glance when he grunts approval at the assortment of negligées and lingerie hanging from racks. He stops at one and I feel a stone form in the pit of my stomach.

"Hey Steph come over here for a sec."

I look around with horror to see if anyone noticed my dad beckoning me towards a red get-up complete with uncomfortable bows and ribbons placed conveniently around the lacking fabric. No one. The busiest shopping day of the year and there's no one around. Perfect.

He turns and threatens me with his eyes, and I move quickly to where he's now shifting through the different sizes. Looking at me again, he pulls one off the rack.

"This seems to be your size, right?"

I stare at him disbelievingly before I hear a throat clear behind me.

"Can I help you two with something?"

I turn quickly, too quickly, because I recognize the voice. It's her. The girl from outside the school. My face goes pale and I see the recognition flash quickly in her eyes before she plasters a smile on for my father. I can't even remember how long it's been since I've seen her, but...it's her. I know it. She's...changed. Neat. Clean. Her hair is combed and her nails, once filled with dirt and cracking, are manicured. I catch myself staring and my dad elbows me in the ribs.

"Um...we were uh...just looking for my mom." I shift my gaze quickly to her and then just as fast move them to study my fingernails. Again.

She scratches above her ear and the space in between her eyebrows crease for a split second before she pushes past me and focuses on my father, but not before surreptitiously tweaking me on the arm with her fingers. I catch her gaze and she moves her lips while my dad's staring at some teen girls in a nearby section.

Dressing room.

He turns right as her message reaches me and I bite my lip to keep from showing anything on my face. She starts laying on the saleswoman pitch pretty thick for my father, and points him to some pretty expensive floor length silk sleepers. He's not buying it, though. His gaze keeps going back to the more revealing teddies lining the wall. Not caring how weird it sounds or awkward it seems to other people passing by, I walk over to a bright blue number and find my size.

"This'll work for mom, dad - but let me try it on just to make sure."

Something shifts in his eyes and I turn to find a mom with her daughter, looking aghast at my comment. I smile and shrug.

"We're the same size. Makes it easy."

The mom nods but her uneasiness is unchanged. Good. Maybe she'll be so unsettled she'll do something. Raising an eyebrow I scan the store to see where the dressing rooms are before motioning to my father where I'm headed. He slips me a camera and I know his intent. My stomach churns and my shoulders automatically go tense when I walk past him and feel a pat on my rear end. I know without even turning around the look on my father's face. I hide a smile knowing I have my own little secret in the works. For a brief moment, what lay immediately before me wasn't as overwhelming as what I knew I would have to face.

Twenty-Nine

I HAVE MORE THAN ONE THING GOING FOR ME: BEING A WOMEN'S DRESS-ing room, men were stationed outside. This gave me ample time to breathe as well as a safe space to meet with the girl who disappeared so long ago. I close my eyes and focus - not believing my luck.

Perhaps this is it! Perhaps this is my rescue.

She comes almost immediately.

"Are you in here?"

I hear her whisper and I motion which stall by sticking my hand above the door. I open it a crack before she walks in and sits down on the chair. Before I even know it, the tears are starting to fall. I don't even try to stop them. She studies my face and plays with the edges of her hair.

"How long has this been going on?"

Her question is pointed, her eyebrows raised and her hands moved from her hair and tapping an unsteady rhythm on the arms crossed over her chest.

I sniff, taken aback by the suddenness of her question. "What? I mean...I don't understand. I don't even know you outside a conversation a couple months go where you totally unleashed on me and now you're asking me a question about how long something's been going on? I don't even know your name."

I feel indignant. Outside of Emma, no one ever pays such close attention to me. No one ever spots the warning signs. Or, if they do, they take the route of my pre-Cal teacher and the lady out shopping with her daughter: denial.

"It's Kristi."

"What?"

"My name. It's Kristi. Now what the hell is going on with that guy out there? Is he really your dad? And how long have you been held captive?"

Her last question is a statement and forces me to choke on my words. I sit there staring at her for a few minutes and she waits, a small smile playing on her lips. It's obvious I'm not going anywhere without coming up with some kind of answer.

"He's really my dad," I whisper.

Her head pops back in encouragement.

I glance at the door - wishing for escape and feeling incredible awkward. Staring at the latch I suddenly remember the last time I was in a dressing room, laughing with Emma about Kevin and feeling carefree and beautiful. A tear falls unwillingly down my cheek and I swat at it, poking my eye in the process.

"I'm not a captive," I say under my breath.

A curse flies out of her mouth as she raises an eyebrow.

"You're lying."

Her language surprises me. My eyes go wild for a split second and I take a quick breath at the smile playing on her lips. Something inside me recognizes the quiet chaos in her words - I feel a warning start to go off in the back of my mind but I ignore it - ignore the timing, the change in mood, everything about seeing her. I feel the anger grow again and my finger finds refuge in pointing dangerously close to her face.

"You don't know the first thing about me,"

"Oh yeah? What's on the camera?"

Her head moves toward the camera dangling from my arm and I silently curse. I'd completely forgotten I strapped it there to keep it from falling. Which begged the question: why do I always try and protect my father? This camera gets out and he's immediately guilty with a number of crimes. It'd be over. A sudden thought pops in my head and my stomach twists, repulsed by the idea.

Oh God. Do I want to be here? In some sick universe do I enjoy captivity?

I sink to the ground and pass the camera to Kristi. She turns it on and doesn't last very long before her breath grows ragged. I lift my head to try and see her reaction. A sick smile is playing on her lips and I feel my stomach start to turn. Something's wrong. I gather my strength and use the wall behind me to stand upright, reaching for the latch on the door as secretly as possible. A cough in a nearby stall captures Kristi's attention and her head jerks up just in time to see me fumbling with the door. She slams into me and pins me against the mirror.

"Oh no, sweetheart. You aren't going anywhere." Her voice is sing-songy and her eyes seem distant. She leans in and whispers in my ear, "Your dad told me you'd try to fight."

She starts to giggle then while reaching for buttons on my shirt. I rear back and slap her as hard as I can on the face, leaving her cheek red and swollen. She steps back in shock and I burst from the door, mad with confusion and rage. I thought I could trust her. I thought she was clean because she escaped. I thought she was like me. I guess I was wrong.

I don't even see my dad blocking the entrance to the dressing room and I run straight into him, staggering back and losing my balance, I fall to the floor. He turns and catches my gaze and smiles.

"So it went well with Kristi?"

My face darkens and I trip over my limbs to stand up again. "You. Are. Evil. Evil. What kind of father does this," I wave my arms around, motioning to my body, "to his daughter? What kind of father gets her involved in getting other girls? A good-for-nothing man, that's who. You call me a waste of space? You're a waste of humanity. You have no soul. No emotion. You just seek your own pleasure and that's sick." I wipe my nose on the back of my hand and run toward him, beating his chest with my hands. "You're sick. Sick. I hate you. Hate you!"

My throat hurts from screaming and my head still pounds from the pressure. It's not until security pulls me away from my father that I realize how loud I was yelling. There's a group of people gathering - uneasy at my display. My face is red, and I breathe deep to shallow my breathing. Kristi steps around me, holding her cheek. "Gentlemen, this is my sister. She's...not feeling well. Thank you for coming but we can take it from here."

One of the officers looks at me and my welly eyes, still trying to catch my breath, and turns to Kristi reluctantly.

"Are you sure, miss? Did she hit you?"

Her head dips with false gentleness and she hides a smile, "Yes...but like I said - she's not well. I was helping her with trying on some clothes and she got angry with an outfit I chose for her and started to hit me." Shrugging her shoulders she looked around at the audience forming. "It's all really quite embarrassing. My father and I will take it from here, though. It's really best."

And just like that, the officer loosens his hold and hands me back over to my abusers. The irony isn't lost on me that those who choose to go into a profession where they protect others often hand-deliver people to the biggest perpetrators out there. Like this girl.

I watch their retreating figures and rub the raw spot on my arm where Kristi's nails dug in to my skin earlier in the dressing room. Breathing deep through my nose, I close my eyes and hope to open them with no one staring - my dad and Kristi not standing next to each other gloating. I catch Kristi eyeing a teenage girl looking through a rack of clothing and reality hits deep. She's a pimp. She's clean now not because she escaped but because she started doing to others what was done to her for so long.   I think I might throw up.

I don't have time to think through my emotions, though, because both my father and Kristi are taking one of my arms and leading me out the door into the food court, away from the whispering crowd. "She must be crazy's" and "poor girl" and "did you see she hit her sister?" trailing after me like word-ghosts. I hang my head and fight their leading, tripping over my own two feet. Let the crowd think I'm crazy. It's better than them knowing the truth.

Thirty

WE STOP AT A TABLE IN FRONT OF A HAMBURGER SHOP AND MY DAD pushes me into one of the chairs.

"Don't try and escape - there's about ten men gathered around here watching just in case you get any wise ideas."

I sink into the chair and stare at Kristi. I only slightly notice the men trying to be casual sitting in particular spots around the food court watching us. To be honest, I'm still reeling from the betrayal. Even though I don't know her, even though we've only had one conversation that was highly one-sided, it stings to find an assumption you had of someone fall to pieces in front of you. She catches me watching her and raises an eyebrow. I want to pull off every single brow hair and sit on my hands to avoid jumping across the table. I can't help but ask questions.

"What happened to you?"

"What do you mean...what happened to me?"

"I mean...since that morning you told me about...you

know...."

She smiles and maneuvers to where she's leaning forward across the table, "When I told you about my own father? Is that it?"

Her eyes sparkle as she leans back and crosses her arms. The table is silent for awhile and her smile grows bigger- triumphant even.

"Have you ever thought about where you hide your diary?"

My blood runs cold.

"What?"

I chance a look at my dad and he's rocking on his feet - chuckling under his breath and shaking his head.

"Oh Stephanie. You're so naive, you know it? Kristi's been working in the school for awhile. How do you think we got Marisol to convince the cheerleaders to join her?"

My eyes cloud over and my breath grows shallow. *What is he saying? Is he saying...*

"Did you steal my diary?!" I glance at Kristi, "Were you... were you saying stuff you read out of my diary?! To gain my confidence? To make me believe you?"

I could feel my voice starting to shake and I stopped talking, digging my nails into my hands. Nothing was sacred. Nothing. I owned absolutely nothing that was solely mine.

My life - my words - my thoughts - everything belonged to him.

Kristi laughs and shrugs her shoulders, "You'd be amazed at how useful your diary came to be for us. You see, I work for your father. I know how to befriend girls - get them to trust me." My eyes widen and she shakes her head, "I mean really Stephanie. Did you think you were the first to think of the idea to befriend girls and bring them in? Hardly. It's because of your brilliant idea - and your need to pour out your feelings on a sheet of paper - we knew you were headed to Kevin's for Thanksgiving. It's why your dad didn't wake you up that morning. He was too busy beating you over to the Matouse's to have a little chat with Kevin's mom. Did you ever wonder who told her about your past? About how you...make money? Who would want their son to date a prostitute?"

My vision blurs and my head sinks into my hands.

"Oh and another thing. Your friends. You know we realize they're onto us, right? This Chad person Jude sent your way? We took care of him. He won't be getting involved anytime soon."

Kristi starts giggling and my blood runs cold.

I look at her and try to find my voice, "What do you mean, you took care of him?"

My dad starts chuckling and drops his head as if I just asked the stupidest question.

"Oh sweetheart. We have our ways." He smiles big at my widening eyes and maneuvers himself to where he's close enough to whisper, "Don't worry. We didn't do anything too bad. Just scared him a little. Let him know what happens to people who don't mind their own business."

He pulls his wallet out of his jeans and rummages through the plastic picture covers before pulling one out. Throwing it on the table between us, he places his hands behind his head and grunts with approval.

"I gotta say. My guys are getting purty good at scaring the hell outta people."

The picture will haunt me for awhile. I see Chad - but it's not really him. Both of his eyes are bloodied and swollen and his front teeth are missing. His shirt is stripped off and there are bruises along his rib cage - probably indicating broken bones. His legs twist in unnatural ways and his two pinky fingers are tilting the wrong way. I bite my lip against the hatred burning in my chest.

My father is a monster. I close my eyes against the reality

of my day and fight for something - anything - other than the rising feeling of throwing up every bad thing that ever happened to me. I put my head down on the table again in order to stay away from the gaze of Kristi and my dad. If anything I can escape in this way - closing my eyes to the truth of my life. Everything is a lie. Everything I've built my life on - this need for hope - I really was all alone this whole time. And then, as if a force outside myself is pulling my head up to look at my surroundings, I feel someone watching me. I casually shift my gaze around the food court as if I'm people watching. I almost miss him. Hidden behind a tree, sitting on a bench, is Kevin. He's watching me. My heart stops for a split second before crashing into a million pieces. What I've lost is so painfully obvious as I notice him watching over me. I have to drop my head before my dad or Kristi sees me. The last thing I need is Kevin's cover to be blown. And then something else catches my eye. A woman is walking up to his bench. Her gait looks familiar - her blonde hair flowing behind her with the breeze coming from the nearby windows. The sunlight coming from behind gives her an almost ethereal look and I fight the emotions welling up inside - jealousy, confusion, hurt. My mind jumps to conclusions before even focusing on what's really going on. I can't help but think I've seen her before, though...

I breathe in deep and quick - it's Natalie. The nurse from the hospital.

What's she doing here?

Within seconds, she's standing next to Kevin, leaning over and whispering in his ear. He remains still, as if she's not even there. As if her hair isn't falling across her face in his vision. She whispers for awhile, and it's not until she tucks her hair behind her ear and stands upright that his expression changes to a determined glare. Without showing any recognition of the girl in front of him, he raises his head and sticks his cell phone in his pocket. Getting up, he finds my gaze and nods his head and so quick I could have missed it offers me a small smile before turning around and walking away. The woman remains, arms crossed and standing firm by the bench. She turns her head from watching Kevin walk away and I jump as she catches me staring.

Kristi and Dad notice, and turn and look to see why I'm reacting so harshly. They look right at the blonde but say nothing. My dad turns back around and stares at me as if I've gone crazy.

"You look like you've seen a ghost."

My eyes fly to his own and then away like a skittish colt. I haven't seen a ghost, but I may have heard one. I wasn't about to tell them this though - because as soon as Natalie turned and looked at me, I heard her voice quietly in one of my ears, as if she wasn't across the mall but leaning over me whispering.

"Rescue is coming, sweet girl. Hold on tight to hope. Hold on tight to what you know."

Her words echo within and find a home in some of the deepest and darkest places of my heart. Without even trying, I feel a tremendous calm. I close my eyes and breathe deep the feeling of rest. As Dad begins pointing out various girls hanging out in the mall, I can't help wonder how long the peace will last.

Confident with his choices, my dad looks at Kristi and asks how long she thinks it will take before the girls can be used within the business. They begin talking about logistics: whether to continue posting on Craigslist as salon services, whether or not the other website serving as a back door would suffice, whether or not the local police department will continue supporting them with customers.

"It's only a matter of time before they stop supporting us. They can turn on us in any moment and who would authorities believe? We can't really hang it over their heads that they've been involved because as soon as they decide to wipe their hands of this situation we're in for it." Kristi's words echo around me and I tune out my dad's response.

I swallow against the words and disgust rising in my throat and look away. Natalie is still in the background, watching. I feel safe with her there. I don't know what connection she has with my situation, but just as certain as my dad sits in front of me, I know she's working to set me free.

Kristi's voice cuts through my thoughts and I realize both of them are looking at me. I rub my eyes and fake a yawn.

"Sorry. I almost fell asleep. What'd you say?"

"I said if I had your help it wouldn't take as long." Kristi shrugs and moves her head to find my eyes. "Would you consider helping if I told you it meant less customers for you? Less work - more sleep - less men?"

I search her face and clear my throat against the thick bile of distrust. Turning my head for a split second, I find a piece of hair and start twirling it.

She mistakes my hesitation for consideration and adds, "It would mean your dad re-enrolling you at the high school. Probably after Christmas. All you would need is to pay attention. Make some girl friends - especially the quiet ones. The ones who just broke up with their boyfriends or who have no father are even better. Leave our wordless business cards lying around for the boys to pick up." She smiles, "Trust me. Their dads will know what the business cards mean when they bring them home."

"Kristi, I wouldn't help you if my life depended on it."

Her face blanches and dad shifts his weight and settles deep into his boots. He leans forward so his hands rest on the table inches from my body.

"Don't tempt me, sweetheart."

I allow him a grin before rolling my eyes.

"Trust me, Dad. Offing me will be the least of your worries. It may even be doing me a favor."

Kristi groans and moves her hands through her hair.

"Honestly, Stephanie? You're one of the whiniest brats I've ever met. Your dad may not get the privilege. I may beat him to it."

And my dad starts laughing as if she made a joke about the latest political embarrassment and not my life. I grimace as he locates the nearest trash and spits his chew, wiping his mouth on the way back to the table. Still chuckling, he motions toward me.

"I'm going to take her home and upload those pictures to the website." Glancing around the tables, he picks at his teeth with a leftover fork and nods his head. "You think you can get one of these to me today?"

Both of them focus on one girl in particular. She's alone and focused on the screen of her phone. Every once in awhile she moves her hand to wipe her cheek - like she's crying. Kristi stretches confidently and points the girl out as an easy target.

"Oh yeah. She's alone and vulnerable. Give me three hours."

My dad nods his approval and pulls me away from the table. I can't stop thinking about the girl - about what she's getting ready to face. I have to do something. I'm willing to try anything. With one last push, I find myself out of his grasp. His eyes go wild for a brief second before I put my hands up in defense.

"I think I forgot the camera."

He stands still - not thinking through the statement enough to remember Kristi giving it back to him. I walk over to the table, my eyes on Natalie the whole time. I don't even have to capture her attention - she's already walking over to the girl with the phone - already whispering in her ear.

I turn around and throw my arms out in wonder, "Never mind. It's not over here."

Before I reach my dad, the girl is already gone.

Natalie catches my gaze and smiles.

My dad's driving is erratic at best. Even though the mall is about forty miles from our house, with my dad driving we get home in less than twenty. He's been on the phone the entire time - wheeling and dealing with who-knows on the end of the line and getting progressively more frustrated and angry. I dread the schedule coming - the expectation Kristi and Dad will have of me. I can't help but wonder how long I will last. Something upsets him again and he starts spitting out a list of cuss words as we careen into our driveway. My head bounces against the ceiling of the truck. I open the door as soon as we come to a halt and begin walking to the front door, rubbing my scalp the entire way. I reach for my keys and remember my bag - as well as everything else - is still in my room. Impatiently, I wait for my dad to get off the phone so he can unlock the door.

"Don't tell me the feds are hot on our tail. Do something about it or I will."

His voice threatens. I know all too well what waits for the person who refuses his suggestion or disappoints him in any way. Without any warning, pictures of Chad fill my memory and I grimace. I close my eyes and pray for strength and for some sort of relief. *Please. Don't let him take his anger out on me.*

I see him come around the corner and question whether or not to meet his gaze. I choose not to, and keep my eyes on the doorknob as he unlocks it. I can still feel his breathing

- heavy and labored. He hasn't gained control of his anger yet, and I refuse to bear the brunt of his fists. As soon as he opens the door, we're hit with the stench of stale trash and spilt alcohol. I wrinkle my nose and fight a sigh. Stepping into the house, I continue my silent treatment and head to my room. I almost make it to my door.

"Hey Steph."

I cringe at his voice and slowly turn - not knowing what to expect. He's still picking his teeth with the fork from the food court, "You may wanna get some rest. Busy night ahead of ya. No falling asleep this time." He then smiles and the grin doesn't even reach his eyes - the evil radiates from every pore, "I mean...I would hate to have to tell Kristi. Who knows. You may get lucky. You may even catch a sunrise."

Without waiting for a response, he turns around whistling and heads to the back door.

My stomach turns and my blood starts racing. For the second time in twenty four hours, I nearly make it to the bathroom before puking.

I stay in the bathroom for nearly half an hour - my insides quivering with rioting upheaval. Stumbling into my room, I collapse on my bed and stare mindlessly into space. Regardless of the message I heard today from Natalie, I'm feeling hopeless. I notice a bottle of pain pills given to me last time I was in the hospital sitting innocently on a nearby shelf.

Perhaps Natalie meant my rescue would fall into my own hands. Perhaps my rescue would mean me taking my own life.

I think about everything I'd leave behind. Pacey had Emma and Jude. My relationship with them is cut off because of my father - no telling what he said on the phone the night before, and what he told Kevin's mom. Kevin. My heart twists at the thought of him - all of the memories crashing into each other and begging for space. Running from trains and splitting cinnamon rolls and piggy back rides - all something from the past, things I'd never experience again. I squeeze my eyes shut against the realization of beauty never again existing within my memory and the pain grows so intense I can't take it anymore. I reach for the bottle and decide to end this hell - once and for all.

People will understand. The truth will come out - eventually.

I wonder, if only for a brief second, if authorities will connect my suicide with Marisol's death. In a strange way, I believe maybe, just maybe, sacrificing myself will perk the attention of the media - two suicides in a week? Both the same way? The plan seems foolproof and I silently hope the message I've been trying to send will be loud and clear. Unscrewing the lid, I pour out the rest of the pills and stare at the pink and blue flecks of color. I grab the glass of water left on my nightstand and breathe deep. I hear my dad in the living room - talking on his cell phone. His voice is getting louder and louder but I only make out a few phrases like "getting things ready" and "knowing when to break and head east." I hear a door slam but think nothing of it. My mind, my heart - everything is focused on finishing the pain once and for all. I look again at the pills and swallow any fear or doubt left behind.

I can do this.

Just as I'm about to throw the pills in my mouth, I hear a tap on my window. My head jerks up and I toss the pills underneath my bed as if I'm caught. I wrinkle my brow at the interruption and make my way to the window. Pulling back my curtains, I notice two things: my dad's truck not in the driveway and Kevin staring at me from the other side of the window.

Thirty-One

My heart's pounding as I make my way to the front door - thoughts of *why is he here?!* mix with exquisite glee - seeing him does something all together different with my emotions. Different than anything I've ever experienced. I panic as I briefly remember the pills strewn all over the floor of my room, but then remember he's never even seen the inside of my house, and probably won't tonight.

I open the door and see Kevin. Without thinking, I collapse against the wooden frame.

"You," I manage to squeak out. He raises an eyebrow and pulls an envelope out of his pocket.

"Hi, Steph," he whispers.

I notice the visible grief on his face and look away. I wonder if he's coming to talk about seeing me at the mall.

"I saw you earlier today. Are you following me?"

He smiles and shrugs his shoulders, still fingering the envelope in his hands. "Why was Natalie there? Are you guys planning something? Kev...please don't do anything stupid. Please. Remember what I said."

Translation: I'm sorry. Please don't leave me forever.

Kevin looks at me and tilts his head.

"Natalie? Steph...what are you talking about? No one met me at the mall..I just saw you with your dad and some girl..."

"No...I saw - I saw Natalie walk up to you and whisper in your ear. Right before you left. She walked over to you at the bench and..." It's obvious he has no idea what I'm talking about so I bite my lip and look away. *Be strong, Steph. Remember. You're dirty. Ruined. He's better off without you complicating his life.*

He hands me the envelope and I look at him questioningly. "What's this?"

"Remember you putting my information as your own in your college application? Well. This came in the mail today from USC."

I glance down at the envelope and "Office of Admissions" catches my eye. I lift my head to meet his gaze and widen my eyes. My heart starts beating rapidly and I thrust the papers back toward Kevin.

You've gotta be kidding me. There's no way I can open this - no way I can know. Not right now. Not when my life is hopeless. I think again about the empty pill bottle on my nightstand and shake my head.

"I-I can't open this."

I chance a look at him and cross my arms against my chest, shielding myself from the cold wind scraping against my heart. My hands grab either side of my shirt, but I know he notices the way they shake.

"Do you want me to open it?"

He asks and I simply nod, not trusting my voice for anything. I can't help but notice his distance - by now he's usually wrapping his arms around me to keep the cold away. He must think I'm disgusting, I can't help but think. He smiles, a half-hearted attempt compared to what I am - was - use to coming from him. He moves to open the letter and reads the piece of paper tucked safely inside and I wait. My mind going crazy with conflicted thoughts and feelings -

Please be an acceptance. Please be an acceptance.

-and-

Don't get my hopes up. Don't get my hopes up.

I don't even notice my hands moving close to my mouth, clasped in anticipation. I don't even know why I'm so anxious when seconds ago I planned on ending everything.

Kevin hides his reaction well; I can't read his face at all. He looks at me and holds my gaze for what seems like eternity before opening his mouth.

"Steph..."

A low voice growls from the driveway and I freeze.

Crap. Crapcrapcrapcrap. Dad.

"What the hell are you doing here, punk?" his voice slurs and I close my eyes against the fear. He's been drinking. Upset about the earlier phone call, he must have gone to the local bar to toss back a few before working on the website like he told Kristi. I glance at Kevin, who surreptitiously places the letter with my fate in his back pocket.

"Hello, Mr. Tiller." He's covering any sort of apprehension well - but I know he's scared out of his mind. Catching my eye ever so slightly, he nods and turns again towards my father.

"I know you don't like surprise visitors, but Mrs. Peabody mentioned Steph was withdrawn for medical reasons, so I wanted to stop by and bring her a card from the class."

My father doesn't even notice the blatant lie - doesn't remember Mrs. Peabody as the one who stopped us this morning in the mall parking lot. There's no card - my arms are still wrapped around my chest - barely reining in the thundering of my heart.

"Kevin, just go."

My voice draws the attention of them both. Kevin shakes his head slightly and I just turn away - once again reminding myself of the dangers of affiliating with me. He slowly gets the idea and walks away. My dad holds my gaze until Kevin is out of eyesight. I try not to think about seeing Kevin pull out his cell phone as he rounded the corner. As sweet as rescue would be, I'm in this one alone - of this I am painfully aware.

"You taking customers behind my back, you whore?" His steps prove uneven because of the alcohol and he stumbles against me.

"No. Dad, I told him to leave. He was just dropping off the card."

He grabs my arms and gives me a shake. "Lemme make this clear. You are mine. I see that jerk again and I will kill him. You understand? I shoulda done something when he was here. Let him know I mean business."

Tears come to my eyes and I blink in order to get them to disappear. It's too late. He sees the emotion and stops cold.

"You've gone soft on me." Sneering, he spits on my shoes and glances back at me from the top of his eyes - barely focusing. "Maybe you're not as well-trained as I thought."

He pulls me by the hair and my hands fly up to try and wriggle free. He rears back and slaps me across the face, and for a split second I see double. It's all he needs to overpower me and he takes advantage of the opportunity. He pushes me away and kicks me in the ribs only to pull me close. My lips curl against the stench of his breath as he leans forward and whispers in my ear.

"Let me make this easy for you." Pulling out his phone he dials a number. "Hey, Frank - it's me. I have another job for you."

A moan escapes my mouth and I shake my head in disbelief...*not Kevin. Please not Kevin.*

"Yeah. This one should be easy. He's a kid. Just walked away from the house - he's down the street now. Name's Kevin Matouse." My dad catches my eye and winks, "Give him the Tiller special. Hold nothing back for this one. He owes me quite a lot of money for hanging with my daughter while she could be workin'." He hangs up and places his cell in his pocket. Pointing at me he sneers and spits at my feet. "Let this be a lesson to not get yo'self involved. I warned ya. Now he pays."

I collapse against the grass and start to rock back and forth - not knowing what to do but wanting to escape from everything - Kevin. Run. Hide. I don't know how to stop them but...please. Not Kevin.

"Don't try to escape, princess. I would hate to see you black and blue for the customers waiting for you out back."

I groan and shake my head, and my dad just laughs.

"Did you think you'd have a day off? After yesterday? There's makeup to cover those bruises, sweetheart."

I find the strength to look at him square in the eyes and wipe the tears staining my cheeks.

"I hate you. Even though you hurt me, you will never break me. And one day, I will escape. One day, you will pay for what you've done. You won't find Kevin. He has people who protect him. One day you won't be able to hide under the protection of your precious pawns in the police department. I can't wait to see you brought to justice."

I push him away and start walking towards the house, surprised at my words. I'm not able to think too long, though. Out of the corner of my eye I see my dad pick up a bat Pacey left in the yard a couple weeks ago. There's not even enough time to run. The bat comes flying towards my head and I fall to the ground with a cry. Within seconds I'm unconscious from the blow.

❄

When I wake, I'm out back. My ankles are spread apart, tied to each side of the bed. I try to move my arms and find I'm spread eagle - unable to make any sharp movements with out any pain. I hear the shuffling of feet outside the door and freeze. Maybe they won't try anything if they think I'm still knocked out? The door opens and laughter fills the air along with the stench of alcohol and stale smoke.

"Here's your prize, gentlemen. You've paid well, so she's free for whatever you desire. Oh and, the camera is over there on the table. Remember to take pictures for the website."

I don't even recognize the voice, but I've learned to not be surprised at the lengths my father will go to grow this cycle of crime.

The mattress shifts and I feel whiskers on my cheek.

"She sure smells purty."

The smell is almost too much to bear. My eyes struggle open and the man breaks into a smile.

"Well there you are, gorgeous. Ready to have some fun?"

I narrow my eyes and spit in his face. He jumps back and wipes his face.

"Oh boy. You're gonna wish you didn't do that, sweetheart."

He motions for the other men to help him out and they form a half-circle at the foot of the mattress. I'm completely surrounded. I see one of the men grab the camera and run over, barely able to turn the camera on in his shaky excitement. He holds it up and presses the button repeatedly, flashes going off incessantly. Every time my eyes blink in protest.

"Keep your eyes open, girl. You know you want this. You're gonna be famous. You know that, right?"

I rear back and the tendons pull to their breaking point in my wrists and ankles. I cry out in pain when one of the men grabs my hair and pulls my face towards him.

An unadulterated groan escapes from his lips and he

whispers against my neck, "Oh yes. We're gonna have some fun tonight."

He leans forward and I can hear the cheers of the men in the background. The flash of the camera continually blinds me and the tears threaten to spill. I can't do this anymore. I can't. I breathe in only to taste this man's scent, I open my eyes only to see his frame on top of me. I close my eyes against the pain - separating myself from what's happening I find myself in another place entirely. Afternoon walks with Kevin. Watching the stars collapse against the sky. Laughing with Emma.

It's only then I notice color out of the corner of my eye. I turn as best I can and see another girl - bound and wild-eyed. One of the men take to untying her and carry her over to where the rest of the group is - the tears flow freely down her cheeks, her whimpers quiet against the choke-hold of the fabric against her mouth.

The hatred I feel for these men - for this space - is deafening.

"Hey men....this must be the newbie we was told about. Look how young she is!"

His breath turns guttural and he shuffles his feet with anticipation. The flashes of light from the camera are blinding and I fight to hold the gaze of the girl.

Just hold on, just hold on....

I feel myself slipping when I begin to understand their plan for us. One of the other men pulls out a flip video camera and smiles.

His voice is low - his lisp strong, "You two beauties gonna show us some action?"

And then I hear something. Shouting. It's instant chaos outside and there's banging on the door. Suddenly, the door to the shed bursts open and men in uniforms and guns come rushing in with force. The lights from their flashlights blind me and I close my eyes against the contrast. I don't under-stand what's happening and fear the worst...

"Don't. Move."

A low voice barks from the doorway and I whimper against the weight of the man on top of me. He's suddenly pulled off of me and I gasp.

"Kevin?!"

He wastes no time. The rope is untied from my wrists and ankles and for the second time, he pulls me from the bed and carries me out of the shed in his arms. I notice his black eyes and have only a small fraction of ability to remember my father's threat. I see my street covered in flashing lights and official looking men running around with guns and uniforms. I hide my head against Kevin's chest and fight against the questions. Once we escape the noise and commotion, Kevin slows and pulls me closer to his embrace. I lift my head just long enough to make sure the other girl got out - and I see another uniformed man carrying her in a different direction. I don't even know where my dad is - don't even know if he's come home since he left earlier in the afternoon - and I see my mom making her way with a uniformed officer to a nearby police car. People are beginning to come outside - once again watching the show outside the Tiller home. This show is all together different, though. This show is the truth - what's been our reality for far too long. Kevin senses my tension and leans down to kiss my forehead.

"It's okay, Steph. You're safe now. It's over."

My eyes fight for life - for awareness - but my mind takes over. My body bounces with the rhythm of Kevin's cadence and I smile despite the way my muscles protest against the jostling. My rescue is here. He's holding me against his chest and running with me in his arms like a knight in shining armor. I feel myself go limp - and for the first time, I know the feeling of true protection.

Thirty-Two

I SHIFT IN AND OUT OF CONSCIOUSNESS FOR THE NEXT FEW DAYS. MY dreams have the ethereal fuzz to them - bright, echoing, hard to focus...I know I'm in a hospital, and I hear different voices. Jude. Emma. Pacey.

Kevin. Oh, Kevin. The one who rescued me - time and time again. The one I pushed away. I don't even know how he managed to pull off the raid - and I don't even know if I care. Does he even still want me? Does it even matter? Tears come unwillingly and I feel hands wiping them off my cheeks. The hands are soft and smell of citrus. Must be Emma, I think and silently wonder at her ability to love in the face of trauma and disaster.

I have so many questions - How did they rescue me? Has anyone found my father? Does Pacey know what's really going on? But mostly I still have pain. It settled itself deep in my chest and feels like a hot ball of hardened coal taking up space where my heart should be - something happened in the shed that night - I gave up something...hope perhaps? Whatever it was, I haven't found it. Even with the rescue. Even with those I care about most holding my hand through the haze.

I wake up one moment and see Jude and Kevin talking in hushed tones. I hear things like *the agency is looking at you for a permanent position* and *there are threats worldwide we're taking into account.* It doesn't make sense to me. Threats? What threats? Add it to my list of growing confusion. I think I may have made a noise, because Kevin looks at me and catches my gaze. His eyes widen in surprise - and then fear - almost as if I wasn't supposed to hear. It doesn't matter because before I even begin connecting the conversation the pain meds take me under yet again.

I wake up in a field, but given the glowing breeze I know I'm dreaming. I can still hear Jude and Kevin talking, but they're mere echoes - a figment of my other life. I close my eyes against the cool wind and feel how it refreshes me. When I open my eyes I see a man standing before me - smiling. He walks slowly toward me and I take a step back - not knowing yet if this is a nightmare or simply my subconscious working out some wrinkles. The memories still haunt me and I know they always will. But this dream is different. My other dreams have been dark and involve me running toward the bright light never to find it. In this dream, I'm in the middle of the light and it's blinding. I barely see the man's robe blowing in the breeze. His eyes hold my own and I'm captivated. *Be still,* He says and His voice washes over me. I pause and tilt my head. I've heard this voice before - usually in the middle of my dad's shed when I would shut my eyes against the pain. This voice would echo in my ears to hold on. It was always soft then - dim. I could barely Him above the grunts of my abusers. Here, in this moment, the voice is strong and sure. He walks up to me and places His hand under my chin. *You are beautiful my child. Beautiful and whole.*

I laugh, then. So I really am going crazy, I think. I look at the man and shake my head.

"You must be mistaken. I'm anything but whole. And beautiful? No. Not me."

I glance at my clothes and step back in horror - I'm still wearing the costume from the other night. My tights are torn and there's a piece of cloth hanging from where my shirt should be - I don't even know who this man is and I feel completely bare. Naked. Exposed. I search for a way to cover myself and find nothing. I can't believe he's seeing me like this. I look disgusting. Used. Broken. There has to be be something to cover me...there has to be a way to hide. I finally collapse on the ground and rock myself into a ball.

He leans down and looks at me *I've known you for awhile*, He says. *Before the foundation of the world I set you apart. You are chosen. I chose you.*

I shake my head and place my hands over my ears.

"Stop it. Just stop it."

My heart pounds and I fight for consciousness - away from this man's penetrating gaze. Away from his way of disarming me with His love. Before I know it, He's sat down beside me and taken me into His arms. I'm cradled against His chest and I can hear His heartbeat. It's beating my name. No really. *It's beating my name.* My breath catches and I slowly meet His gaze. He smiles and nods, *you are My child - you always have been in my Hand.*

I feel the confusion well up inside - the questions and the hurt and the doubt and rejection pouring out from my life.

"But it doesn't make sense!" I cry, "Where were you?! Why does this hurt so much? Where were You when they took it all away? Where were You when no one bothered to look at me? How can you say I'm whole when they took everything?! Everything! Where were You? *Where were You?!*"

I'm screaming now - pounding my fists against His chest like a little girl with her father. All I feel is rage - all I see is red. The anger wells up and spills out unbidden and uncensored. I cry until I can't cry anymore - until my eyes sting and my head pounds from emotion. He's rocking me, holding me, caressing my head slowly and gently.

My screams die down to a hoarse whisper, I cling to His robe and He stops to look at me.

"I have nothing left. Nothing."

Oh but my child - You have everything in Me. And I was here all along - in the sunrise taking your breath away and Emma fighting for you and using Kevin and Jude as My instruments of justice. I was there when you held Pacey tight and I was there by your side when you let him go. I was there when Natalie reminded you that rescue is coming and I was there when they found you bound and used. And I can make you new. I was always there and I will always be here - I will never leave you or forsake you. I will make your stone heart flesh. Your ashes will become a crown of beauty and justice will shine forth like the most stunning sunrise. Out of this mess I will bring forth life.

My breath evens out in exhaustion and I lean my head against Him. I feel my heart turning - pumping - and an all together different kind of pain enters my chest. Here, resting in His embrace, I realize my protection has been here all along. Rescue was coming because Rescue was already here - waiting. I reach for His scarred hand and realize I'm leaning against the arms of my Father - the one I always searched for and never found. He was here - in this moment.

And He was for me.

I feel His hand shift and I look at His face. He takes my chin in His hand once more and smiles, *All you need to do is believe, beautiful one. Believe in Me and I'll make you new. Believe in me and your past will be white as snow.*

I process this for a moment - thinking of everything I've seen, everything I've been through, everything I've experienced. All my past - all my dirtiness - gone? All my shame - all my fear - gone? I look Him in the eyes and I smile through the tears,

"Oh, Father. I believe," and then I close my eyes and fall asleep to Him singing over me.

Epilogue

STEPHANIE SLEEPS QUIETLY IN THE HOSPITAL BED AND I FIGHT FOR A space on the couch in the room. Pacey and Emma and Jude left for the night, but I won't leave her side. I can't. Not when her dad still managed to escape the raid. By the time we got to the house, he was long gone - all of his belongings thrown about his room as if he left in a hurry. There wasn't much left in terms of evidence of Daddy's Little Girls, but we still had the shed. My heart drops and I wipe the tears threatening themselves yet again, being careful not to push too hard on the bruises from Fred teaching me a lesson. I wasn't worried. The shed was more than enough to put him behind bars for a long time. We just had to find him. One of his guys - Joey I think - mentioned something about him somehow getting a tip before we got there - before I even walked over to give her the letter from USC. The letter. I smile, fingering the piece of paper in my pocket and imagining her reaction when she reads it for the first time. Hearing someone walk in the room,

I sit up and look around the corner.

"Kevin?"

"I'm right here, Jude."

He looks at me and shakes his head, "Kid - you really took a beating from Tiller's guys. You okay?"

I sniff and nod my head, "I'll be fine. A little sore but nothing..." my voice cracks and I clear my throat, "nothing like she's faced."

Jude watches Steph, a look of love and rage flashes across his face. I understand because I recognize the ferocity within myself - the absolute need to protect her. I don't even know when it happened. He jingles the keys in his pocket and looks out the window.

"He got away."

"I know."

"Two years...two years searching and building evidence and watching Stephanie..."

I watch the snow continue to fall and shake my head. It's hard to think of it being that long. No one knows my involvement - not even my parents. Somehow, my name was leaked to Jude's agency after the party where I was pinned with raping the girl. Because I came forward, because I tried to fight the injustice, my name was smeared. His black-ops noticed though and mentioned it to Jude. I've been on the case ever since. For awhile, I just watched Stephanie. Got to know her movements. Knew her favorite coffee before I knew anything else. Then the more I got to know her father - the more I got to see the idiosyncrasies of her family - I was dumbfounded. We thought we knew in the beginning. We thought he was working to build a trafficking ring - we had no idea the roots. Until Stephanie told me the truth, we had no idea the inner-workings and how much her father had accomplished in such a short amount of time. How anyone survived that environment for so long...her resiliency moves me. Watching her now I fight the urge to hold her in my arms. Seeing her tonight - broken and bloodied - something inside me shifted. Her past means nothing to me. Her safety and worth everything.

Jude curses under his breath and runs his fingers through his hair. His voice is low...a whisper...

"Sometimes I feel like justice will never be found. Like...all this work is for nothing. Sometimes I wonder when good will finally win out in the end."

My blood runs cold as I remember my conversation with Steph earlier. Jude notices my reaction and stops his pacing long enough to ask me where my thoughts are going.

"It's nothing...just something Steph said."

Jude walks over and sits next to me on the couch.

"What'd she say?"

"You remember when you asked me to follow them to the mall? Well, Steph saw me. She asked me why Natalie met me there."

"Natalie?"

"Yeah...that nurse she talked about when she was in the hospital the last time."

"She saw her? At the mall?"

I nod my head and rub my face with my hands, "Yeah. She said Natalie walked over to me and whispered in my ear right before I got up and left."

Jude looks at me out of the corner of his eye and shrugs.

"Well did that happen? Did you see her?"

"No. I was there watching Stephanie. I didn't see anyone else. But right before I walked out of the mall I felt like someone was whispering in my ear. Like I heard this voice speaking to me and it hit me deep in my chest, you know?"

"What'd the voice say?"

"The fight is not yours. Rescue is coming. Trust in His hand."

Jude cursed under his breath again and popped his neck. "Wow."

He catches my gaze and we look at each other, not needing any words. We hear movement on the bed and see Stephanie opening her eyes. I'm by her side within seconds - my heart breaking into a thousand pieces from the color in her eyes.

"Hey beautiful." I whisper.

She stretches and offers a shy smile before looking around with confused eyes, "Hi."

There's something different about her. I can't put a finger on it. I brush some hair out of her eyes and Jude grabs her hand.

"Are you okay? Do you know where you are?"

She looks around and her eyes glaze over for a second - as if memories are finding their way back into her view. She finds my gaze and I can see the fear in her eyes. I want to wipe it all away - every last doubt. As soon as the fear appears it vanishes, replaced with an inner peace I've never seen her possess.

"My dad? Where's my dad? I saw my mom get in one of the police cars but my dad?"

Jude and I look at each other and he clears his throat.

"Steph, your dad got away. We're still looking for him but we don't really know where he might have gone to hide."

"He said he'd go east."

Her voice is a whisper. Her throat still dry from sleeping for so long. Jude looks at her and tilts his head. I move in closer and rub the side of her hand with my thumb.

"What'd you say?" I ask.

"The night you guys came...I was in my room. I heard my dad talking."

She starts coughing and we wait until she's done - I offer her some water and she accepts, drinking for awhile. Once she's through she takes a deep breath and continues.

"I heard him say something about heading east....needing to break free." Her eyes brighten and she tries to sit up - only to grimace in pain and fall against the pillows again. Looking at me she squeezes my hand, "I think I may know where he went."

Jude turns and looks for paper and comes back to her bedside. My heart is pounding at the thought of maybe catching him - I silently pray I won't be around when he's brought in because of the hatred I feel toward him. We look at Stephanie and she tells us about this place east of here where they use to go when she was younger. A cabin against the river. Jude walks out in the hall, already on his phone talking with the team.

I look at Stephanie and smile, "You missed Emma. She came by earlier with Pacey and Benjamin."

Her lips move into a small smile and she swallows slowly - still trying to come awake against the medicine pumping in her veins.

"How is she? Is she worried?"

I laugh and place my hand on her cheek.

"Steph. Leave it to you to be concerned about someone else."

She maneuvers her head and her eyebrows lean in as if in question, "Kevin...how'd you know where I was? What happened...your eyes - they are black as if someone beat you up. I don't understand how this all worked." She lifts her hands and stretches out her arms, "Is this real? Am I really rescued?"

I lift my head and study her face - the bruises slowly starting to show. For a long time I've debated telling her what's really going on - how Jude and Emma knew all along and how I've been her built in body guard - watching, waiting, sharing. I clear my throat and look out the window.

"Steph...there's some things you need to know." Her face

grows pale and I smile in reassurance - knowing her fear of abandonment and rejection, "Ever since I first saw you, there's been this magnetic pull. I can't stay away from you. And...I've told you the first time I saw you was in the coffee shop, but that's a lie. I watched you long before then."

She laughs then, "What do you mean? I saw you before then too...Kevin, we go to the same school."

"Yeah but...do you remember me telling you about that party? The one where the blame went to me?"

She nods slowly and hesitantly - unsure of where the conversation is going.

"Well. Other people heard about my reaction to the case and contacted me about working with them. Other people who know you and love you. Other people like Jude. Emma. Chad."

She shakes her head in confusion.

"What? Kevin...you aren't making any sense."

"Jude works for an agency who studies patterns in human trafficking. The past few years he's been studying your father - not knowing you were involved in the ring he created. He knew the abuse but didn't know the roots."

Her eyes widen in understanding and her breathing starts gaining speed, "All this time...they...knew?"

I nod my head, "Yes...and technically...so did I. But I didn't know for sure how deep you were involved until you told me. That's when things got serious. When we started moving fast to get you out of there."

She looks away from me for awhile - studying her hands and occasionally wiping her cheeks. I lean forward and cautiously pull some hair away from her face and she glances at me out of the corner of her eye.

"So...all this was a ruse? You really weren't my boyfriend?"

My heart plummets and I reach for her hand. This is what

I was worried about - her thinking we staged the whole thing - including our relationships with her. I gingerly cup my hand underneath her chin and lift her face so she sees me,

"Stephanie...absolutely not. I was - and am hopefully - your boyfriend. I didn't set out to fall in love with you - I set out to protect you. Watch you. When we ran into each other in the coffee shop something changed. Everything since then? It's all real. I was just more involved than you realized."

She studies my face, her eyes searching for the truth I know is there.

"He was right. You protected me."

"What?"

"The man from my dream." She smiles at my look of hesitation and grabs my hand, "It's a long story. I'll tell you all about it later. But...He mentioned this whole time my protection has come in different forms...including you."

"Yes. That was my job. Watch out for you at school. Follow you home. Keep an eye on the house at night. I was always somewhere nearby. I didn't think I'd fall in love with you. You just made my job easier when we started dating."

I can tell she's overwhelmed with the information. Her hands are clinched tight, bunched underneath her covers. She closes her eyes - a habit she has when she tries to think of something or is processing information.

"All this time...I ached for someone to rescue me. I wanted protection. I wanted someone to see. And all this time...I had it. I just didn't have any idea."

She turns toward me then and takes a deep breath, "Well I've had my own secret for awhile now too."

I raise my eyebrows, "Really."

She nods and tries to hide a smile.

"Yes. Really. Kevin Matouse...I made the biggest mistake when I broke up with you. I don't know why you want me. I don't know what you see in me. But I do know I love you

- regardless of me trying to push you away time and time again. You're still there - always." She closes her eyes and tears start to fall, "I love you, Kevin. I've known for awhile."

I breathe deep her words and lean forward to kiss her - gently - on her cheek. I know she'll need time - lots of it - before she's fully recovered from what's happened. But she's right. I am here. Always.

We're interrupted by Emma running into the hospital room. Her eyes are wild and she seems about to burst with information.

She rushes over to Stephanie and kisses her forehead.

"It's so good to see you awake!"

Stephanie leans back and studies Emma.

"What's going on? You have something you're not saying..."

I smile at how perceptive Stephanie is and watch Emma's reaction. She grabs Stephanie's hand and squeezes it.

"It's over, Steph. You're free. Completely. They just found your father. He's been taken into custody and will be placed in prison this evening. He's gone. Forever."

Jude walks in then and I turn and catch his gaze. He's visibly more relaxed now and he nods in affirmation when he sees me question the information. I breathe a sigh of relief I didn't even know I was holding in and I laugh. *Rescue is coming* the voice said when I was in the mall. I suddenly realize just how true this is - and just how beautiful trusting in His hand can be when you do it completely.

Jude makes his way to the side of her bed and squeezes her toe.

"Hey beautiful, how are you feeling?"

She moves her gaze from me to Emma to Jude and begins to relax. Looking out the window her smile turns radiant as she notices the sun's rays streaking across the night sky. Her sunrise. She happens to wake just as light seeps into the darkness and I recognize the significance. I think about when we watched the stars - when I told her beauty can sometimes be found in darkness. I look out the window again and notice how the sun's colors play hop-scotch across the freshly fallen snow. It's breathtaking - perfect for Stephanie - as if someone created it just for her. I squeeze her hand and repeat Jude's question. She looks at me and her eyes grow big with wonder and amazement and relief.

"I feel like I've come alive."

Author's Note

I wish I could accurately describe the process my heart has taken in writing this book. Throughout the course of crafting Stephanie's story, I've felt the steady wooing of One who seeks to rescue that which was lost. I was able to have multiple conversations with Rob Morris, co-founder of Love146, and heard his heart echo that of God's for these girls caught in slavery. I befriended the Springer family - the masterminds behind SheDances - and shared with them the first chapter as soon as I wrote it. I felt moved - stirred - to write. I couldn't stop. Stephanie's story just came and no matter how busy I was or what I was facing the words still flowed. It wasn't until I got to the ending that I realized I hadn't experienced my own freedom - hadn't believed in my own rescue - and so I didn't know how to write it. I set the manuscript down on my dresser and went about my life as if I hadn't just written a full-length novel minus the ending.

Because of some amazing friends, divine conversations

and an incredible therapist, I was able to breathe deep and dive back into Stephanie's pain after more than a year of separation. And it was painful. Writing this story was emotionally taxing and there were moments I had to step away from the words because I couldn't see through my tears. But I kept pushing through because I knew. I knew how to end her struggle because I believed in the end myself - knew that restoration truly was possible for one who was destroyed by life's monsters.

And this is where I want you to rest.

Life is messy and we're a bunch of broken people. But I hope what you get out of this story is more than just a realization of brokenness. I hope you see the Beauty. I hope you recognize the footprints of One who pursues us at any cost - even when we don't see it. And I hope, just like Stephanie, this realization will help you come alive.

Connect with Elora

 facebook.com/eloranicolewrites

 @eloranicole

Other Books by
Rhizome Publishing

Find Z at:

Samuel is headed down the path of mediocrity and regrets, and
his annual summer trip to Cloudland Camp only reinforces this
when he finds himself stuck on the newly created Z troop - specifically designed for the boys who:

"show apathy in the face of adversity"

But when their counselor, David, gets ahold of these boys,
Sammy will discover the power that lies in self-belief, the
strength that comes from never bending to the establishment,
and the courage that comes from taking the first step.

But can one summer really change the course of   someones
life?

BARNES&NOBLE
BOOKSELLERS

amazon.com

janetober.com

amazonkindle

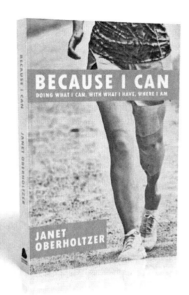 iBooks

One moment, she was savoring life on sunny Malibu Beach and the next she almost lost her legs and her life.

Janet Oberholtzer is not a celebrity or a superhero, instead she could be your mom, your wife or your daughter, but her story will give people hope to heal if they find their world has become dark and hopeless due to a life-changing event.

Because I Can chronicles Janet's struggle after a horrific accident while she was traveling around the country with her family.

After being trapped in a wrecked motor home with her legs decimated, her pelvis shattered — paramedics and firefighters rushing to save her life — her struggle wasn't only to survive her physical injuries, she also had to learn how to live with her new normal.

This included the struggle of keeping her marriage together, fighting through anger and depression and liberating herself from physical limitations to run again. Why?

Because she can.

CPSIA information can be obtained at www.ICGtesting.com
Printed in the USA
LVOW121528230812

295668LV00010B/24/P